Ellen Withers has a gift for creating dual time mysteries.

> — Beth Westcott, award-winning author of
> The Three Sisters series.

I am carried away with the descriptions of that time in history—Ellen makes it come alive ...

> — Julia Wilson

Ellen's characters are like old friends. You can't wait to get together and share some tea.

> — Linda Vamprine, retired insurance fraud
> investigator

SHOW ME SKULDUGGERY

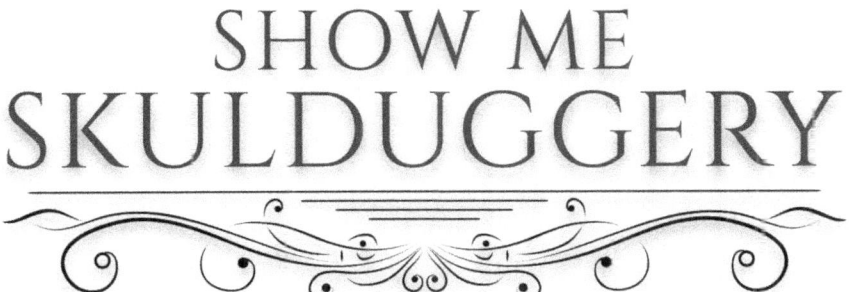

SHOW ME MYSTERIES – BOOK THREE

ELLEN E. WITHERS

Scrivenings
PRESS
Quench your thirst for story.
www.ScriveningsPress.com

To Susan Erdel Atkins and Nancy Erdel Oliver, beloved cousins among many beloved cousins, and to my lifelong friend, Joy Oliver Keith.

Chapter One

The Angel of Justice

Katherine Mull was blissfully unaware she was going to depart this earth before the next sunrise. A smile tugged at the corners of my lips. I would serve that vengeance.

She strolled out of her modern three-story mansion right on time. The only positive habit she possessed was her punctuality, and it would factor nicely into my plan.

The sundress she wore was figure-enhancing and eye-catching, precisely the fashion statement she tended to make. A salute to a 1960s-style patterned print of orange and blue. Katherine always stood out—a tier or two above the masses.

Her hair, transformed into sun-streaked blonde tresses by a skilled stylist with high-tech coloring solutions, was twisted into a messy knot at the back of her thin neck. Rhinestone studded sandals completed her look and brought attention to her manicured toenails. Genuine diamonds sparked at her earlobes and on her right wrist.

With a quick glance toward the blistering morning sun, she adjusted her sparkling sunglasses, then walked to her mailbox. The large stucco replica of her home was unrecognizable as a receptacle for official mail delivery by the United States Postal Service.

Everything about Katherine was an ostentatious display of affluence, from her mailbox, her acres of property, to her *palace* with an attached three-car garage. If her goal was to establish a grandiose demonstration of wealth accumulation, she'd succeeded.

She bundled the gathered mail under her arm and made her way to the silver Corvette parked in her driveway. Soon, the engine purred to life, and she completed a three-point turn, picking up speed as she whipped onto the road.

I stood sucking in air, clearly visible on the sidewalk of her neighbor's home, but she didn't spare me a glance. Typical. I was no one to her. Just a jogger with ear buds. She focused on what actions she could take to increase her wealth or how to make herself appear richer and more fashionable.

When her sportscar disappeared from my view, I spun and jogged with energy into the woods along her property line. I retrieved the final two gas cans I'd hidden among the bushes. Although the cans were large and cumbersome, I'd made several trips through the thicket this week and had learned how to handle them.

For two weeks, I'd been dropping off plastic cans of gasoline inside her garage. Because she appeared to focus only on herself, I figured she'd never notice.

Reaching the house, I hid in the overgrown landscaping beside the garage and accessed the code to open the door. The main garage door slid open soundlessly when I overrode the security system.

Katherine hadn't disappointed me. As planned, the red gas cans were in position, ready for use this evening.

I hustled the recent additions where the previous cans awaited. Once satisfied with their placement, I exited the garage, shut the door, and restored the security system.

My ease at accessing Katherine's castle and treasures would horrify her. She'd find out later, and I'd get to see her surprise. Now, to sprint home and change. My next stop was her bank. I wanted to witness the stink she'd create there.

Who would dare mess with her money? Who was brave enough to take away the golden idol she obviously cherished more than God?

Me.

Must. Run. Faster. Can't miss the fireworks show she will put on at the bank.

Little did she know, this was only the beginning. The relocation of her funds launched her punishment for being worthless and uncaring.

Death loomed on the horizon.

I was through waiting for God to right the score. Why had He allowed her to continue her horrible ways for so long? Now I would stop her cruel behavior.

My mission would make her understand she could no longer hurt people. Her actions would have consequences.

Chapter Two

Liesl

Liesl Schrader smiled as she pushed through the revolving doors of Community One Bank's downtown branch. This morning's mission would be a delightful surprise to share with Mr. Barnaby, the bank's president.

Sparks of excitement surged through her. Today, she'd set into motion this phase of her plan for a Community Center. She and Mr. Barnaby, one of her favorite people, would start a special project for the citizens of Mexico, Missouri.

Liesl waved to a teller, who smiled as she made her way to the teller line. Mr. Barnaby's office sat behind their counter.

Several people were queued up for service in the teller line. Liesl stood on tiptoes to see if Mr. Barnaby was free. She glanced at her watch. Still a few minutes until their nine o'clock meeting. It wouldn't do for her to barge into his office if he was busy.

Barnaby's office was a glass-sided cubicle. Liesl recognized the person sitting across the desk from Mr. Barnaby. Katherine Mull. This recognition wiped the smile from Liesl's face and drew sympathy for the sweet banker. Everyone pitied those forced to deal with Katherine.

Katherine was a tall, birdlike woman with chemically induced blonde hair, enhanced monthly by her stylist, and a nose too big for her face. A nose that peered down at other people.

Liesl turned left and walked toward the loan officer's desk. Miranda Marquette glanced up. A grin replaced her former business-like concentration. They'd been friends since grade school.

"Hey there, Liesl. How're you doing this morning?"

"Great, until I saw Katherine with Mr. Barnaby." Liesl shook her head. "Poor man."

Miranda was always chipper. Yet even her smile faded when Liesl mentioned Katherine. "I know. Sad, isn't it?" Miranda gestured toward the chairs at the front of her desk. "Please have a seat."

"Thank you." Liesl sat and placed her purse and leather briefcase on the chair beside her.

"Katherine didn't have an appointment. She just stalked in and made a tremendous fuss. Mr. Barnaby ran out to help her, and then she shouted at him, right here in the lobby."

"Shouted at Mr. Barnaby?"

"Sure did. Luckily, he herded her into his office before she made too big of a fuss. We don't need such things happening in front of our other customers."

"Katherine is certainly mean, but I didn't figure she was malicious enough to yell at such a nice man. Why would she do that?"

Miranda shrugged. "Apparently Katherine has a reason." She rolled her brown eyes behind her cute glasses.

Liesl gripped the arms of her chair. "That makes me furious. She should relate with people the way God intended us to act. Everyone in her path gets hurt."

"I know." Miranda bent toward Liesl and whispered, "No one ever wants to assist her. She's always so crabby and threatens to report us for poor service, no matter how hard we try to please her." Then, in her normal speaking voice, added, "Aren't you scheduled for an appointment with Mr. Barnaby now?"

"Yes, but I'm considering rescheduling. I don't want to apply any additional pressure on him. His posture and face telegraphed his misery."

"I'm sure he's uncomfortable."

They both glanced toward Mr. Barnaby's office, which was visible from their side of the lobby. Although the conversation behind the glass was inaudible, Katherine's angry countenance and flailing gestures told an obvious story.

Miranda turned back toward Liesl. "It appears his hands are full right now. Could I help you with something?"

"I wanted to talk to him about an extensive project. My plan was to run it by Mr. Barnaby first." Liesl turned to gather her purse and briefcase. "I might as well wait. I want the project to start with him, but I'm sure we'll get you involved eventually."

"I look forward to working with you on it," Miranda said. "In the meantime, I'll take your appointment off his schedule." She turned to her monitor and taped on a few keys. "Would you like an appointment this afternoon?"

"No, I have to set up for that fundraiser tonight at Simmons Stables. Could I reschedule for Tuesday morning?"

"Nine o'clock?"

"Perfect. I have things I need to do before the fundraiser

today, anyway. Putting off our appointment will benefit me in the long run."

Liesl pulled out her phone and added the rescheduled appointment to her calendar. "Please give my apologies to Mr. Barnaby. Tell him I look forward to talking with him on Tuesday."

"Thank you for understanding, Liesl. Katherine's a handful." Miranda's sunny smile was back. "We look forward to seeing you again under better circumstances."

When Liesl turned toward the exit, she spotted one of her former Sunday School instructors in the teller line. She said hello to Mr. Mansfield. Before she left, she'd spoken to several other acquaintances in the lobby. A benefit of small-town life, friends could be almost anywhere, anytime.

When Liesl stepped onto the sidewalk, she transferred her briefcase to her left hand. With her free hand, she groped in her purse for sunglasses. Either the sun was always beating down in June in Missouri, or rain poured on its citizens. She preferred sunshine any day. The local farmers might choose the precipitation.

A black police sedan pulled to the curb. Detectives Kurt Hunter and his partner, Hector Vega, emerged from the car. Kurt was tall, with an athletic build. Hector, several inches taller than Kurt, had bushy black hair that added even more height to his appearance.

Kurt grinned at her, causing her stomach to do a quick flip.

This was the first time she'd seen him back on regular duty. He'd completed restricted duty following a recent knife wound to his shoulder, and the happiness shining on his face displayed his pleasure to be back at work.

Kurt strode toward her. "Doing a little banking this morning?"

She gave him a lazy smile. It was hard to resist the urge to toss her briefcase and hug him in the middle of downtown Mexico. "I was supposed to meet with Mr. Barnaby today, but Katherine Mull changed my plans."

Kurt's eyebrows raised. "What happened?"

Liesl shrugged. "I don't know the details. Apparently, she waltzed in and yelled at Mr. Barnaby until he whisked her into his office. From the little I could see through his glass walls, she's still in there ranting."

Kurt and Hector frowned.

"Interesting," Kurt said. "We're to report on an incident here."

"The bank reported her behavior? As threatening or something?"

Hector shook his head. "No. We've been told there might be an issue of fraud. What exactly did you see in there?"

"From the lobby, Katherine's face was flushed, and I saw her gesturing angrily at Mr. Barnaby. I couldn't hear their conversation, but I witnessed him taking a beating with her words. He seemed crushed."

Hector and Kurt exchanged a look of dread.

If they were heading off to deal with a furious Katherine, she felt sorry for them. The girl was a monster.

Liesl said, "I wish I could tell you more." After a pause, she added, "I don't understand why you've been called in. Isn't bank fraud a federal matter?"

"It depends whether the bank is a state charter or a federal charter," Hector said. "Community One Bank is a state charter." He turned to Kurt. "We gotta go."

Kurt winked at her. "I'll see you at the fundraiser."

She nodded. "I'm heading there now. It's going to be a long day. And a long evening. Are you bringing Ross?"

"No. My parents took him to the Lake of the Ozarks for a couple of weeks.

"I'll bet he was thrilled." She was fond of his son, who was nearly eight years old. Kurt had been a single parent since Ross was born.

Hector patted her on the shoulder. "Hey, I know you'll miss Ross, but I'll be there too. See you tonight."

She watched Hector and Kurt push into the bank.

Possible fraud? What could have happened to Katherine that might have been fraudulent?

Kurt took his police duties seriously, so he wouldn't provide her the answers. But she and Nicole could conjecture all about it. She and her best friend would be spending the afternoon setting up the fundraiser. Plenty of time for speculation about why Katherine jumped onto the anger bus. Liesl resented the woman trying to crush Mr. Barnaby beneath its wheels.

She prayed that Mr. Barnaby wouldn't suffer any negative consequences. Poor man.

And poor Hector and Kurt.

She pitied *anyone* who crossed paths with Katherine Mull.

Including herself.

Chapter Three

The Angel of Justice

Miraculously, I beat Katherine Mull to the bank.
She must have stopped somewhere along the
way. Maybe she stopped at her attorney's office
to report the incident and was sent here to make an official
complaint. I would have loved to have been a fly on the wall for
that conversation, but her whirlwind entrance was just as
enjoyable.

I stood in the teller line, patiently waiting to make a small
withdrawal from my account. Mr. Barnaby ushered her to his
office, tucked in behind the tellers. Thankfully, my height
allowed me to watch them through the glass walls.

My vantage point gave me a view of her facial expressions
and body language. She wasn't just angry—she was livid.
Exactly how I wanted her to be. It was hard to hide my delight
at vexing her so deeply.

Pride welled within me at causing her so much angst and

anger. Any former feelings of inadequacy and doubt melted away.

During the planning stage, I'd hoped she would take her accounts elsewhere so Mr. Barnaby and his people wouldn't have to deal with her attitude again. But she never switched banks, forcing me to act on Community One Bank.

Those who witnessed Katherine's actions in the bank stared and whispered. I joined them, acting as shocked as the others. The crowd felt sympathy for Mr. Barnaby and fury at Katherine. They were seeing the real Katherine, and she wasn't pretty.

Was I worried about the maneuvering I did to wreak havoc with her finances? Not a bit. When they try to figure out what type of fraud caused this conundrum, all fingers would point to Katherine.

This attack was only the first step in my mission. I stifled my chuckle, imagining the look on her face when she realized everything but one single dollar had been removed from her accounts.

I wish I could have seen her discovery that something had happened to the golden idol she cherished—her precious money. I hadn't expected her to notice within hours of the transfers, but she did. She must watch her money like Midas.

Had she asked Mr. Barnaby where the money had gone?

The answer was at her own fingertips. I made it look as if she moved the money herself.

And her money went to a very worthy cause.

This revenge took months of planning, but I knew I must mess with her money. It was hard to gain access to the information I needed to transfer money from her account and into the account of a well-intentioned charity. Now her fortune would help people instead of hurting them, as she did.

She helped no one in need unless someone was watching,

like at a fundraiser. She gave the impression she was generous, but her actions were only a false gesture.

Sadly, the bank officials couldn't leave her money with the charity, but it was a nice statement to make. She should have already donated thousands of dollars to help those in need, but her assets are solely for her own comfort and enjoyment. Never for others.

The Butterfly House, a shelter for women and children to escape domestic violence, could have done so much with her generous contribution. Since their accounts were at the same bank, the transfer was easy.

Too bad Mr. Barnaby had to take the brunt of Katherine's wrath. I couldn't figure out a way around that. In chess, sometimes the Queen must be sacrificed to capture to the King.

This was just the first step.

By midnight tonight, Katherine Mull would know her fate.

Chapter Four

Nicole

Nicole Smith brushed back her long, wavy hair. It was a hot day, and her hair stuck to her neck. She should have put it in a ponytail.

Why did she always let Liesl talk her into volunteering at these events?

Deep down, she liked it. It was hard to admit, even to herself, how much fun she was having. Her mission was to transform the renovated historical Simmons Stables into a magical venue for a fundraiser on behalf of its preservation society. She was succeeding.

Weeks ago, her bestie Liesl placed her in charge of decorating for the event. After agreeing to a budget, they shopped for items and scrambled to design a plan for transforming the former horse stable into a beautiful event venue. As a real estate agent, she often had to make things pretty, to craft and design, and she enjoyed it. The transformation left her energized.

Liesl had no sense of style. Planning and organizing were Liesl's superpowers. Thanks to Liesl's poor decorating skills, Nicole had been roped into assisting.

Nicole placed the final decorative centerpiece she'd created, then stepped back to admire her work. Fantastic. With a glance at the main entrance, she'd finished just in time. Guests were arriving.

She'd planned ahead by wearing a dress that was a decent length for reaching, leaning, and squatting. Its peachy hue also looked great against her brown skin tone. Perfect for the day and for all the duties performed.

The venue was beautiful, thanks to the continued improvements made possible by funds raised by Simmons Stable Preservation Society. The stable was an enormous historical structure forty-two feet wide and two hundred forty-two feet long. Its wooden exterior was painted white.

Inside, stone tiles lined the eighteen-foot-wide center aisle, dotted with guest tables. Festive lights adorned the stables' doors. The exterior iron gates recently added to the parking lot entrance were a stunning new feature.

Nicole liked to imagine what the stables had been like when the structure had been filled with expensive horses, along with their grooms, trainers, and stables boys. More than one hundred years of prized horseflesh had passed through this building.

Nicole walked to the front. She gave a critical eye to the aisle where heavy wooden crossbeams were interspersed with twinkle lights, but they were perfect. She smiled at the rainbow glow of stained-glass colors shining on the tiles.

The sun's rays streamed through the entrance's fan-shaped stained-glass window, previously restored by the Preservation Society. This window was original to the structure when it was built in 1887.

She was excited to spend the afternoon and evening with adults. Her parents were keeping Claudia before they left for vacation.

At Nicole's approach, Liesl glanced up from her clipboard. Silent auction items dotted tables at the front of her. "Hey, girl, you look nice. Even in mid-summer temperatures."

Nicole preened. "You like this?

"That peach color looks fantastic. Are you and Claudia wearing matching outfits tonight?"

"She's having an overnight with my parents tonight."

"Nice. I'll be able to keep you and Lee working even later this evening."

She chuckled. "Not if we can escape first. With your eagle eye, I doubt that will be possible. Good thing Claudia's entertained because she would want Ross here. Do you know why he's out of town?"

"He's at the lake with Kurt's folks."

"Ross is such a sweet kid." When Liesl and Kurt dated in high school, Kurt had a one-night dalliance with a girl that produced Ross. The girl wanted nothing to do with Ross, so she'd terminated her parental rights soon after he was born. Liesl and Kurt had a big breakup, but now, years later, they were dating again. "I'm glad you have moved forward with Kurt."

"Me too." Liesl turned, then sucked in a breath. "Oh, my."

Nicole glanced around but saw nothing, "Oh, my" worthy.

Turning back to Liesl, Nicole studied the distaste displayed on her face. "What's wrong?"

Liesl bobbed her head toward the parking lot. "Over there."

Nicole scanned beyond the enormous front door of the stable, which was open for guests.

The tall, thin figure of Katherine Mull strode into the stables. Several other guests spotted her and reacted. Some turned their back to Katherine. Others moved in a sideways crab crawl, obviously avoiding her.

Nicole spun back to Liesl. "I knew it. You have the same look you had when Mrs. Newman's German Shepherd vomited near your front door right before you hosted Sally Newman's bridal shower."

"Believe me, I remember." Liesl chuckled. "I can forgive a dog for almost anything, but I'm less tolerant of Katherine Mull. Could you believe she chewed out sweet Mr. Barnaby this morning? No matter what the issue, he didn't deserve that."

"What are you talking about?"

"Sorry. I meant to tell you earlier. I got distracted. This morning, Miranda Marquette relayed the ugly scene of Katherine coming into the bank and shouting."

"Whatever for?"

"I haven't found out yet. Maybe Miranda will know on Tuesday, when I go back. I had an appointment with Mr. Barnaby, but ..." Liesl nodded in Katherine's direction. "I rescheduled."

"Was she mad at him personally or mad at something involving the bank?"

"I don't know. Surely it was something the bank did. All I witnessed was her expression and waving hands. She was giving him an earful, and I felt sorry for him."

Nicole sighed. "It's not Christian of me to say this, but I prayed she wouldn't be able to come tonight."

"Of course, she would be here. She RSVP'd she'd attend."

"I know, but I was hoping for an emergency. Or some business matter to keep her away. You know she'll offend someone or even make someone cry. The person who cries will probably be me."

"Or me." Liesl laughed. "That woman! What are we going to do?"

"Is flogging illegal?"

"Yes. Go speak to her."

"Me?" She pointed a finger at Liesl. "Hey bossy boots, it's *your* turn to take one for the team."

"My turn? Why?"

"You *voluntold* me to take part in this fundraiser. I'm the unpaid worker bee here, whereas *you* are management."

Liesl blew out a big breath of air. "Let it be known, I'm going under duress. And can you believe she's early? I'm sure that was on purpose. I bet she wanted to catch us unprepared so she can sneer about it."

"That would be my guess. She likes to sneer. Now, go say hello to her. No one else is willing."

Liesl's expression at the approaching Katherine caused Nicole to grin. "A word of advice, Liesl—tell your face to use its inside voice."

Liesl pulled her lips into a forced smile and took a deep breath. "This is a fundraiser, and she's a prospect for contributing funds. I can't allow her to leave in a huff, offended by my face, can I?"

"No matter what you do, she won't contribute much. Is the sacrifice worth it?"

Liesl nodded. "Every dollar counts. It's a good cause."

Nicole motioned her head toward a group of attendees. "Look at them. They're ripping Katherine to shreds with their words."

"She asked for it by draping herself in diamonds today."

"See?" Nicole expressed her frustration by spreading her hands, palms up, at Liesl. "She simply *begs* for people to ridicule her. Why would she bedazzle herself to attend a fundraiser in a barn?"

"It's not a barn. Technically, this is a stable and has been for more than one hundred thirty years."

"Whatever. It's a shelter formerly used to house animals. No matter what you call this structure, her fashion priorities need adjustment. Go straighten her out."

Liesl crossed her arms in front of her chest. "I will not address her fashion priorities."

Nicole studied Katherine as people drifted left and right around her. Katherine resembled a bowling ball scattering pins. Kristen Hanish passed through the entrance, pushing a stroller that held her darling daughter, Sutton. When she spotted Katherine, Kristen spun the stroller in the opposite direction and almost mowed down her approaching sister, Kate Keith.

"You're right," Nicole said. "There goes sweet Kristen in a panic to get away from her. No one has acknowledged her presence, and she's nearly halfway through the stable. Look at her staring down her oversized nose at the rest of us."

"Not just that. She wrinkles that protruding nose as if registering something odoriferous."

Nicole stifled a giggle. "Odoriferous. You and your words."

"Why is she this way?"

"You mean, why does she find fault with everything and everyone except herself? Why is she the type of person who thinks the world revolves around her?"

"Yes."

"I don't know, but I'd like answers. Get going."

Liesl didn't move. "I'm scared."

With an unladylike snort, Nicole said, "I know how to work her type. When she deems you worthy of conversation, she'll treat you as if she were your best friend. Be smart and just nod at her, compliment her appearance, and then excuse yourself."

"Does that really work?"

"You bet. I do that with difficult real estate clients. It's about sixty percent effective. These types of people don't realize the compliments are insincere. Their egos feel they deserve every bit of praise."

"She brings misery to many low-income families," Liesl said. "Her landlord's business lets her have the power to rule over half of the town. Her tenants need help the most, yet get the worst from her."

Liesl stomped her foot lightly on the stones. "We need to stop her. Somehow. There has to be a way to improve conditions for her renters." Then she walked toward Katherine with a fake smile plastered across her face.

"I'll think about it," Nicole called out to Liesl.

Nicole watched as her bestie dealt with the scrunched, oversized nose of Katherine Mull. In a moment, she'd have to go rescue Liesl. No one could take Katherine's self-directed conversation for longer than a few minutes.

Katherine's presence at a party quickly revealed true friends. Loyal friends would take pity and come to the rescue, while casual friends sat back to watched the all-about-Katherine soliloquy.

Nicole straightened, gathering her inner strength as she moved toward Liesl and Katherine. She was a genuine friend. When she tightened her lips on the way, she asked for Divine help.

God, please support me to keep impolite words from escaping through these sassy lips.

Chapter Five

Arden Rahn
Summer 1920

Sounds of laughter pulled on Arden Rahn's heart. The open field was still out of sight, but that didn't stop the giggles from reaching his ears. He wished he had time to play.

What were the boys doing? How long since he'd yelled and squealed in delight like that?

Too long. Everything changed when his father died.

Regardless of whether he could play with these boys or his own brothers, he'd love to experience the freedom of a game midweek. Were these boys worry-free? He'd almost forgotten what that felt like. So long since he'd been carefree.

Arden pushed the handcart beyond the tree line and spotted the improvised ball field. A torn and frayed saddle blanket was their first base. The bottom of a broken bushel basket was home plate.

They were using a real baseball.

Imagine.

His eyes and a surprising desire lingered on the wooden bat the boys were swinging. The bat appeared professional, similar to what Ty Cobb or Babe Ruth might have used. Arden smiled.

The boys were about his age. Their clothes indicated that they were not much better off than his family, but at least they didn't have to work.

He sucked in his breath when the biggest player hit their ball into a cornfield to the left of the diamond. The game paused as everyone searched for it. He considered helping them, but his delivery could wait no longer.

He wasn't surprised he didn't recognize any of the players. The only kids he knew were either his relatives, attended his country school, or children of business owners who bought his vegetables. These boys likely lived in town and attended a local school.

A yearning crawled over him as he remained motionless, eyeing the boys as they teased the big boy who knocked the ball into the field. If only Arden could play.

He frowned at his silliness. There was work to do.

The big kid turned toward him. After a moment, he asked, "Wanna play?"

Arden smiled but shook his head. He gestured toward his cart of vegetables. "Thanks, but I've got a delivery to make." He could hear the lecture sure to come for delaying his delivery of vegetables to Mr. Morris's Grocery.

Arden turned his back on the fun and pushed his cart toward his destination. The ache in his heart lessened when he realized his skills, compared to these fellows, would be poor. Had he taken up their offer to play, he'd have made a fool of himself.

After he made his delivery and had coins jingling in his pocket, he pushed the empty cart a few blocks askew from a straight path home. Mother might not approve, but he'd take a moment to catch the horses training at the stables.

He walked toward the roads in Mexico lined with grassy fields outlined with split-rail fences that appeared to run for miles. Long barns, most painted red, dotted the landscape. These long barns were not for pigs and cattle but for handsome horses. Expensive horses.

Arden imagined men and boys of all shapes and sizes treated these animals like royalty. He veered toward the fencerow. The horses were the most beautiful creatures he'd ever seen.

These weren't ordinary plow horses. No. These seemed like they could fly like an angel. He'd seen a picture of Pegasus, and these beauties were similar.

They didn't have wings like Pegasus, but these thoroughbreds had the same curved imperial neckline. A mane flowed atop their arched necks. When they walked or trotted, their manes fluttered in the wind like water rippling across stones in a creek.

Their stature and bulging muscles made them appear as if they were the strongest creatures on Earth, and their coats gleamed in the sunlight, brushed to a perfect shine. The only mar to perfection occurred from exercise, when their powerful necks lathered.

Arden dropped his cart and took in all the colors—black, brown, chestnut, gray, and white. Some horses even had a snowy streak down their noses or white socks running along the pastern area. All were extraordinarily shiny and muscled compared to an ordinary horse.

Their eyes were enormous and gave the impression they noticed everything. Their ears and noses displayed their feelings toward humans. If their nostrils flared and the ears lay back, watch out.

Movement caught his attention, and Arden leaned against a fence rail, holding his breath as a horse and rider emerged from the stable. After waiting for a few minutes, he couldn't believe his luck. They were going to work the horses. He squinted, trying to identify the man. Was it the famous trainer, Mr. Tom Bass?

Arden realized the man on the horse was not Mr. Bass. Arden studied the men on the backs of the spirited animals, taking them through their paces. "Trainers," Arden muttered to himself. "Only the stable owner is higher up than a trainer."

Watching a trainer work a beautiful horse was something Arden enjoyed. The beast stepped around the ring. The trainer tapped his heels against the horse's belly, snapped the reins, or clucked his tongue to run through the different gaits that made these horses famous and unique.

Time was irrelevant as Arden became lost in admiration. Their high knee action fascinated him. Trainers became one with their animals. A fluid motion from man to beast was a fantastic sight.

Viewing them as they moved through their paces around the corral filled him with excitement and drama created by the horse strutting. These horses showed their pride in themselves through their smoothness, changing from one gait to another.

Approaching steps interrupted Arden's daydreaming. He turned and gawked at a man who was not only famous locally but across the country.

Tom Bass walked toward him, his stride quick and sure, even though he was an older gentleman. He had light brown skin, a square jaw, and a flash of humor in his eyes, partially hidden beneath his Derby hat.

Arden stumbled away from the fence. "I-I promise I hurt nothing, Mr. Bass."

A smile spread across the older man's dark face. "Son, don't be concerned. I want to talk to you, is all."

Arden's cheeks flushed. "Please, sir, I was just watching."

"Yes." Mr. Bass bobbed his head. "I know. I noticed you doing just that. I'm also aware how much that view appealed to you." Then he chuckled. "Aren't you one of Fredrick Rahn's boys?"

"Yes, sir." Did Mr. Bass really remember him? This man, who some say was well-known around the world? He shook his head in disbelief.

"You used to bring wood for my stoves in the winter." There was kindness in Mr. Bass's statement.

Arden lowered his head. "We had to quit cutting trees when Papa died. None of us knew enough about logging to continue."

"I was sorry about his accident." Mr. Bass glanced down and kicked the dirt with his shoe. "He was a good man."

"Yes, sir. He was." Arden moved to leave, but Mr. Bass put a hand on his shoulder.

"I perceive your admiration for these horses."

"Yes, sir." Arden watched as the horse and trainer trotted along the nearby fence. "They are such a sight."

Together, they stood silently and observed as the magnificent beast passed.

Eventually, Mr. Bass turned toward Arden and asked, "What is your first name, son?"

"It's Arden, sir."

"Would you like an opportunity to work with horses? It's obvious you love them."

Arden's mouth fell open, speechless. "I ... can't imagine anything nicer, but I don't know much about these fancy creatures. We only have a mule and a workhorse at our place."

"It's not considerably different to care for these. It's the

27

love of the animals in your heart that's important. That can't be learned. It must be there from the beginning. It's what helps you learn to nurture and train animals."

"I'd be able to work ... work for you? Around these horses?"

Mr. Bass hesitated. "I already have enough help at my stable, but earlier, Mr. Will Lee mentioned he's shorthanded right now."

"Do I just go on up to the stables and tell them I'd like to work here?"

Mr. Bass chuckled. "I believe I'd better come along. They may want someone with experience. I'll convince them your heart for the animals is more important than years of familiarity."

"You'd do that for me?"

The older gentleman patted Arden on the shoulder. "It's hard work. You'll be mucking out stalls, putting in new straw, bringing in fresh water. That sort of thing. The owners, Mr. Will Lee and George Lee, won't let you touch a horse for a long time."

"But I'd get to see them. I'd be near them, even if it's only for a few moments."

Mr. Bass nodded. "Yes, that's true."

"I've heard tell that sometimes boys will sleep in the stables with the horses, just to be on hand for any emergency?"

With a shrug, Mr. Bass said, "Happens sometimes."

"It would be an honor to work there, sir." Arden grinned. "Will they trust your recommendation of me?"

A laugh tumbled from the lips of Mr. Bass. "Why don't we find out?"

Mr. Bass led him around the fence, and they entered the front door of the stables. Arden's head moved back and forth, completely absorbed in the sights, smells, and noises of the stable.

This differed completely from anything he'd ever seen before. He watched the stunning animals, heads bobbing out of stalls, their enormous eyes following him. Arden resisted the urge to reach out and pet them as they passed.

Mr. Bass stopped abruptly, and Arden nearly ran him over.

"Sorry," Arden said as he stepped back.

"See that man there?" Mr. Bass pointed to a portly, middle-aged man wearing a weathered skimmer atop his head.

Arden nodded.

"That's Mr. Will Lee. He and his brother, George, are the owners I told you about." Mr. Bass glanced around. "I don't see George, but I'll go talk to Will. Keep quiet unless he asks you a question."

"Yes, sir."

Mr. Lee was bent over, feeling the upper part of a horse's leg, when he spotted Mr. Bass. He straightened and smiled. "Did you forget something?"

Mr. Bass smiled. "No. I came back to introduce you to the son of one of my friends. His father passed on from a logging accident."

Mr. Bass gestured toward Arden. "This is Arden Rahn. You said you needed more help."

Mr. Lee frowned. "He's a tad small, isn't he?"

"The boy is young. He'll grow."

Mr. Lee eyed Arden from tip to toe. "Won't you have to go to school?"

"Not until fall. This boy will be worth your time and trouble. You can work with him all summer and see how he does. He has a love for horses that can't be taught. I think once you get him trained, you'll keep him. Once school starts, he can work before and after school."

Mr. Lee turned to Mr. Bass. "You expect me to trust him simply due to your recommendation?"

"I'm not wrong about him, Will."

They both stared at Arden, who felt his cheeks redden by their scrutiny. He shifted his weight from foot to foot.

Mr. Bass smiled in encouragement.

Mr. Lee still appeared unconvinced, but he eventually nodded. He skewered Arden with a look. "I'll take you on a provisional basis. You prove to me you're a hard worker, and I'll give you more training and teach you skills you'll need to move up in the world of Saddlebred horses. You can start tomorrow."

"Thank you, sir. What time do you want me?"

Mr. Lee furrowed his brow. "Can get here before sunrise?"

"Yes, sir."

"Once you've cleaned the stalls I assign to you and get the horses watered, you'll be fed breakfast. Then I'll use you for various duties until late afternoon. By supper time, you're home. Pay is three dollars a week."

A surge of happiness ran Arden's length. He would be paid well. "That money will help my family. Thank you, sir." Then he stepped close and held out his hand to Mr. Lee.

Mr. Lee stared at it. It was as if he wasn't sure what to do for a moment. But he took Arden's hand and shook it.

Surprisingly, Mr. Lee had calluses to match his own. "Thank you, sir."

"You're mighty welcome, son."

Mr. Bass added, "You know I can pick a horse. I think in a few months, you'll be thanking me for picking this fine young man for you."

Mr. Lee put his hands on his waist. "Time will tell."

Arden and Mr. Bass walked out of the stable and back to the fence.

"How do I thank you?"

"You owe me nothing. Treating their horses and mules right is payment enough. I'm confident you'll always do that."

"Yes, sir. I promise."

The two stood as the horse and rider ran through the training. Once the trainer handed the horse to someone else, Mr. Bass turned to Arden.

"That horse is heading for a cool down. I'd best be off now. I'll bump into you whenever I stop by the stables."

"Thank you again, sir."

"Doing right by these animals is all the thanks I'll ever need from you."

Arden waited as Mr. Bass walked toward his own stables. Then he ran home to share the news.

Chapter Six

Arden
Summer 1920

A rden could not believe his luck ... or was it a blessing from God? He was working around the most magnificent horses in the world, with the best trainers in the world.

The sounds of the Saddlebreds, carts, and workers mingled into a delightful song. Arden breathed in the combined aroma of animals, leather, soap, manure, and grain. It smelled heavenly. He labored hard, but because it was his dream, he didn't complain.

Arden's position was the lowest rung on the stable's workplace ladder, but working hard would allow him to move up one day. The important part was that he was here, working for two of the successful owners and trainers in an area filled with them.

With this opportunity, he needed to learn everything he could from all the people here, but especially the Lee brothers.

Mr. Will Lee considered his employment provisional. This haunted Arden. He couldn't stomach being forced to walk away from these beautiful animals. To be hired permanently, Arden made sure he arrived earlier than everyone and left last. He prayed Mr. Will and Mr. George noticed this while they both scurried around, rushing every moment of their day.

In his first week of work, while Arden was cleaning a stall, a voice startled him.

"Hi, ya."

He turned to see a tall, black-haired teenager standing at the stall door. The boy held a bridle in his hands. Arden had noticed him around the barn, but they'd never spoken.

Arden smiled at this unexpected visitor. "Hi yourself. I'm Arden."

"Albert's my name, but I go by Bert. How old are you?"

"I'm twelve."

Bert nodded. "Figured I was older'n you, since I'm almost a foot taller. I'm fifteen."

Arden grinned. "I'll catch up one day." He faced the ground and pointed to his oversized rubber boots. "Seems I need my feet to grow too. These were the smallest pair I could find."

"They're probably my old pair." Bert matched his grin. "Do you live around here?"

"My mother has a small farm out of town. My Papa died about two years ago, so my older brother helps her take care of the animals. We grow corn and a few vegetables. We sell the extras in town, when we can." Arden continued to rake while they talked so no one would think he was slacking or taking a break.

Turning his back to Bert didn't cause any pause in the boy's conversation. "I don't have a father either, but I never had one. I was a shame birth, so it was always just me and my mama.

But we get by." He straightened. "I add to our purse by working here in the summers."

Arden glanced back at Bert. "All my money goes to my mama too. My oldest sister works for a wealthy family in town and comes to visit on Sunday afternoons. We older kids help Mama feed the four young ones."

A look of wonderment crossed Bert's face. "Wish I had brothers and sisters. It's lonely being the only one."

"Come home with me sometime. I'll introduce you to all of them."

"That'd be real nice."

While Arden continued to ply his pitchfork cleaning the stall, Bert explained it was a Mr. Clark and his brother-in-law, Mr. Potts, who built this beautiful stable in 1887. "They are the owners of this stable, and the Lee brothers lease it from them. Most likely, the Lees will want you on the painting crew for next spring. The red paint is only bright for a couple of years and so we paint every other year."

Arden shrugged. "As long as the Lee brothers keep me on here, I'm happy to do whatever they want."

"They'll hang onto you. You're proving to be a hard worker. It's already making some of the other guys mad, 'cause you're showin' them up."

"Mad? I don't want to make anyone mad. All I want is to keep this job."

"I'll say a word for you if they'll listen to me. You appear to be a decent fellow."

Arden winked at him. "I am. Thanks."

Bert fiddled with the bridle in his hands. "It's not easy to work here. Every day is hard, but it's worth it if you like money."

"No doubt about hard work." Six days a week, Arden woke up, washed, and then rushed to the stables on foot. Once there, the head groom told him what stalls he was to clean. And that was only the beginning of his chores.

"But you like the money?"

"My family needs the money. I give it all to them. My favorite part is leading the horses out of the stall before having to hand them off to someone else. The family gets my coins, but the pleasure of working here is all mine."

His job was to clean stalls, replace the straw bedding, and refresh the water. Grooms were in charge of the food for each horse. Many had a special diet. Working tirelessly before and after dawn, Arden finally took a break, sitting at the workers' table for a substantial breakfast. After that, it was back to the usual tasks—running, fetching, and cleaning saddles, bridles, and tack.

"Sometimes we get important people visiting here," Bert said. "John J. Pershing, the Commander and Chief of the Great War, was here once."

"You're joshing me!"

"Nope. Eyeballed him with my own two peepers. He was stiff, but you could tell he loved horseflesh. I peeked at him through the slats in a stall."

"Seeing someone famous must have been exciting."

"Famous?" Bert snorted. "Heard tell it was Mr. Bass who marched in here with you, insisting the Lees hire you."

Arden stopped and turned to him. "It wasn't that way. Mr. Bass saw me admiring a horse being trained. The Lees had just told him they were shorthanded."

"I'm just messing with you. Mr. Bass is the most famous person we see regularly around here."

"I don't really know him."

"Heard tell Mr. Bass was born in nearby Boone County, the son of a slave and a white owner. He moved to Mexico before he became famous."

"I thought he moved here from Kansas City."

"When he was younger but had made a name for himself, he was enticed to move to Kansas City to work. He started a huge horse show called the American Royal, or the Royal American, or something similar."

Arden chuckled. "These horses are comparable to royalty. It makes perfect sense to use 'royal' in the name of a show featuring them."

"Mr. Bass moved back here because Mrs. Bass liked it here. So, Mr. Bass bought a stable to continue to train. It's just a block from here."

"I know where it is. I've watched the horses there too. He never noticed me when I was over there." Arden returned to work. "This is a special place. What else do I have to learn? I'm pretty good at cleaning stalls and water buckets."

Bert scuffed his boot against the wooden gate. "Not much changes in our routine here. Clean stalls, then the horses are fed, then they're brushed and exercised, then cooled down with walks, then fed again, and finally bedded down in their stalls overnight."

"Do you ever stay overnight with an ailing horse?"

"Nah. The grooms usually do that. I don't think they trust us to care for any of them that are ailing. I have stayed when there are exceptional horses here being trained, and the trainers want someone with them day and night."

Arden grinned. "I'd like to do that sometime."

"I'm sure you will." Bert backed out of the stall entrance. "I'd better get on with it. Good to meet you, Arden."

Arden called after him, "You, too, Bert."

Other than Bert, the workers ignored Arden, but the barn dog, Jess, took a liking to him. The dog was a large, hairy mix of breeds. He was sleeping, slobbering, or following Arden around most of the day, hoping for a bite of toast Arden occasionally slipped to him.

Like everyone else associated with the stables, Jess had a job to do. He was housed in the barn overnight to alert the Lee brothers to any threat or disturbance.

There were plenty of barn cats too. Most were feral, but a few would rub against Arden's legs and allow a bit of petting. Their job was to kill the mice that always haunted any structure where grain was spilled.

The constant movement within the stables amazed Arden. Rarely did anyone stand and talk, unless they were diagnosing an injury or watching a foaling. From sunup to sundown, workers had jobs to do, and they rushed to do them.

Workers interested in moving up the ladder could be trained in higher-level skills. A stable boy could become a groom. A groom needed lots of experience working with a trainer, but they could eventually become a trainer. Some exceptional grooms and trainers moved on to other employment opportunities. With the town of Mexico having an abundance of everyone who worked around Saddlebred horses, including breeders, jobs were plentiful, and personnel bounced around.

Before working here, Arden's experience with horses was limited to draft horses and mules. Both were almost the size of the horses trained here, but most farm animals were calm and easygoing.

Arden learned the hard way that some of these particular beasts were bad-tempered and moody. Some would bite or crush toes. Others danced around and pinned him against the walls of their stalls.

Horses are prey animals and can be skittish if they are afraid. Fight or flight for them is flight. Arden learned never to be trapped inside a stall with a horse when it became frightened. These horses wouldn't hesitate to kill him to get to freedom.

Arden's plan was to learn what each horse liked. If he could please the animals he was assigned, perhaps he could move up to the better horseflesh.

Whenever the opportunity arose, Arden did his best to set up his work area in a sight line with the horses' training areas. The tack room was next to the side door, which offered a view of the west track. If he was positioned at the right angle, he could clean and polish tack while watching the horses run on the track.

He'd place his wooden stool to take in the best angle, then situate his cloths, saddle soap, and tools within reaching distance. Perfect.

Arden watched with interest as a trainer worked a chestnut stallion with a cart. When Bert approached with a saddle blanket draped over his arms, Arden called him over.

"Can you tell me why they're working that horse with a cart?"

Bert glanced at the stallion as the animal passed by, pulling the trainer in the cart. "That's Firecat. He's new here, and you can see he's young, can't you?"

Arden nodded.

"That cart teaches them to walk in a straight line. Sometimes, the young ones shift around when they walk." Bert twisted his hips. "The shafts keep them from wiggling and so that keeps them straight."

"How clever."

Bert resettled his cap. "You find all this interesting, don't you?"

"I do."

"I've got to go." He held up the blanket. "Can't let Queenie get cold."

"Thanks," Arden called after Bert as he raced away. For the life of him, he couldn't remember which horse was Queenie, but a cold horse was never good.

For nearly an hour, Arden accomplished his cleaning duties and tried to pay attention to every detail of the training he watched. His position kept him away from the special animals, but his goal was to move up to groom and actually care for them one day.

His dream was to be a full-fledged trainer. One who trained saddlehorse breeds, sold them to an eager public, and showcased them at nearby and distant shows.

Arden disregarded the fact that being a trainer could be dangerous. When a horse misbehaved and dropped its shoulder, trainers could be thrown from the saddle. No trainer enjoyed being the target of laughter while struggling to avoid the horse's hooves and weight.

A horse's strength and power displayed during training captivated Arden's attention. The most challenging horses to train were those with fierce temperaments. One was acting up now, so Arden observed how the trainer responded to the horse's antics.

Suddenly, his stool fell out from under him, causing him to crash backward on the ground.

He felt a sharp pain at the back of his head, and everything turned blurry.

Chapter Seven

Nicole

As the fundraiser evening progressed, Nicole believed it was turning out a success. The venue was full, and everyone appeared happy. The only dark cloud was Katherine Mull's attendance.

When Liesl announced the silent auction items were open for bidding, Nicole spotted someone walking away from the crowd, heading toward the exit.

It was Katherine, making an escape. In stealthy moves, Katherine slid around the corner at the main entrance. With her brightly colored dress and sandals that sparkled in the setting sun, Nicole marked Katherine as a failure in the inconspicuous bracket.

Just as I predicted, that woman came this afternoon to make sure everyone noted her presence. Then she slipped out of here when it was time to donate. That girl!

Once Liesl finished her announcement, Nicole caught her

eye and gestured with her head at the departing back of Katherine Mull.

She and Liesl shared a silent friendship communication that conveyed Nicole's unspoken "I told you so," and Liesl's reply of "I should never have doubted you."

Actually, Liesl's facial expression may have expressed sentiments more like, "Give me a break, girl. You think you're right about everything."

Regardless, Nicole's prediction of Katherine's appearance, then disappearance once money was to be spent, turned out to be correct.

When Liesl later approached Nicole and asked her to "do her magic" in raking in money for the organization, Nicole pondered her next action. Kurt was helping Gretchen at the money table so, she wasn't needed there. Nicole hovered near the silent auction tables. She could encourage people to bid, raising the bid with each signature.

Someone called out, "Hey, Nicole."

Nicole turned. It was Justin Frazier. She wrapped him in a quick hug. "Oh, I'm so glad you came."

Justin was her current real estate client and Liesl's former main squeeze. He was a blond, tall man who was personable and fun.

He pushed aside a lock of his hair that had strayed across his brow. "I don't know if the timing is right, but I have to move on, don't I?"

Nicole nodded. Sympathy rose within her for his situation. "Liesl told you she had to work things out with Kurt. That must have hurt."

He frowned. "It did."

A trace of anger crossed his features. Then he took a deep breath and sighed. "She was so kind about letting me down, I couldn't stay mad at her. That's why I wanted to come."

"Rip off the bandage?"

With a nod, he said, "She's given me the shove. Either I can be resentful of my broken heart or move on and make the best of a sad situation. I'm going to be bumping into her all over town. That's the way it is here in Mexico, isn't it?"

"You better believe it. I bump into more acquaintances in the grocery store than when I'm walking around in my neighborhood."

Justin shifted his weight. "This should be a good place for that first awkward meeting. To get it over with."

"Good of you to not hold a grudge about it."

"I still admire her. I'd like our first encounter after our breakup to be a good one. Not awkward. This way, I've chosen a place where I won't be surprised. After this, we can move on as friends."

"Are you still interested in finding a house?"

He nodded.

"No pressure, Justin." She held up a hand. "I just wondered if you plan to stay in Mexico after ... ah ... circumstances changed."

"Of course I do. Keep looking. Something is out there for me. Something that needs a little renovation."

Nicole nodded. "Will do. My greatest skill is to match people with their perfect house."

Susan and Alan Atkins approached the bidding table. Nicole exchanged greetings with them, then motioned for Justin to follow her.

She stepped back from the table, and in a dramatic whisper said, "I assumed your job with Lumber City would force you to move."

"I love this town. There have to be other management jobs here or in a nearby community. I'm tired of being relocated. I'd like to set down roots."

Nicole's eyebrows rose. "That's wonderful. I'll tell every businessperson in town you're available for a management position. I can talk you up to all my connections. In no time, you'll soon be interviewing for openings."

He grinned. "Sounds great."

She was happy to help him. He needed a boost after what Liesl handed him. "Do you need it to be in retail or construction? I assume you know about both of those topics."

"I do, but I have other skills. Like computer skills, customer service, and such."

"Why don't you come to my office on your next day off?"

"I'm off on Tuesday if that works. Are you going to show me more houses?"

"I certainly will but bring your resume with you. I can look it over. Maybe add some suggestions or improvements. It's important for me to know what skills you have. Then I can to *sell* those to my contacts."

He grinned. "Would I owe you a retainer fee?"

She laughed. "No, sir. My payment would be your time volunteering at fundraisers once you're a permanent resident."

"Consider it done."

Nicole glanced at her smartwatch. "It's time for my handsome husband to arrive and enjoy the fundraiser until he has to help us clean up, pack up, and transform this space back into a stable. Unless you desire to be put to work, I suggest you find Liesl."

They agreed on a time for Tuesday. Then Justin said, "Any idea where Liesl is? I'd like to talk to her about my plan to stay. I hope she won't mind." A sadness behind his beautiful light blue eyes wasn't expressed by his words.

"She'll be delighted. I promise."

"I hope you're right. See you later."

Nicole winked at him as she teased, "You can't go yet. Not

until you make a bid on something at this table. That's my job tonight."

He chuckled and began perusing the items offered.

As he did, Nicole watched him. How proud she was of him. She wasn't sure whether he'd started loving Liesl, but he'd certainly been fond of her. He was suffering but pushing through it. How painful love and falling in love could be.

Nicole said hello to Mr. Mansfield as he joined Justin at the bidding table.

She purposely had not told Justin her other plan. She'd introduce him to all the local single girls of an appropriate age. Clandestinely, of course.

God, regardless of the extent of Justin's pain over Liesl breaking up with him, please help his heart to heal. Lead him or help me lead him to the right woman for him.

Nicole chuckled when she realized she couldn't tell Liesl about her matchmaking plan for Justin. Liesl would say it's none of her business or that she's not a matchmaker. Neither of these statements were true. For years, she'd told Liesl that Kurt had never stopped carrying the torch for her. Recent events proved her prognostication correct.

Who would be right for Justin? This little conundrum made her romantic heart pound with excitement. She loved being a matchmaker. God had a plan. She hoped His plan was to allow her to lead Justin to his *true love*.

Chapter Eight

Liesl

What a night! A nice turnout made all their effort worthwhile.

When she'd checked in at the financial table, Kurt grinned at her. Gretchen was too busy to tell her anything. When the accountant at a fundraiser is too busy to talk to, it usually means money is flowing.

After what happened at the last fundraiser here, Kurt volunteered to sit with Gretchen. Police protection might be over the top, but it stopped a previous theft. They wanted no opportunity for another.

Liesl noticed Jimmy Reed, a Missouri State Highway patrolman, who was a friend of Kurt. She chucked to herself when she remembered the first time she'd seen him. Her first impression had been that he was a *bad guy* at a previous fundraiser. She couldn't have been more wrong.

Now, she walked over and chatted with him. Jimmy's wife was a *horse person,* and he was just along for the ride.

After their conversation, Liesl decided to sit. If only for a moment. She spotted a chair in the back left corner, across the room from Gretchen's payment area, and strode to it with speed in her step.

Liesl slid into the chair and sighed as she slipped off her shoes. She swiped the sweat from her neck with the back of her hand and bent to rub her throbbing feet. The crowd blocked her view, which she decided was a good thing. More people meant more money spent. At least, she hoped it did.

She needed to talk to Nicole about her plan to buy the city block for her Community Center. The commission Nicole would make would thrill her. Liesl grinned just thinking about it. However, they'd both been so busy setting up for this fundraiser, they hadn't discussed it.

The nearby crowd parted, allowing Liesl to see Justin hurrying past Alice Leonatti. Was he striding toward her? His presence at this event was unexpected.

She plastered a smile on her face as she experienced several emotions. Sadness from the hurt she caused him in their last conversation, a spark of excitement at seeing his handsome face, an ounce or two of dread about speaking with him.

Did everyone experience such emotions? She'd been through the torture of talking with Katherine Mull, and now she faced a different torture by Justin's appearance.

Justin smiled and then veered to grab a folding chair. He snagged it and carried it over toward her.

Her eyes darted toward the finance table. Was Kurt seeing this? She couldn't tell, thanks to the people gathered between them. What would he think about this?

She scrambled to locate her shoes and get them back on her feet. "Hello, Justin. Thank you for coming. I apologize for you having to scrounge for a chair." Heat from embarrassment climbed up her neck to her face.

He smiled down at her. "No worries."

"Other than a disgraceful lack of chairs, have you enjoyed the fundraiser so far?"

"Yes. It's full of people bidding on items, which is good." He held the chair but didn't move to sit down. "You're in a perfect spot for us to have a conversation. I'd like to talk to you, if that's okay."

She blinked at him in surprise. "Really?"

"If you're not ready to talk, I can leave."

"It's fine. I'm just …" She searched for the right word. "Surprised you'd want to speak with me."

"When you broke off things, I wasn't pleased. But no matter what, Liesl, I want us to be friends."

She nodded. "I'd like that."

"Our breakup was kind, and I appreciate that. You want to make a go with Kurt. That's reasonable."

"I'm happy you understand."

"I've had time to think. There are things I'd like to discuss. Will you hear me out?"

"Of course." She gestured toward the chair. "Put that chair next to me, and let's talk."

He grinned, and she relaxed. He'd been upset and stiff when she'd broken things off a few weeks ago. Not that she blamed him. She'd hurt him. Hurting people, especially someone she cared about, felt terrible.

Once settled in the chair, he said, "I wish only the best for you and Kurt."

"Thank you. It's a difficult situation to have put you in. Again, I apologize."

"It's fine. Just don't ask me to be friends with *him* right now. I resent him. It's not related to anything you've done. That's on me."

She chuckled. "That's a reasonable request. Don't blame

you for not wanting to cozy up to Kurt."

"Besides being fond of you, I'm fond of this town. I'd like to stay."

"Like permanently?"

"Yes."

A surge of genuine delight ran through her. "That's fantastic news."

"I'll have to find a different job, but I've talked to Nicole about it tonight, and we have a plan."

"Nicole has wonderful business connections. She can be a big help to you. I'll do everything I can too."

He met her eyes, then glanced away. "I'd hoped you would be okay about this. I wasn't sure, considering ...."

Liesl reached over and patted his upper arm. "Trust me. I'm pleased about your decision."

When he smiled at her, Liesl's spirit lifted. She hadn't wanted to hurt him. But her powerful feelings for Kurt forced her to be honest with Justin. Anything less would have been cruel.

"With our friendship intact, I'll plan to stay in Mexico."

Liesl grinned. "I want to remain your friend."

Justin relaxed into his chair. "You can always call or text me for anything."

"Same goes for me. What if I ask you to do charity work? Is that acceptable?"

He chuckled. "Of course. I admire all the charitable work you perform."

"I appreciate that."

Within moments, they transitioned to having a natural conversation.

The sound of someone clearing his throat caused Liesl to look up. Kurt stood in front of her, but he was looking at Justin.

The men stared at each other, neither looking pleased.

Kurt pulled his face into a neutral expression and turned to her. "I'm sorry to interrupt, but Gretchen is ready for the next table to close out bidding."

Liesl stood abruptly. "Thank you, Kurt."

She turned to Justin, who was now also standing. "Excuse me. Duty calls."

"Of course."

When she turned around again, Kurt was gone.

Liesl walked to the auction tables, praying for the three of them to get along.

One day. Obviously, not today.

Chapter Nine

Liesl

Liesl sighed as the headlamps of her SUV illuminated her garage's exterior. It had been a long day. After she'd parked her car in the garage, her tension seeped away. She was exhausted, but home.

The fundraiser was a success, but it had drained her energy. Now she understood why no one did it more than twice a year. A big job that paid big rewards. Worth it, thanks to a tremendous volunteer effort.

Bless Lee Smith, Nicole's husband, for overseeing hauling away all the rented tables and chairs. He, along with her, Kurt, and Nicole, had packed them into his truck so they could be returned tonight. Kurt rode with Lee to help him unload the tables and chairs. They were coming to her house with boxes of Aunt Suzanne's china, silverware, and serving dishes, plus the boxes of decorations to be stored in the attic.

She would ask the guys to leave the dish boxes on the kitchen table. Washing, drying, and storing them in the butler's pantry could wait. Mrs. Zimmerman wouldn't mind helping her with them when she came to work on Monday. The decoration cartons could be stacked in the attic. Then she could collapse in her bed.

Lee and Kurt deserved special kudos for their labors, but also for their patience tonight. Both had listened, as neutral as Switzerland, while she and Nicole debated the future use of the table decorations Nicole had made. Should they be kept for another fundraiser or party? Or donated for use at the Butterfly House?

Liesl made an argument for the Butterfly House. "They can make the women there happier. Those traumatized ladies and children need every bit of happiness we can provide."

Nicole fisted her hands on her hips and dug in for a fight. "These fabulous decorations, plus the dishes and silverware you inherited, should be part of a party business you run from your beautiful home."

Liesl waved at the white flag of peace. "I'm too tired to argue about this now. Let's compromise. How about we store the decorations in my attic for now? This discussion can be saved until both of us aren't so tired. Agreed?"

Thankfully, Nicole had nodded her head. "Deal."

With both sides happy, the four of them loaded Lee's truck in peace.

An unfamiliar stiffness assailed Liesl as she climbed out of her SUV. Why should stiffness surprise her after the workout they'd put in this afternoon and evening?

As she walked to the back of her car, the sound of an opening door interrupted her musings. She spotted Joey entering the garage's side door. Joey lived in an apartment Liesl added to the garage after there had been a fire.

Joey wore his signature blue jeans and plaid shirt. His normal, neutral expression scrunched in concern.

Her stomach tightened. "What's wrong, Joey?"

"I thought about calling you. Some men came here."

Liesl studied Joey's puckered face as she walked toward him. Joey was an elderly man with birth defects but functioned well. It was rare to see him upset.

"What men?"

"They drove three white Chevrolet Silverado fifteen-hundred pickup trucks. The two white ones were both twenty-twenty-one models. The silver one was a twenty-twenty-four." Joey liked cars and trucks and never forgot a vehicle.

"You didn't recognize any of them?"

He shook his head.

Odd. Joey knew a vast majority of people. Although he had other disabilities, his brain remembered details, including vehicles, people, and their names.

"I wasn't expecting anyone."

Joey nodded. "You were at Simmons Stables."

"Yes, that's right." Something about these men disturbed Joey. She'd have to ask the right questions until she could identify the problem. "What did they do that caused you concern?"

"One went up the steps of your porch. Another walked all the way around to the Boulevard side of your house. The fence stopped him. The third one walked over here and rang my doorbell."

Loud noises bothered Joey. *I need to have someone disconnect his doorbell since it's truly torture for him.*

"Did you answer the door?"

"No."

"What did the man do when you didn't?"

"He touched the flowers in my flower box." The pucker of Joey's face and the disgust in his voice made Liesl's heart hurt. Joey didn't like anyone touching what he'd planted. They were for him to care for, beautifully lined up in boxes under his large picture window.

"I'm so sorry, Joey. What happened after that?"

"He walked all the way around the garage. The other guy, the one on your porch, came back down the steps. Together, they walked to the back of your house, opened the gate, and went into your backyard."

Liesl gasped. "Are you kidding me?" Even as this question escaped from her lips, she was well aware Joey could not tease or skew the facts. He only stated the truth, as he witnessed it.

Anger surged within her. "That's trespassing."

Joey's gaze dropped to his shoes. "It wasn't right."

"That's correct."

Joey's shoulders slumped. "I should have called you."

"You could have, but I might not have been able to get here before they left. Don't worry about that, Joey. How long were they in my backyard?"

"No more than a minute."

"Can you describe the men?"

"One of them was really tall. Like Mr. Sonny Dillard. He had hair the color of your cousin Gretchen but less curly."

Mr. Dillard was a tall drink of water, on the thin side. Gretchen was red-headed with German roots but appeared as if she'd just arrived from Ireland or Wales.

"One was young. About the same age as Guy Peterson."

She nodded. Guy was about seventeen, still in high school, and worked at Kentucky Fried Chicken. Since Joey loved fried chicken, he ran into Guy frequently. "What about the third guy?"

"That one was shorter than the tall man, but had the same hair. He was older than the tall guy. And he bossed the other guys around, pointing out things to them."

"What did he point out?"

"After they come out of your gate, they stepped back and looked up at your roof. He pointed to it twice. Then, when they walked back to their trucks, he motioned toward the driveway."

These strange visitors mystified Liesl. She hadn't asked anyone to inspect her property. They didn't sound like they were from Mexico, either. With Joey's failure to recognize them, odds are they were from out of town. He'd remember area workers, their vehicles, and their uniforms.

"I stayed in my apartment since they didn't look like nice people." He turned his faded blue eyes to her. "You always let me know when someone is going to do work around here or might need to talk to me. *Always.*"

She nodded. "I try to keep you informed about repairs and construction."

"Two reasons something was wrong." Joey counted on his fingers. "One, you didn't tell me they might come. And second, I didn't recognize them."

"You did the right thing by staying inside. If anything similar ever happens, please call me or Kurt, or call nine-one-one."

He frowned. "Nine-one-one is for emergencies. It wasn't an emergency. I can call you or Kurt if it happens again."

"You're right. However, if you're uncomfortable with a situation, you can reach out to the police. You know Miss Roxy?"

He nodded. "She drives a blue twenty-twenty Honda Civic EX, works the front desk of the public safety building, and attends First Baptist Church."

"Good to know." Liesl smiled. "You can call the direct police number instead of nine-one-one if it's not an emergency. Someone on duty, like Miss Roxy, will answer that call. Then you can ask them to send someone here to check out whatever is causing you concern."

Joey stared at her, appearing to consider the validity of this option.

"I'm never too busy for you, Joey. Call me anytime, no matter what I'm doing. As for the police and nine-one-one, if you are afraid, then that is emergency enough to call for help. You choose whether to call nine-one-one or their main phone number. Okay?"

He nodded.

"Do you want to talk to Kurt about these men? He'll be here in a few minutes."

"No." He turned and walked away.

"Hey, Joey?"

He stopped and swiveled his head in her direction.

"Thank you for protecting me and my property. I know I'm safer with you here."

He almost smiled before he disappeared through the garage door.

The light breeze that kept the day's temperature bearable had stilled, replaced by the mugginess of the evening. Cicadas sang their tune as Liesl stalked toward the fence in her backyard. *What were those men doing here? What were they after?*

After checking to ensure the gate was securely closed, she glanced around. Nothing appeared missing or out of place.

At the front of the house, she found no advertisements or door hangers the men might have left.

Once inside, she punched in the code to disable the alarm while Barney, her adopted beagle mix, jumped in excitement at her arrival. Tonight, she was happy to have an alarm, cameras, and a dog.

She set down her purse and went to the back door. With Barney trailing along, she crossed the backyard and locked the gate. Unless someone could scale that high fence, she and her dog should not have any more *visitors* in the backyard.

Back inside, she tapped out a text message to Mrs. Zimmerman to come in through the front door on Monday, saying she'd explain later.

Thank the Lord for surveillance cameras. She had them running, and now she could look at everything that had happened earlier. Her instincts told her Joey related the important events. But, if he missed something, the video should cover it.

Chapter Ten

Kurt

Kurt stared out the passenger window as Lee drove to Liesl's house. The sounds of a Cardinal baseball announcer calling the action of the ninth inning rang through the radio speakers, but Kurt had no interest in the view or the baseball game.

He'd felt uneasy since he walked up and found Liesl talking with her old boyfriend tonight. His stomach churned. Was Justin still a *former* boyfriend, or was this guy back in the picture somehow?

"Something wrong, Kurt? You've been quiet tonight."

Kurt debated about discussing this with the husband of Liesl's best friend, but Lee was his friend. He trusted him and could use his opinion.

Kurt turned to Lee. "I walked up on Liesl, deep in conversation with Justin tonight. They were smiling at each other. I didn't want her to see how angry it made me, so I left as soon as I gave her the message that caused me to hunt her down in the first place."

"You think something was going on between them?"

Kurt shrugged. "I don't know. They both looked so happy. To be fair, I have no idea what they were discussing. Think I should be concerned?"

"Like I'm some expert on women?"

Kurt smiled. "Well, you are married to one."

"That probably makes me even less of an expert, but I will tell you not to jump to any conclusions. Talk to her, man. Push your fear to one side and find out what happened between them. I feel like you're borrowing trouble. No need to stew about it until you know the truth."

When they arrived at her house, Liesl ran out the door to help them unload.

Kurt climbed out of the truck with dread. Lee was right. He needed to talk to her. In private.

Over the top of arms full of packed boxes, she filled them in on her unexpected visitors. The more Liesl explained what Joey said about them, the more Kurt worried. Something was off about these guys.

After three trips to various areas of her house, including the attic, their work was complete.

"I was going to have Lee drop me back at my car tonight," Kurt said. "I left it parked at the Stables. Are you okay if I send him home while you and I review that video footage? I want to see it. Now. You can take me back to the stables when we're through."

He also thought this might give him an opportunity to ask about Justin.

Liesl turned to Lee. "Go on, Lee. You and Nicole have done so much to make the fundraiser a success. Thanks for all your help. I'll get Kurt back to his ride after he checks out the video of my trespassers."

Lee gave her a big grin. "We're always glad to help with a worthwhile charity. If you need protection from those *visitors*, you know I can take 'em out."

"Hey, buddy." Kurt grinned. "Leave this to me. I'll take 'em out."

Although Kurt prided himself on being an athlete, Lee was a more imposing figure. Tall, broad-shouldered, with a build developed as a high school athlete. Since then, he'd never let his physical condition slide. He was a high school social studies teacher, plus he coached soccer and wrestling. All that kept him in top shape.

Lee flashed him a grin. "See you guys later. Never figured you'd have a movie date involving surveillance video."

He gave Liesl a hug. "Don't stay up all night. You look as tired as I feel."

She nodded. "I promise. I am tired."

Kurt clapped Lee on the back when he turned to leave. "I didn't think of this situation as a movie date, but I'll take time with Liesl, regardless of the circumstances."

When Lee left the house, Liesl surprised Kurt with a quick hug.

"Thank you for staying. I'm glad you want to see the tape. These men kind of scare me."

He reached for her hand. "Not to worry. We'll get it figured out."

Liesl's security system was upstairs in the smallest spare bedroom. It didn't take long to pull up the footage of the early evening visitors.

Kurt stiffened when he watched the strangers enter her backyard. "I'm glad Joey had the sense not to open his door to these guys. Do you have a spare external drive I could use? I want you to copy this for me."

"Sure. But don't watch anymore until I get back." Liesl disappeared and returned with a thumb drive and her laptop.

As they watched the events play out, Liesl commented, "Joey described them perfectly."

Kurt nodded. "He's right on the money with these guys. They're definitely acting suspicious."

"He didn't say so, but I think they scared him. He instinctively knows who is good and who is bad. I don't know if it's because he observes all the details or whether it's his special mind, but I trust him and his impressions."

Together, they made notes on her laptop. Liesl typed a list of details about the men and their vehicles. The recording was black and white, but thanks to Joey, they had hair color and estimates of their height to log.

Kurt then made a copy of the pertinent digital materials, isolated several images of each man, and copied these and his and Liesl's notes onto the thumb drive. The closest shots were of the man who approached the front door. The video was not clear enough to pick up the number and state of the license plates of the trucks, but he could tell the state of Missouri did not issue them.

He pulled out his phone, thumbed through his contact list, and then made a call. After speaking to his CI, he hung up the phone and said, "I'm embarrassed."

"Whatever for?"

"I should have guessed their identity. I've had training about them."

"Who did you call?"

"One of my CI's."

"What? You're doing that *cop-speak* stuff again."

He shook his head. "Sorry. I called a confidential

informant. We call them CI's. This one has a nose for dirty work. He's as accurate as a bloodhound. He said the men on your video are likely part of a nomadic group."

"A nomadic group? I don't understand."

"People mistakenly call them gypsies."

"Like a fortune-telling gypsy?"

"Long ago, maybe. Not so much now. They can also be called travelers. Some of these groups are Middle Eastern Europe immigrants from Poland, Yugoslavia, and Romania. Others are of Irish, Welsh, or English descent."

Liesl crossed her arms. "That's all good information, but what are they doing in my yard?"

"This group appears to be construction workers who follow storms from state to state. They offer services like roof repairs, painting, and asphalt for driveways, tree trimming, and such. Sometimes they do a good job."

"And when they don't?"

"They can be scam artists. They might increase their prices after they've given a verbal estimate and then demand the difference. Or do shoddy work. It depends upon who you hire."

"So, they're from out of state?"

Kurt nodded. "One reason for the group to be nomadic is to make it hard for law enforcement to pin down to a residence. Even an identification is difficult. Families share the same name and use a nickname. Like a variation of Edward, can be Ted, Teddy, Ed, and Eddy."

"Just first names?"

"Last names too. Like the surname Stuart. It can be spelled S-t-u-a-r-t or S-t-e-w-a-r-t and other variations."

"I didn't know." Liesl took Kurt's hand and led him toward the staircase. "How about we discuss this over a glass of iced tea?"

"Good idea." Maybe he could ask her about Justin before

she dropped him at his car. Although she wasn't acting any differently toward him, he couldn't shake his feelings about Justin.

Once seated at the kitchen table with glasses of tea in front of them, Kurt returned to the subject of her visitors.

"My advice is to have nothing to do with these characters. Mexico has plenty of licensed and bonded workers from the state of Missouri. They'll do any storm repairs you need."

"Why are these *travelers* in Mexico now?"

"Could have been that storm.

"What storm?"

He sipped his tea. "Back in March or April, we had a hailstorm."

"But that was tiny hail. How could it have caused damage?"

Kurt shrugged. "I think it's funny they showed up at your house. With your slate roof. That roof can last a hundred years. You'd have to have a Storm of the Century, with huge hail, to break your slate."

"Well, *that* didn't happen."

"No. But seeing them gesture toward your gravel driveway, they may come back to talk to you about asphalt."

Liesl crossed her arms. "I wouldn't use anyone but a local contractor for my property."

"Other people might get conned into thinking they're getting a bargain. These groups are notorious for soliciting homeowners. They sometimes offer *leftover materials* at a discount from a *previous job*. Innocent citizens will pay too much or receive poor-quality work. Possibly both."

Liesl rose and opened a cabinet. "Care for a cookie?"

He hesitated and then gave in to the urge. "Just a couple."

Liesl returned to the table with cookies on a small plate. Could you stop it?"

Kurt snagged one. Between bites he said, "I'll talk to the Chief about reaching out to the media, warning people about using unknown and unlicensed workers. He can encourage them to use local, licensed and bonded contractors and skilled labor."

"I'll tell Nicole to get the word out to all the realtors in town. They spend their days talking to renters and homeowners."

He ate another cookie, finished his iced tea, and patted his pocket where he'd placed her thumb drive with the photos and video of her visitors. "Ready to drop me off? Your exhausted self needs to go to bed."

"I do need sleep." Liesl smiled. "Thank you for making me feel better about those men."

"Just doing my job." He leaned across the table and pushed a stray lock of her hair back behind her ear. "I have one question before we go."

"Shoot."

"Should I be worried about seeing you and Justin in deep conversation at the fundraiser tonight? You both were all smiles."

Liesl frowned. "I knew you weren't happy to find us together, but you have nothing to worry about. He wants to stay in town and remain friends with me. But that's it. Just friends."

He struggled not to show his displeasure at this news. His thoughts tumbled. *He wants to stay in town. Like forever? This man will never be out of the picture.*

Liesl narrowed her eyes. "Is that going to be a problem for you?"

Kurt sighed. "Him staying in town isn't great news from my point of view. I thought he had a job where he moved every few years."

"He does. But he wants to settle down. To move here permanently."

His stomach fell. *This man was never leaving!*

Liesl patted his hand. "I promise you, he and I will just be friends. Nothing more."

He entwined her hand in his. "I want us to make this work. For the long haul."

Her eyes filled with tears. "So do I."

With a rush of emotion, he leaned over and kissed her. When they pulled apart, he said, "We'll discuss this in more detail after you've had some rest. Ready to take me to my car?"

She squeezed his hand, then released it and stood. "That ride to your car might cost you more kisses."

Kurt strode to her and wrapped his arms around her. "A welcome price to pay."

Chapter Eleven

The Angel of Justice

Oranges and pink peaked over the stable as I walked out of the fundraiser. First goal of the night, establish an alibi. Fulfilled. Now to head home and prepare for my evening excitement.

My pulse raced as I drove through town. Each block brought me closer to putting my plan into action. Closer to rendering justice.

Once home, I dressed in black from head to toe, including black rubber gloves and charcoal on my face. I should be all but invisible to a normal citizen going about their business.

Next stop, Katherine's swanky neighborhood.

She had departed from the fundraiser long before I did. It was a no-brainer she'd make a beeline to her car once she'd made an appearance. Of course, she'd want no part of actually handing over her precious coins for a charitable cause.

Her only charity was "The Enrichment of Katherine Mull Fund."

Hopefully she was rushing to a *meeting* I set up for her at the Pearl Martini and Wine Bar rather than straight home. Last week, I left a letter in her mailbox that promised to enlighten her about saving money for her rental properties. She believed one of her accountants wrote it.

If she cared about the people who worked for her, she would have known the letter was a ruse. The accountant I urged her to meet was on vacation with his family in Kansas City.

I needed her to wait at least fifteen to twenty minutes so I could get to her house first.

I jogged up to her luxury home and waited near the extensive bushes near the garage door. No need for me to put myself in plain view. Right on schedule, the purring engine of her Corvette Stingray broke through the night's silence. She was home.

Once Katherine opened the garage door high enough, I rolled under and scrambled under her Hummer, parked in the adjoining slot.

With its large tires and elevated frame, I had plenty of room to maneuver. I need only wait until the time is right.

After months of surveillance, I knew her habit was to close the door before she exited any of her vehicles. Tonight was no different. This safety feature of hers would block anyone outside from seeing inside the garage. And seeing me.

When she opened her driver's door, I slid out from under the Hummer. Staying low, I crept closer. As she exited the car, I made my move. I hit her head from behind with the small hammer I'd brought with me.

She melted like chocolate on a hot day, sliding toward the floor. I confirmed she was unconscious.

Leaving her there, I verified that the house door was unlocked. So many foolish people didn't lock their houses—

Katherine was one of them. They didn't realize how easy it was to override an electric garage door.

Her security alarm warning sounded, allowing thirty seconds to enter the code. I punched in the correct 6-digit alarm code on the first try. This wasn't the first time I'd disarmed this system.

If things went according to plan, it would be my last time.

From the garage, I pulled Kathrine's limp body through the back door and into the mudroom area. This was a challenge. I may have maintained my military running habits, but I'd neglected my strength training, and she weighed more than I'd expected. With great effort, I drug her into the kitchen area and deposited her into a nearby wooden kitchen chair.

Working with speed, I stuffed a small dishcloth in her mouth, then looped a large dishtowel around her head, securing it with a plastic zip tie. Perfect. No one would hear any sounds from her.

I zip-tied her wrists together and secured her lower arms to the armrests of the chair. Her eyes fluttered, and a few moaning noises escaped her gag.

When she opened her eyes, I would be there for her to see. She'd recognize me.

When the dullness in her eyes was replaced with confusion, I moved in front of her. She stared until anger replaced her confusion.

I slapped her, wanting to knock the anger out of her. I was the angry one now. Not her.

How long had she deserved to be hurt? How long has she needed punishment for all the gut-wrenching pain and grief she'd caused me and my wife?

Although I yearned to pummel her until she breathed no more, I pushed down these feelings. Impulse wouldn't do. No. The way I'd planned was a better way for her to die.

For the first time, Katherine Mull was not only looking at me but *seeing* me. The surprise and disgust she displayed as she comprehended her circumstances brought life back into my veins.

Fear painted her face as my ability to harm her registered. Those slanted eyes were wide open in shock.

"You scared?"

Immediately, she narrowed her eyes and stared darts at me.

With a grin, I said, "You should be afraid. Retribution has arrived for all the wrongs you've accumulated in your miserable life."

Katherine's eyebrows, visible above the gag, knitted together. She struggled to free her wrists from the zip ties.

"Are you unsure about all the evil things you've done? Need me to list them for you? Theft, breach of contract, deception, malicious mischief ... murder."

Her eyes widened at the last crime. After a pause, she fought for her freedom again.

This visible panic displayed by her filled my heart with joy. Witnessing her fruitless efforts to escape created a smile. I'd almost forgotten how good such things felt.

The self-inflicted injuries she caused were a surprise. The ties cut into her wrists, causing blood to drip onto the seat of the chair, slowly pooling on the floor. Her struggle increased as fright overtook her.

Watching that blood flow made me laugh aloud.

Anger flashed in her eyes.

"Did you think you could mistreat innocent people and never be punished for your sins? Charge your tenants' multiple rate increases related to property worse than most doghouses?"

She mumbled into her gag.

"Your rentals don't meet the basic needs to maintain human life. You provide roofs that leak and toilets that won't flush, then you refuse to repair them. These things cause your renters to bend under your costs until they are broken. Did that stop you?"

She shook her head from side to side, the gag keeping her silent.

"Ding! Ding! Ding! You are correct. You did not stop."

I yanked a nearby chair around to sit in front of her. "Instead, you wait until a tenant leaves, have the shack cleaned, then rent it to some other unsuspecting soul who can't afford it. Of course, you sue the tenant who left for breach of contract. What about your duty to provide a decent property? Do you care that people have died because of your mistreatment?"

Her squirming stopped. She stared at me. *Was she upset people died because of her actions? Did she have a heart, after all?*

"You balance on a tightrope between following the law and mistreating human beings. No one has stopped you."

She renewed her efforts to escape the chair.

When I grew tired of watching her, I said, "I'm stopping you now."

Katherine ceased her struggle. Her poison dart eyes glared at me.

I laughed again because she could no longer hurt me.

"Do you only care about money? Or is it power you love? Are you really powerful when you only hurt weak people who can't fight back? Do you enjoy profiting from misery?"

She remained motionless.

"The only love you experience is self-love. Your renters mean nothing to you except to make more money and increase your own wealth."

She fought her bindings with renewed vigor.

"You're wasting your time, sweetheart. This is the end of the line."

I stood up, kicked my chair out of the way, and paced back and forth in front of her.

"Your tenants' demands for necessary repairs have been ignored for the last time. Their health and welfare depended upon you to fix the leaks in their roofs, to clean up the mold and mildew inside the homes, and to provide protection from the elements."

I stopped pacing anticipating her reaction to my next statement.

"Katherine, my dear, someone else will inherit what you own. Soon. They'll do a better job of taking care of your renters. They will have a conscience."

Her eyes grew wide when my meaning sunk into her ice-cold soul.

"You're out of time. I waited for God to bring justice. When it didn't come, I took control of your destiny. Now I'm going to kill you."

She made muffled sounds in her gag while she squirmed. Fresh blood dripped from her wounds.

"You're dying in the most miserable way I could imagine. For the first time in your wretched, greedy life, you'll understand what it means to suffer. To die in agony."

Tears fell from her eyes as her body racked with sobs. Her hair hung in clumps around the gag, and black mascara left trails down her cheeks.

Did I feel pity?

No.

For safety, I shut off the electricity to the house and the pilot light to the water heater near the kitchen. No sense blowing myself up while creating an inferno for her.

It took a few minutes to open and unlock every window on

the first floor. It was time well spent. A fire needed oxygen and my efforts should provide plenty.

Fires also needed a fuel load, something to burn. I glanced around at all the thick wood floors, gigantic pieces of furniture, and scattered finery. Plenty of items here to add to the fire.

Then, I disabled every heat sensor and smoke alarm in the main area.

As I walked the house making the necessary preparations, the temptation was great to pocket objects of value. Her jewelry alone was worth a fortune.

I resisted.

The fastest way to get caught was greed.

The sheer terror on Katherine's face when I sloshed gasoline around the house was worth all the effort I'd put into this plan.

Finally, she understood.

She had been sentenced to death. Now death was staring her in the face, moments from occurring.

The fear she displayed lifted my spirits. I'd been down in a pit of despair for such a long time. Then, I'd been actively planning this revenge. Now I'd reached the payoff, and it was worth it.

I poured multiple cans of gasoline around the lower level of the house. When I was down to the final can I poured half of it around her.

Time to go.

I verified the now blubbering Katherine was still tied to the chair.

"Good riddance, Katherine."

She looked up, then swung her head toward me.

I jumped out of the way, splashing gasoline on my pants thanks to the puddle around her.

With the last of the gasoline in the can, I poured a trail

from the kitchen, through the mudroom, and out to the garage, leaving all doors wide open. The fumes smelled strong.

Then I opened the side door of the garage, carefully lit a Zippo lighter as far away from me as possible, and flung it on the gasoline trail.

When the flame jumped and ran along the gasoline trail, I laughed. Chills ran through me as I watched the flame crawl into the house.

"Enjoy your time with the devil, Katherine! Earth doesn't need you here anymore."

I hoped she could hear me over the sound of flames eating away at her home, dancing their way to her.

Chapter Twelve

The Angel of Justice

I silently passed into the bushes at the corner of Katherine's garage and paused. The cul-de-sac was dark and void of people. Only the cicadas chirped in the night. This neighborhood had enormous houses built on large lots. As a result, very few people were nearby. Few were active this late at night.

Once I was sure the flames were leaping inside Katherine's house, I made my way, bush by bush, into the acres behind her home. In my dark attire, I would not attract attention. I'd been doing this for weeks and no one spotted me.

When I reached the end of her property line, I stepped out and jogged along the plowed fields, as would a normal jogger. It was darker out here, away from the lights of the neighborhood, but I made good time.

Once I drew near to my chosen hiding place, I entered the tree line. About 60 paces in, I found the tallest tree. This was where I'd hidden the gas cans. Now, I had different tools in this spot.

A few days ago, I'd dug a hole. On my way here, I'd buried a bag with face wipes, a pair of jeans, a pair of sandals, a T-shirt, and a baseball cap. I located the bag in the dark with no problem. Once changed out of my dark clothes and running shoes, I cleaned my face, removed my black knit cap, and changed into these fresh clothes and sandals. Everything I had been wearing was reburied.

As I walked back to town, the small hammer I'd used was thrown in a handy pond. I dropped the leftover zip-ties along the side of the road and made my way into my neighborhood. Although I no longer looked like I'd been out for a jog, I now looked like I was out for a night walk.

For months, my neighbors have seen me setting off or coming back from my nighttime jogs. Even changed into street clothes tonight, no one in my crummy neighborhood would give me a second glance. I was known as the man who couldn't sleep.

My neighbors knew my story and the grief I endured. Instead of being worried about me, they were scared of the criminal element and riff-raff who wandered the streets at this time of night.

Chapter Thirteen

Arden
Summer 1920

A rden's sight was blurry. He rubbed his eyes and shook his head. After a moment, his environment came into focus.

He glanced up as peals of laughter surrounded him, emitted by the stable boys who encircled him. No one asked if he was hurt.

With his wits gathered, Arden pushed himself to his feet as the laughter faded.

The giddy face of a redheaded groom named Toby was inches from his own. "Welcome to the family, boy."

Several grooms laughed at the greeting.

Toby had never spoken to him before. Bert warned him to stay away from Toby as much as possible. He had a reputation for being mean.

Toby appraised the grinning faces of those gathered. The

reactions encouraged him even further. He shoved Arden. "You're new here, ain't ya?"

Arden regained his balance and nodded. Although he wanted to push back, to release the anger inside of him, he decided instead to remain mute. Anything he said might fuel a fire within his attacker.

Toby shoved him again, this time forcing him to trip backward over something at his feet.

More chuckles erupted.

When he landed on his backside, Arden realized he'd fallen over the stool he'd been using. When he stood again, he grabbed the stool and held it like a shield, its three wooden legs aimed toward Toby.

Toby eyed the stool. "You need some protection against me?" Then he snorted again. He swept a hand at the circle of smirking faces. "Anyone else?"

"Stop!" The sharp command echoed down the stables, along with the sound of boots hitting the cobblestones. "What are you doing?"

An older groom named Slim arrived with a rake in his hands.

Bert was fast on his heels.

"Get on back to work. All of you." Slim swung the rake at the circle of onlookers. "Go on. Git!"

Amid grumbling, the group scattered.

Arden remained rigid. The stool remained in his hands until everyone but Slim and Bert left the area.

"Thank you, Mr. Slim."

"It's just Slim. And don't thank me." He pointed his rake in Bert's direction. "Thank your friend here, who came to get me. I swear if I see a gang around you again, I'll actually use a rake on 'em."

After Slim returned to his duties, Arden thanked Bert for

his help.

"No need to thank me, Arden. It's what friends do."

From that day forward, Arden stayed as far away from Toby as possible. Although Toby had never struck or pushed him since that first week, Arden suspected Toby was behind certain bad things that happened to him and his work.

One day, he'd cleaned a saddle to a glossy sheen. Arden stepped away to retrieve another one and, when he returned, found the first covered in manure. When he moved to clean the saddle for a second time, someone's laughter echoed through the stable. Arden gritted his teeth and persevered.

Another time he found dirt thrown into every bucket of fresh water he'd delivered to the stalls. Arden fought the temptation to push back at Toby. Even with no doubt who was behind these things, he felt powerless to make it stop.

Bert and Slim were aware of these events. Since his encounter with Toby, Arden noticed one or the other was with him or working near him most days. He appreciated their protection and their loyalty. More than likely, Toby also picked them on for being friends with Arden, but they never let on.

He'd been working at the stable for about six months when he noticed several of the same workers would gather and talk when only grooms and stable boys were around. His first impression was they were just jawing, taking a break from all their hard work, but he became concerned the more he watched them. Toby, his nemeses, was the leader of the group.

Such goings-on raised Arden's hackles. He didn't have a good feeling about these impromptu gatherings when the bosses were away. If Toby could pick on a kid like him, imagine what other mean things he could do.

Once, when Arden and Bert were cleaning stalls side-by-side, their conversation turned to Toby.

Bert walked to the middle of the stables, glanced around,

and then called over the wall. "I've been told that Toby served in the Great War and returned different."

"Interesting," Arden said, his mind whirling. "Different how?"

"Some of the guys said the fighting changed him. Said he was a calm, easy-going groom before the war. He was nervous and impatient, angry, like, after it. They noticed he lost patience with the horses. He used to help take care of mules, but he'd get so frustrated with them, he'd throw buckets at them."

"Mr. George's prize mules?" There was a mule breeding aspect to the stables. Mules were strong, and brought a good price at the sales because farmers needed them. Bred for toughness and a calm temperament, these mules were trained solely for human interaction, to pull plows or wagons, and to respond to verbal commands.

Farmers had reins on the mules when they used them for plowing, but paid more for a mule that would respond to "Gee" or "Haw" to get them to go left or right when working in the field. Mule training was part of the Lee Brothers' operation.

"Yep. Toby was saved from being fired, but they moved him to the horses. He said he couldn't work with the mules 'cause they were stubborn and stupid."

Arden pictured the one and only mule belonging to his family. Bucky was a pet, and they cherished his power. No one considered him stupid. Rather, the opposite. "Does Toby ever talk about what happened to him in the war?"

"Never."

"I'll pray for him. But in the meantime, I'm scared of what he'll do to me. I'm trying my best to stay out of his way."

"Me too. He knows we're friends. He's left me some ... let's call them pranks ... to show his displeasure with me."

Arden stopped working and walked over to Bert's stall.

"I'm sorry he's picking on you too. I hope being friends with me is worth the trouble Toby is causing you."

Bert gave him a good-natured pat on the shoulder. "One day, we'll both be big enough to stop Toby from picking on us. In the meantime, you need to get back to work, boy."

A few days later, Arden was cleaning tack. He'd finished with the first saddle and strode to the tack room, where the smell of leather and saddle soap engulfed him.

The tack room was home to saddles, rugs, bridles, and all the other equipment used on horses. Brushes, straps, and bandages dotted the shelves, circling the room. Hooks were fastened to the ceiling for hanging bridles for ease of cleaning.

In the back corner of the tack room was an old stove. It wasn't for warming their backsides. Instead, it was to dry damp and wet blankets and prevented mildew from forming on anything leather.

After Arden hung the saddle and left the tack room, he spotted Toby and his group gathered again. He came to a halt. This was trouble.

Arden glanced around, then crouched behind the open door of a nearby stall. He was hidden from view but could overhear Toby's conversation.

"You see, boys, I'm gonna make a bundle on this."

Chuckles from the men gathered around him followed Toby's declaration.

"You laugh, fellows, but it'll work."

Someone asked, "If you get caught, you'll lose your job here and won't be able to work for any other trainer in town."

"Don't matter," Toby replied. "I can go to California or Virginia and get a job. Probably have better weather there."

Arden listened with growing concern. What terrible thing was Toby planning? Somehow, he had to find out what Toby was organizing. He couldn't report him to either Mr. Will or

Mr. George until he discovered what Toby was doing to make money.

The sound of footsteps and murmurs alerted him of the group's dispersal. A moment later, Arden walked out of the stall with a bridle in his hands and made his way toward the tack room. It appeared no one had spotted him.

When Arden reached the tack room, the farrier was in there. His arrival was the likely reason Toby and his group had returned to their tasks so suddenly.

Arden spent the rest of his day wondering what bad thing Toby was planning. What kind of scheme would make money? Whatever Toby was planning, it was wrong. Arden's worry made him sick to his stomach. What could he do to stop it?

As the days passed, Arden kept watch for workers gathered in conversation and, when he found them, did his best to eavesdrop. He prayed he could put bits of information together well enough to figure out Toby's plan. It would be easier to go up to the other men and ask them, but they'd give him the back of their hand for being nosey and wouldn't tell him anything.

One day, he undid the girths to unsaddle a horse while eavesdropping on a conversation Toby was having with another lad. Arden listened for as long as he possibly could but when forced to walk away, they'd talked about nothing concerning. How was he going to find out what Toby was planning when he could never overhear anything useful?

A week later, the barn manager gathered the workers together.

"Fellas, we're going to be shifting several of the horses around to different stalls this morning."

After a moment, murmurs of surprise filled the silence. Horses liked routine. Changing stalls might upset some of the more high-strung animals.

The manager held up his hands. "I know this is unusual. But we have a special horse coming for training and he's going to be treated as special as Rex McDonald, if he were still alive."

The men nodded.

Bert turned to him and whispered. "Rex was the most famous Saddlebred horse in the country during his lifetime, and when he died, they stuffed him."

Arden nodded. "I know. He was on display at the Ringo Hotel when I helped my father deliver firewood there."

The manager continued. "This horse is coming by rail car. I'll need some of you to go to the depot and make sure he's unloaded properly. A groom is coming with him, but he'll leave after the horse is settled."

While the manager gave specific instructions to the grooms, Arden scanned the faces of the crowd. When he spotted a smirk on Toby's face, he grew concerned. Could this new horse be related to Toby's scheme?

He studied the other men. He recognized a handful as Toby's *gang*. They smiled at Toby.

Yes. The plan has to be about this horse. Toby must have learned or overheard it was coming. Now what horrible thing was he planning to do?

Chapter Fourteen

Arden
Fall 1920

Grooms worked six days a week and rotated working on Sundays. The animals' needs were the same every day, but it was the Lord's Day, so about every fifth week a fellow had to work.

Trainers and the Lee brothers occasionally stopped by to check on an ailing horse or mule, but otherwise, the stable kept the Sabbath. No training or sales of animals occurred on Sundays.

Arden's homesickness crept up on him during the week when he worked Sunday and couldn't have time off with his family. Although he went home every night, there were chores to do there, then early to bed. He returned to the stables before dawn.

As much as he loved his work, he felt sad at times. Occasionally, he was afraid he'd burst into tears in front of the other fellows. He wouldn't allow that to happen. They'd never let him live down the shame. Their teasing already made him so angry he thought he might explode into pieces.

Once convinced Toby was planning something terrible, it seemed to take forever before Arden was off on Sunday. Thanks to his low pecking order at the stable, he had no other option but to wait until it was his turn.

Arden yearned for a relaxing time with his family. There were eight of them. His older sister's only time off was Sunday afternoon, but when he was off, she was there.

Seeing his family lightened his burden and brought a smile to his face. Even though his siblings were annoying, he loved each one of them in a special way. He'd spent his life surrounded by brothers and sisters fighting for biscuits and for attention from their mother and father. With their father in Heaven, he appreciated the rest of them even more.

He also wanted to see Pastor David. Pastor David was family—both Arden's mother's brother and the family pastor. Arden grew up calling him Uncle David at family gatherings and Pastor David during worship and at church-related activities.

Uncle David had a unique way of understanding his flock. Arden hoped he'd relate to what Arden was going through. Life hadn't been easy for Uncle David, either.

The day finally arrived for him to go home after supper on Saturday. Time seemed stalled, like a horse unwilling to cooperate. Although he'd been busy that Saturday morning and time passed normally, the afternoon stretched on for an eternity.

Today, like every day, Toby did his best to aggravate Arden. Arden cleaned and shined a saddle until there was a luster and sheen rarely achieved by other grooms. He walked away after he'd hung it in the tack room as Toby hadn't been around.

But Toby fooled him. When Arden returned, he found it

covered in dirt and manure. When Arden spotted that saddle, he wanted to grab it, hunt down Toby, and beat him senseless with it. Instead, he sighed and cleaned it again.

When everyone was finally called into dinner, Arden ran to the table. He gathered the three one-dollar bills under his plate, then twitched in his chair until everyone else arrived and the blessing was asked. He ate as quickly as he could, then made a request to be dismissed.

Mr. George Lee was aware it was Arden's turn to be off, so he nodded at the request. "Go enjoy your family."

As Arden raced toward home, he imagined his burden about Toby was what being an adult must feel like. Was having a problem he couldn't solve mean he was turning into an adult? If so, he wanted no part of it.

When he drew near home, the golden glow of the fireplace shone through the only window and lit his path to the door. The sight of it made him smile. Then he spotted lamplight coming from the barn, so he turned toward it. He'd help his older brother finish whatever he was doing so they could both come in for the night.

The following day, the family walked to hear Pastor David. Their church was about a half-mile walk toward town, but time passed quickly for Arden when his family surrounded him.

All eight of them crowded onto the family pew their father had built with his own hands. When Arden sat down, his heart lifted. God and Uncle David had the answers he needed. He must listen to the message.

Uncle David, as Pastor David, delivered a message taken from Matthew's scriptures about the Sermon on the Mount. Arden hung on every word and speculated how he could relate to Toby righteously.

After the service, Pastor David walked home with them,

along with his wife and their cousins, to have dinner. Mama's poorest laying chicken had been sacrificed to make chicken and dumplings as their Sunday feast.

Once the meal was blessed, consumed, and the dishes washed and put away, Arden asked for a moment to talk to Pastor David about Toby.

Once he'd finished telling Uncle David about his troubles, Arden sighed in relief. "I don't know how you're supposed to help me, but I feel better just sharing this with someone."

Uncle David reached over and grabbed Mama's Bible from the mantle. "Keep in mind, Arden, what the Good Book says about evil."

"There are so many passages."

"Yes, but I'm thinking of Romans, chapter twelve, verse twenty-one. He turned to it. '*Be not overcome of evil, but overcome evil with good.*' It means you must keep doing good to rid yourself of the evil of those around you."

"I'm finding that hard."

"Of course you do. Being a servant of the Lord can be extremely difficult. Remember the suffering Paul endured in order to faithfully serve Christ. Think also of how Job's faith was tested. Perhaps this is a test of your faith."

"It is truly testing me. Not so much of my faith but of my patience. It's hard to turn the other cheek."

"God has blessed you with a type of apprenticeship you enjoy. Every day you get to take care of those animals you love."

Arden nodded. "It is a blessing."

"Your love poured out upon those animals is a blessing to them. Cherish what is good in your daily life. Pray about those evil things you haven't been able to change."

"But how can I protect them when there is someone planning something evil?"

"Pray that your love for the horses will help you protect them. Pray that God knows the love in your heart and will move in ways we can't define to protect those you love."

Uncle David turned his head toward Heaven. "I will pray for you. I'll pray for protection from those who are evil-minded. And I will pray someone will help you along your path."

Later that night, or early the next morning, a tremendous crack of thunder awoke Arden. His eyes flew. He shifted on the down-filled bed, then held still to see if his brother was awake.

Another rumble of thunder sounded nearly as loud as the first crack, but his older sibling never moved. Could he sleep through everything?

No. That wasn't a fair representation. Leon reacted to any distress sound coming from the barn, no matter the time of night. Perhaps being the farmer in the family made him deaf to things that didn't bother his charges.

When another bolt of lightning flashed, Arden threw back the quilts and got dressed before the accompanying thunder rumbled. The horses!

Their own farm animals were not so high-strung, but the stable had horses that didn't do well with loud thunder. Since he had to get up in another hour, he might as well get up and go now. The horses might need his help.

As he crept down the ladder of the loft, his mother called out.

"Arden? Is that you?"

She startled him. After calming his nerves for a second, Arden continued to tiptoe down the rungs. "Keep your voice down, Mama. Leon and the rest are still asleep."

His mother lit a nearby lamp and he could see she was still in her nightgown and cap.

She turned to him. "Where do you think you're going?"

"The horses, Mama. Some are terrified of storms. They're going to need my help."

"The horses, the horses," she echoed. "They're all you ever think about." She walked over to the window. "It's raining cats and dogs out there. You aren't leaving. What if it hails on you? Large hailstones from a storm like this could kill you."

He smiled at his mother's concern. "You know, if it's going to hail, it would have already done it. This is just a bad rainstorm."

He walked closer to her. "I have my cap and I'll add my raincoat and run as fast as that blowing wind out there. I've got to go help the horses." He spotted the wavering in her eyes. "Please mama. It's my calling to help them. God has opened this path for me. I must do my best work for Him."

She hesitated, then walked over and pulled a biscuit tin off the shelf. She removed two stale biscuits. "I was going to feed these to the chickens this morning. But you'd better take 'em. Lord knows it will be hours before you see any food."

He grinned at her, grabbed the biscuits, and gave her a kiss on the cheek. "Thank you, Mama."

When he reached the stable, it was still raining hard, but the lightning and thunder had moved east. Every bit of his clothing was soaking wet and covered in mud, but he hurried inside for a different reason. He could hear terrible cries from several horses.

What he'd dreaded was actually coming to pass.

Jess was barking in reaction to the sound of several horses acting up. Voices of various grooms and trainers reached his ears. They were working hard, trying to settle down the upset horses.

A horse in a stall close to him was making a lot of noise. He followed the racket, and when he rounded the corner, the horse didn't appear to have anyone with him.

He ran to the stall. The noise came from Indian Warrior, a gray horse who was smart but skittish. This was one of Slim's horses.

Slim had mentioned at some time or another how Warrior was fond of food. Too enamored at times. He would steal apples from pockets or grab spilled grain from the ground. Slim had his hands full, keeping Warrior on his proper diet.

Arden didn't open the stall door due to the possibility the horse would bolt. Instead, he climbed up and hung over the top edge on his stomach. Then he spoke in a low, calm voice.

"Hey there, Warrior. You don't need to be afraid. I'm here with you."

Warrior stopped jumping but dug at the ground with a hoof, still swinging his hind quarters left and right. Agitation also showed on his rippling neck muscles.

Arden remembered the biscuits his mother had given him. He reached into his pocket and broke off a piece of a biscuit, holding it in his flat palm while murmuring sweet words to Warrior.

Eventually Warrior couldn't resist the offered treat. His soft lips picked up the piece of biscuit while Arden continued to speak softly to him. Although his ears remained back, the rest of him appeared calmer.

Once all the biscuits were eaten, Warrior was as calm as expected under the circumstances.

Arden was ready to slide off the stall gate but froze when Toby led Cumberland out of a stall, three stalls down. Cumberland was a beautiful black stallion that Mr. Will Lee adored and planned to use for a stud.

Arden had no place to hide. He couldn't avoid Toby in this situation, but he didn't want to call any attention to himself, either.

When Mr. Will walked out of the stall behind Cumberland,

Arden was surprised. If Cumberland was upset, getting into his stall was dangerous. Even deadly at such a time.

Neither Mr. Will nor Toby spotted him until Toby reached the stall.

"Why are you hanging there, boy?" Mr. Will walked up and gave him a hand to lift him off the stall door. "From the look of your dripping clothes, you must've come from home. Did you come here because of the storm?"

Arden focused on Mr. Will and his question. "Yes, sir. I was afraid the more high-strung horses would hurt themselves with the noise of the storm."

A smile broke out across Mr. Will's face. "Thank you, son. You calmed Warrior?"

"Yes, sir. I bribed him with biscuits."

Mr. Will threw back his head and laughed. "Smart lad. Thanks for coming."

Then, he hooked a thumb toward the other end of the stable. "If you have any more biscuits, try that trick on Suzanna back there. She's either going to hurt herself or kick down the stall door. Then go find some dry clothes."

Arden spun and raced toward Suzanna, but he could feel the hatred emanating from Toby as he ran away.

Chapter Fifteen

Kurt

Kurt pushed his police sedan faster, siren wailing and lights flashing. He raced across town in the dark. The streets were empty, thankfully.

Another emergency call out. This time, it was a fire.

He was thankful Ross was with his parents.

Kurt's mind turned to the fire. The callout indicated a large blaze reported by a neighbor. A large fire was rare in Mexico, Missouri. And it was unusual for the detectives to be called out to assist.

In addition, the address was in one of the swankiest neighborhoods in town. Although he wasn't sure which neighborhood resident suffered this loss, he questioned why the fire had grown out of control. Mansions in that part of town had surveillance systems, heat sensors, and every other piece of high-tech equipment to alert firefighters and police to any emergency.

Kurt fretted about the lack of alarms until the glow of oranges and reds was visible in the sky to the east.

Oh, my! It was much worse than he'd imagined. He was over a half mile from the address, and the bright colors revealed this was an enormous fire. As he neared, the acrid smell of smoke seared his nostrils. He would need gear before he approached the home.

He parked behind a line of several police cars. All the rolling trucks and equipment available to Mexico's firefighters appeared to be on the scene.

While he stood near the trunk of his car, grabbing his fire gear, a ladder truck from Centralia pulled in. The driver honked to alert others they could not get within striking distance of the flames.

Kurt noticed various law enforcement vehicles blocked the path to the home, so he ran to move one. Several other responders joined him, and they soon cleared egress for the ladder truck.

Kurt hurried back to his car to suit up in his assigned firefighting apparatus. After removing his blazer, he pulled a fire-resistant jumpsuit over his slacks, traded his loafers for fire boots, and put his fire-rated breathing mask over his head, but let it hang from his neck.

It was a sultry night. The gear made him instantly break into a sweat. No way was he adding the mask until they were closer.

Hector pulled in behind him and trotted to the back of his car to don his firefighting gear. Once both men were outfitted, they strode toward the fire together.

Kurt shouted above the noise of fire suppression efforts. "Great night for a wiener roast."

"What everyone wants in the middle of the night. Hot

dogs." Then Hector stepped into a water puddle, splashing both of them.

"We're up next," Hector said. "If this fire is associated with a crime, it's on us to investigate it,"

Kurt nodded. "I figured. Whose house is this? I didn't recognize the address."

"Katherine Mull."

Kurt scanned the handful of people gathered behind the crime scene tape. He didn't spot Katherine, so he turned toward the leaping flames and heat. "If she didn't get out of there quickly, she could be dead."

Hector spun on him. "You're making an assumption, and we don't do that in our line of work. That woman is the devil. She might be fireproof."

Kurt chuckled. Hector wasn't far from the truth. "If this fire is a result of foul play, we'll have our work cut out for us. The suspect list will be endless. Everyone in the county dislikes her."

Hector nodded. "Where is she? Why isn't she yelling at the firefighters and police? She's always telling us we're not doing our job. Her absence makes me nervous."

"I agree. She'd never miss an opportunity to criticize. She proved that at the bank yesterday. What a fit she pitched! At us, Mr. Barnaby, the bank, and to anyone who crossed her path."

"Don't you think it's odd she's not around?"

"Yes."

Hector pointed to the nearest home on the opposite side of Katherine's property. "I may be wrong, but I think that house belongs to Mr. Colby. He may be the resident who reported the fire."

Hector and Kurt strode to the area where active fire suppression efforts were ongoing. Mexico's two ladder trucks, positioned at angles to each other, directed their water streams toward the house's left wing. The ladder truck from Centralia was just getting their water flowing toward the back of the major structure.

Firefighters on the ground resembled strange astronauts in their fire gear. They aimed water at flames in the center of the structure. The right wing and side of the main structure showed the most damage. It had housed the three-car garage wing, which included a second story above the garage. The second story gaped open to the elements. On the ground, debris covered two metal frames, likely what remained of vehicles inside the garage.

The center section of the home was missing the front entry and walls on either side. The left wing appeared in good shape. Fire suppression teams appeared to be successful in their effort to stop the fire in that wing.

Kurt stared at the utter chaos for a moment. "In my amateur opinion, I'd say that garage wing is toast."

Hector nodded. "I don't see how anything but that left wing will survive. However, our firefighting partners have previously pulled off some miracles."

Kurt squinted in the smoke-filled night air, then turned to Hector. "We better jump in. They're going to need all the help they can get."

Hector held up a finger. "Let's talk to the chief."

Plodding their way through puddles of water attributed to firefighting efforts, they found the chief. While Hector engaged in conversation, Kurt watched the firefighting efforts.

Hector moved to him. "We're to help the ladder truck teams. They need a break."

Kurt nodded. "Yes, sir."

They strode toward the ladder trucks. Hector veered left,

leaving Kurt to approach the one on their right. When Kurt reached a group of workers feeding hose to the workers on the extended ladders, he shouted, "What can I do to help?"

One man yelled to another up the ladder. "Go take a rest, Martin. We've got new blood."

Kurt realized the guy coming down the ladder was a new hire to the public safety department. In all the gear, it was hard to identify anyone.

Martin crawled down the ladder. When he took off his helmet, his exhaustion was obvious.

Kurt waved him toward the relief area. "Go take a break. I've got this."

With no argument from Martin, Kurt pulled on his mask and moved up the ladder, taking instructions of "Feed me the hose when I ask for it" from someone he didn't recognize.

After the team rotated out, allowing everyone a rest, Kurt made his way to the chief. "I've just done a full rotation through the ladder truck team. They suggested I come to you for a new assignment."

The chief turned and held up his hand. "Ladder trucks from Columbia should arrive at any moment. See if some of you can get the truck close. Move cars, trucks, people, whatever might be in their way. If we can get them working, we'll knock out this fire."

"Yes, sir." Kurt moved to fulfill orders.

Kurt barked instructions to a group of resting firefighters, and they moved half a dozen vehicles. Once the Columbia trucks were in place, he and Hector volunteered to assist the newcomers.

Three hours of hard work and sweat later, the flames were doused. As the sun rose in the East, wisps of smoke ascended toward the sky from the sunbeams.

Kurt hesitated, thinking the fire was still burning. "Hector. Is that burning over there?" He pointed to what appeared to be smoke.

Hector stopped, then turned toward the direction shown. "No. It's a weird fire phenomenon. Fine particles of ash produced from the active burn become airborne. The light of the sun allows the naked eye to see the floating ash particles, making the observer incorrectly believe this ash is smoke from a fire that has reignited."

"I've never seen such a thing."

"Just ash in the sunlight."

The units gathered their equipment as the assistant chief, Murry Goodgame, now inspecting the scene, changed from firefighting gear to his inspection gear.

Kurt approached Murry. "Sir, Hector Vega and I are the detectives on duty this weekend. How can we help you?"

Murry grinned at him. "You can go home and sleep. It's going to take hours, maybe days, to go through this. I don't want you to mess up my fire site."

"Are you doing it by yourself?"

"No way. I have some light equipment coming and a few men from our local rural fire departments who are fresh and ready to help. We'll be fine." Murry glanced around. "Not that you could mess up this scene any more than all the fire suppression efforts have done. *Comprendo?*"

Kurt smiled. "Yes. Let me give you my cell number. Call me when you're ready for us."

Murry tugged off his gloves, reached into his jumpsuit chest pocket and pulled out his phone, typed in the number, then replaced it. "Now get some sleep."

"I know I'm asking you to speculate, but any guesses why this house burned?"

"I have to keep an open mind about the origin and cause of this fire." Murry turned and glanced at the skeleton of the primary structure. "That said, with the spread of this fire, I suspect it was accelerated. I'm going to be here a long time."

"I understand."

"One other thing makes me suspicious." Murry walked over to a water puddle near the house. "See this puddle? Runoff from the water we put on the fire formed it. Notice anything unusual?"

Kurt stared at the water's surface, spotting iridescent colors shimmering across the top of the water. "A rainbow?"

"An accelerant like gasoline or kerosene can cause that effect."

Kurt's eyebrows rose. "Wow. Interesting."

Murry shrugged. "That's not conclusive. It's just one of a million things I'll note in my inspection. There will be plenty of samples taken to determine if an accelerant was involved. Possibly an accelerant-detection dog may be used. This is a large area we have to cover."

"If you use one, will you call me? I'd like to watch the dog work."

"Sure." Murry held up a finger. "A word of advice. After you sleep, you'll need to find out which insurance company insured this home."

"The insurance company?"

"They'll likely send out their own investigator and expert. With a fire this huge, a second opinion is always welcome. Don't contact them until I'm finished, but you can save time by having that information ready."

"Got it. Thanks."

Kurt's phone indicated it was 5:30 am. The entire night was gone.

He spotted Hector and relayed the good news about their opportunity to shower and then sleep. No clue when their next chance to sleep might occur.

The sharp ringtone of his phone forced Kurt from sleep. It felt as though he'd just closed his eyes. He scrambled to squelch the offensive sounds.

"Kurt Hunter."

It was Assistant Chief Murry Goodgame. "Sorry to call you so soon. We need you back here."

Anxiety gripped Kurt. "What's happened?"

"Found a body. Burned beyond recognition. No clue if it's male or female. I've already called Tony Cappelli. He's headed here and said he'll notify the medical examiner."

Tony was the local coroner. He was an elected official but had the option to involve the state medical examiner's office in difficult or complicated cases.

Kurt glanced at the clock. It was almost nine o'clock. Later than he'd thought. "Where was the body?"

"Under an enormous pile of rubble in the middle section of the house. At this point, I can't tell exactly what room it was. So much debris has fallen. My guess would be the kitchen or an area near the kitchen or a pantry. One of the twisted metal objects nearby could be a refrigerator."

"Was the body on the first floor? Or did it fall from the second story?"

"Only guessing, but I trust it was there before the second story fell. It was under the second level debris."

"Gotcha."

"I've asked the Chief to call for a crane. We'll need to lift what's left of the roof, the rafters, and the second-floor joists off this section of the house."

"Will you need our help?"

"Not right now. I'd rather have our fire crews do it. It was luck I spotted the body."

"I'll call Hector, and we'll be there soon."

"You do what you have to do. I can't let you inside the remains of this house until the medical examiner's office has taken control of the body."

"No problem. My partner and I have many things to do. A body changes everything. Thanks for the information."

Kurt scrambled to dress while talking to Hector on speakerphone. Both strategized about investigating a complicated scene. The fire would have consumed most forensic material, and then water from the fire suppression efforts would have further damaged the scene.

Hector asked, "You think it's Katherine?"

"My guess is yes. Odd that her property burns, and she didn't appear last night."

"I agree. It's not like her to miss an opportunity to criticize the lessor beings risking their lives to save her property."

"We saw her at the bank and then at the fundraiser. Where else could she have gone?"

"No clue. Think you can find out the name of Katherine's dentist?"

"Sure. That's doable. Even if I have to contact every dentist in town. I'm assuming we need that for identification of the body."

"Yes, to identify or eliminate her as a possibility. Any idea who might be her next of kin?"

"Nope." Kurt chose a somber colored tie and looped it around his neck. "Do you remember who she listed as her next of kin in the report we took at the bank?"

"No, but I'll check that."

"So, I'll chase down the dental information and you work on her next of kin."

"Deal."

After a pause, Kurt asked, "You ever work something like this in the past?"

"Closest I've ever gotten to a fire death was a few years ago. Back when the Anderson brothers were working a meth lab in the county. We helped the sheriff's office with that investigation. The oldest brother was the cook. Blew himself up."

"I'm not sure I could stomach such a scene."

"Few of us could. All part of the joy of being a law enforcement officer."

"How are we going to work this one? The scene is essentially destroyed."

Hector sighed. "Every scene tells a story. Some more than others. This one is going to take longer, but it *will* talk to us. I promise. Catch you in a minute."

Kurt prayed he could stomach the scene he would eventually investigate. Even though he didn't like Katherine Mull, if the body was her, he pitied her such a death. Or was someone else in her home and not her?

Was the fire the cause of death of whomever this body turned out to be? Or was there a murder, and the fire was just to destroy forensic evidence? Or did someone suffer a natural death or an illness and somehow the fire began accidentally?

Assistant Chief Goodgame suspected this fire was set. Gasoline? Kerosene? Materials inside a structure that caught fire? How would they discover the truth? He'd leave such conclusions to the experts.

He and Hector would collect dental records and next of kin information the experts needed. He also needed to contact any employees she had. There was a possibility the body was someone who worked for her.

If the body was an employee, where was Katherine?

How would he research Katherine's dentist in this small town without setting tongues to wagging?

Liesl. He'd start with her.

Chapter Sixteen

Liesl

A ping from her telephone's text tone woke Liesl the following morning. She groaned. What time was it? Had dawn even broken yet?

She struggled in the hazy light to wake up enough to locate her phone. Then she peered at the text sent by Nicole.

911 Coffee. Important news.

Ah, oh. The SOS text.
Liesl typed her reply:

Be there in 15.

Another ping followed:

Order for me. Prolly 20 before I get all the 411.

Liesl glanced at Barney, still in his bed but alert to her movements.

"Your Auntie Nicole is paying me back for making her work so hard at the fundraiser. She wants me to roll out of bed for news she thinks is important."

Barney appeared unimpressed.

"At this time of morning, I am equally disgusted, buddy." Liesl threw off her covers. "Let's get you outside for your morning constitutional while I shower and dress. I'm not doing any makeup. That's Auntie Nicole's punishment for making me rise and face the day with the first rays of sunlight on a Saturday."

Thirty minutes later, Liesl walked into Ralph's Doughnut Shop wearing jeans and a T-shirt. She inhaled the delicious scents of doughnuts, coffee, pastries, and all things comprising sugary goodness. There were many reasons why everyone in town loved Ralph's. This enchanting aroma, plus the way the doughnuts melted in one's mouth, were two of them.

She waved at several people in the store as she strolled to the counter and ordered two large coffees, hazelnut for her, and French roast for Nicole. There was no need to check with Nicole for her order. When the Bat Signal went out for coffee, Nicole wanted the strongest brew available.

Besides their coffee, Liesl added a half dozen blueberry glazed cake doughnuts. Neither of them needed such a high-calorie treat, but Liesl had years of experience with these matters. Nicole would protest their appearance and then stuff them into her face as fast as she could talk around them. The aggravating part was Nicole was stick thin and remained that way, no matter how many doughnuts she consumed.

Liesl found a table in the middle of the room—Nicole's preference for seating. As a real estate professional, Nicole's philosophy was to *see people* and *be seen* whenever in public. Many clients and sales contracts had sprouted from her center-of-the-room appearances. She grabbed a doughnut and settled in to wait for her bestie, who always seemed to run late, except for business appointments.

Chapter Seventeen

Nicole

Nicole found a parking spot and rushed inside Ralph's. She glanced at the time. Just fifteen minutes late. Even though it was Saturday, she had an open house later, so she was professionally dressed. Today, she was styling a beautiful, soft yellow pantsuit that flattered her light-brown skin tone. Her face shined with the excitement of her news.

She spotted Liesl at a table that already held coffee cups and a doughnut box. Liesl looked like she'd just rolled out of bed. But to be fair, she probably *had* just rolled out of bed.

Nicole strutted over to her and pulled out a chair. "Good morning, Sunshine."

"You look amazing, Nic."

She grinned. "Some things never change." When seated, she added, "Wait until you hear my information."

Liesl grinned at her. "That's what I've been doing. Waiting

here, with doughnuts, to hear what was important enough to drag me out of bed so early."

Nicole scanned the table, eyed the box of doughnuts, and wrinkled her nose. "Why did you buy so many doughnuts? We can't eat that many." Then, without missing a beat, she grabbed one and took a bite. With food obscuring her diction, she asked, "Have you heard anything yet?"

"Nothing that would qualify as news, but I just stumbled in here a few minutes ago. Spill!"

"There was a big fire in town last night."

"Really?"

"At Katherine Mull's house. Most of the house is ashes."

Liesl sucked in a breath. "What? That monster of a home? It's as big as the Biltmore mansion."

"It was the three E's—Enormous, elaborate, and expensive. But now it's toast."

"I can't believe it."

Nicole nodded. "It's true." She took a big sip of her coffee and sighed as the caffeinated warmth enveloped her.

Liesl leaned toward her. "I need more info. I'm going to snatch that cup out of your hand if you don't start talking." She gave her a warning glance.

"Mary Creason drove as close to it as she could this morning. She said most of the middle section, the three-story part with the columns, is gone. Just rubble. Only one of those two wings appeared to be standing because the garage side collapsed upon itself."

"What about Katherine?"

Nicole took another big bite of doughnut, then mumbled, "What about her?"

"Is she okay?"

She gave Liesl a blank look. "Like we care?"

"Nicole! That's not nice."

"Neither is she. I got my fill of her yesterday."

Liesl crossed her arms. "This is another example of how God works in mysterious ways. This fire leaves the landlord without a place to live."

"Slumlord is a better description. She wouldn't dare live in those horrible shacks she owns. Her lack of maintenance is appalling. I bet she'll rent a hotel room or an apartment in Columbia to find a place suitable for her high standards."

A smile lifted Liesl's lips. "If she's driving drive back and forth to Columbia, we'll see a lot less of her here."

"Good point. A ray of sunshine resulting from the fire." She looked at her phone. "I'm going to have to leave in a minute Open house, you know."

"Do you have an hour for me today? I need to talk to you about something important."

Although Liesl looked serious, Nicole was forced to push her off. "I can't this morning or early afternoon. Hit me after my open house, and maybe I can meet you somewhere. Before the open house, Marc and I are picking out furniture to rent for staging our flip house."

Liesl nodded. "Jim Stubblefield?"

"Yes, he's so good to work with us when our flip houses are ready to sell."

"Is this the bones house?"

Nicole stopped chewing and pierced her with an angry stare. "I wish you wouldn't talk about that horrible incident." She and Liesl had witnessed the unearthing of Civil War-era bones several months prior. Marc had been clearing away a crumbling outbuilding when the bones were discovered.

Liesl shrugged. "You failed to appreciate the history those bones represented. I also suspect you are ashamed you *swooned* during the discovery."

Nicole straightened in her chair. There were some things

Liesl thought were great events for teasing. She could find no humor in this razzing and moved to a related topic. "When are the DNA results coming in on those old bones?"

"Any day now."

She rolled her eyes. "Please spare me the details. I just want to sell the house and forget what happened there."

"You're missing out, Nic. It's fascinating that those bones may belong to an Army officer listed as a deserter. Finding the bones was the first miracle. The second miracle occurred when the historical society tracked down the relatives of the man they believed was the deserter. Fingers crossed, the results come back soon."

Before Nicole could argue with Liesl about miracles, gray-haired, frumpy Margaret Sterling approached their table. Margaret was one of several town gossips. If they rated them, Margaret would land at the top or a close second.

Both Nicole and Liesl sat silent as Margaret paused when she reached their table. Her eyes flashed. Her face had the same look a cat would have after capturing a mouse. "Anyone tell you the news?"

Nicole blinked at Margaret. "Yes. In fact, we were just discussing the fire. Isn't it awful?"

Although Margaret's excitement dimmed at her failure to pass this information, she soon rallied. "I'm told the entire mansion has burned to the ground."

Nicole glanced at Liesl and then shot Margaret a look of pity. "Your source is inaccurate, Margaret. Mary Creason drove by the premises this morning. Only the middle section is gone. One of the two wings was standing and mostly intact."

"Is that so?" Margaret pursed her lips and furrowed her brows. "I don't understand how Janet could have gotten it so wrong."

Liesl interjected, "Janet Cross?"

Margaret nodded. "Janet is Katherine's cleaning lady. Cleans that entire house all by herself. Or, I guess I should say, she used to do that. With that mansion gone, she'll need another job."

Nicole wondered how a sweet person like Janet could have worked for Katherine the Evil. Being Katherine's employee would be a soul-killing job. Janet must have more backbone than she'd assumed. "Was Janet there five days a week?"

"That's my understanding."

Liesl said, "Poor woman. She must have been desperate."

Nicole shot a look at Liesl. "My guess is she's stronger in spirit than we imagined."

"I agree with both of you," Margaret said. "It would be awful to work for someone who hurts a person's feelings for grins and giggles. It's a power thing for Katherine. She feels powerful when she wounds somebody. It's kind of sick, if you ask me."

Nicole fought back the temptation to turn on Margaret with something like, "*We didn't ask you anything. You're over here, interrupting us like the gossipy old lady you are.*" Instead, she asked, "Do you know how long Janet has worked for Katherine?"

"Over a year now. Janet was fearless to stick it out."

Liesl nodded. "You're absolutely right. I'm proud of her. Imagine how Katherine must have treated her."

An idea occurred to Nicole. "When you see Janet, tell her to give me a call. I have an idea for new employment."

Margaret responded with almost as much excitement as the fire news. "Thank you, Nicole. I'll talk to her on my way to work. Saturday shifts aren't fun, but they pay well. Before I go, do you have any other tidbits?"

When Liesl replied, "I do," Nicole was surprised. Was this why Liesl was trying to meet with her today?

"Three dubious men stopped at my house when I was at the fundraiser yesterday. Kurt tells me they are likely storm chasers. Men who want to charge too much to do shoddy work for people. They're from out of state and want to fix damages from that hail and wind we had a while back."

Nicole eyed her with interest. "You mean they put tarps on roofs, do roof repairs, and cut down trees?"

"Exactly. That type of handiwork. Some overcharge for their services or do shoddy work."

Margaret frowned. "The kind who skip town when you realize you've been conned into paying too much?"

Liesl nodded. "Plus, they may offer to paint or do asphalt repairs. Kurt is going to ask the chief to make public announcements about them. The chief will ask citizens to be cautious. It's better for people to hire local contractors and handymen bonded and licensed."

Nicole took a sip of coffee. "I'll get the word out to all the real estate agents in town. We can pass the warning along to our homeowners and potential buyers."

"Good idea," Liesl said. "Kurt and I watched their *visit* on my security cameras, and they were quite creepy. Trespassed in my backyard like they owned the place."

Nicole shook her head in disgust, then peered up at Margaret. "Now you know everything. Have a great day."

Margaret didn't react to Nicole's brush-off. Instead, she glanced over her shoulder and spotted new prey walking into the store. "I wonder if Sheila Swenson knows about the fire." Then she turned back and whispered, "You know her husband had an affair with his co-worker, don't you?"

Through gritted teeth, Nicole snapped, "Whether he had an affair is none of our business. Unless you witnessed the parties in the act, I suggest you stop spreading such a vicious rumor. Gabbing about something that could break a family apart is mean."

Margaret huffed and stalked away, seeking new victims.

Liesl smiled at Nicole. "That's my girl."

"I can't stand it when rumors like that are spread. They only hurt people."

"True. What possible job idea do you have for Janet? If she's put up with the Devil Woman for a year, she's earned an angelic employer."

"Would I be angelic to work for?"

Liesl chuckled. "You'd be better than Katherine."

"Thanks a lot, *pal*," she stated with sarcasm. In a normal voice, she continued, "Marc and I were just talking about hiring a cleaning service for our office. If Janet would consider working after business hours, she could develop her own commercial cleaning business."

Liesl nodded. "If she worked for commercial businesses she wouldn't have to put up with a picky homeowner like Katherine. Great idea, Nic."

"Wonder Woman strikes again. But I can't do anything to save Margaret's co-workers this morning. She's going to run all over the factory gossiping about the fire and the traveling repairmen."

The ring of Liesl's phone provided the second interruption of their conversation. She fished for it in her purse. "It's Kurt."

Nicole concentrated on her coffee and another doughnut while Liesl took the call.

In a few moments, Liesl frowned at her phone and placed it back in her purse. "That was odd."

Nicole finished off the last of the second doughnut. "What did he want?"

Liesl became serious, whispering, "You can't tell anyone. He was asking me for the name of Katherine's dentist."

"I heard you say something about Dr. King at King Family Dental. I assumed Kurt was asking for the name of a good dentist."

"But why would he want us to keep a conversation about a dentist a secret?"

Nicole was confused. "I have to keep your conversation secret as well?"

"He knew you were with me. I blamed you for being the reason I'm awake because you wanted to tell me about the fire. Then he said he helped suppress the fire, but that's a conversation for another day."

"He wasn't kidding?"

"No. He used his official cop voice. And said it was important, and to keep this 'under wraps.' Then he hung up."

Nicole didn't understand. "Why would he need her dentist?"

Liesl's face revealed her understanding as the pieces fell into place. "Oh, Nic." She whispered. "He needs her dentist to identify her body with dental records." Half moaning, she added, "They must think she's dead."

Nicole stared at Liesl. "You really think so?"

After a quick glance around, Liesl narrowed her eyes at her. "I'm guessing. Nothing's confirmed, and Kurt has sworn us to secrecy. They must have found a body in the fire somewhere and need dental records to verify it's Katherine."

"If they found a body inside, that doesn't mean it's Katherine. It could be an employee, like Janet." Nicole didn't enjoy talking about bodies. Time to make a hasty exit.

"You're right. Katherine had Janet for cleaning, plus a yard service to take care of all those acres and extensive landscape spanning the exterior of her house. She may have had other employees too. What time was the fire?"

Nicole grabbed her phone off the table and put it in her

purse. "Mary Creason only talked about the state of Katherine's house. She never mentioned when it happened. Must have been later last night."

"Housekeeping and lawn services would be gone by five o'clock, or at least by sunset," Liesl said. "She left the fundraiser around five."

"That's right. Is there anyone you'd say was a friend of Katherine? Someone she would go stay with since her house is gone?"

Liesl shrugged. "I can't think of anyone who actually likes her. That woman only talked about herself. How rich she is and how stylish her clothes are and how beautiful her home and cars are."

Nicole picked up her coffee cup. "She's always been as mean as a snake. She's back-biting to me and everyone else. The cops will have a hard time finding anyone who knows anything substantive about her."

"I'm sure you're right." Liesl frowned. "Whatever caused Katherine to behave the way she behaved was a mystery to us all."

"Don't even think about sticking your nose in this. After all ..." she dropped her voice to a whisper ... "the object they found might not be who we suspect. It's all conjecture."

"Okay. Then where is she? Why isn't Katherine making everyone miserable about this fire? Kurt wouldn't be asking for the name of her dentist if she'd been seen since the fire."

Nicole pursed her lips. "Good point."

They sat in silence for a moment.

Either the doughnuts or the conversation, or both, was making Nicole nauseous. "My stomach is upset. Even though I don't like Katherine, I wouldn't wish her a death by fire. What a horrible way to go."

"I agree. Like the worst death imaginable. Maybe she passed out and accidentally set the fire?"

"If someone did this to her, they hate her with a wicked passion." Nicole stood. "I'm going to be late for my meeting with Marc." She pointed at the nearly empty container on their table. "Do you mind if I take this last doughnut to him? It would make him happy."

Liesl nodded. "Please tell Marc to enjoy it."

She plucked the box off the table. "Thank you." Then she pierced Liesl with a stare. "Leave this issue to Kurt and Hector. Please."

"Oh, I'm just curious."

"Curiosity killed the cat. If this fire was no accident and—" She glanced around at the other patrons seated around them "—and something beyond property was destroyed, then a dangerous, possibly insane, person is walking our streets."

Chapter Eighteen

Arden
Fall 1920

Arden watched everyone with a suspicious eye. He listened, eavesdropping, to put together the pieces of whatever nonsense Toby was planning.

Whatever meanness Toby planned, it was bad. Arden could feel it in his bones. But he was just a half-grown kid. How could he stop it?

He prayed to God, asking to let him be smart enough and brave enough for the task God had placed in front of him. Then he expressed his thanks to God for Bert, his only friend at the stables. Even though Bert was his only friend, he was exactly the trustworthy and loyal friend he needed.

Toby was a groom, so his duties related to feeding and exercising the horses. Grooms also took care of them during a cool-down and warm-up and virtually all the other responsibilities associated with their training. Many of these tasks occurred outside, when the weather cooperated.

Arden didn't have any business being in or around either of the training tracks unless he had a task to perform there. When he had a chance to volunteer for duties that took him outside, he did—even if it put him behind in his primary responsibilities. He must observe Toby as often as possible.

Every day, the trainer, Mr. Tate, and one or both of the Lee brothers checked on the horses. Regardless whether the horse was boarding or being trained, Mr. Tate touched each animal.

There was a pattern to the touches. It was as if he was asking the horse to relay messages to him through his fingers. Those long fingers were brown from the sun. They were also nimble and knowledgeable.

He'd rub the horse's nose, then its neck and withers. After that, he'd feel the forearm and knee, searching for any heat there from a possible injury. Each hoof and pastern was inspected for problems.

Then he'd run his hand down the animal's back, loin and croup, continuing down the stifle and gaskin to ensure their muscles were strong and well-developed. Mr. Tate always finished by running his hands along the hock, cannon, and fetlock.

As Arden watched him, he prayed to one day develop the same skills as Mr. Tate. On the rare occasion he was in a position to examine a horse, he would repeat the motions made by Mr. Tate, hoping to feel what Mr. Tate felt.

One day while washing down one of Slim's charges while Slim prepared his food, Arden felt some heat and a lump on Filibuster. He'd paused when his fingers ran over it. Was this area hotter than normal? After checking the heat against the other three legs, it was definitely warmer.

Arden threw the towel over his shoulder and dropped the brush back in the in a bucket. Time to find Slim.

After a few minutes of searching, Arden failed to locate Slim but spotted Mr. Tate. He hesitated but approached Mr. Tate. He'd never talked with the man before, but this was important, wasn't it?

The trainer was leaning against the threshold of the door to the west, watching the gait of a horse going through the paces with a cart.

"Sorry to bother you, sir, but I think I feel some heat near the front left fetlock of Filibuster."

Arden waited for a response and watched the training. He remembered Bert saying the horses get used to a cart by having helpers at the horse's head to lead him around, while others followed, keeping the cart from twisting and scaring the animal. Eventually, the helpers at the head encouraged the horse to move into a trot and discouraged him from breaking into a run.

He would love to be a helper one day.

Turning his attention back to Mr. Tate, he tried again. "Sorry, sir, but I'm concerned about the heat in Filibuster's left front leg near the fetlock."

This time, the trainer turned and skewered him with a stare. "You think there is a problem?"

Arden took a deep breath and pulled himself to his full height. "I *know* there's a problem."

"Where is Slim?"

"I can't find him, sir. He probably went to the grain shed. He was working on getting horse feed."

The trainer narrowed his eyes at him. "You better not be wasting my time."

"No, sir." Arden remained steadfast, matching the gaze with his own.

Eventually, the trainer hopped off the barrel. He called out to the rider, "That's enough for today." Then he turned to Arden. "Lead the way, boy."

As Arden guided him to Filibuster, he realized the trainer didn't even know his name. But that didn't matter. This animal needed attention.

The trainer ran his hands down the neck of Filibuster. He moved on to the fetlock in question where he prodded and poked, causing the horse to whinny and step backward.

"Hold him still, boy."

Arden stepped up, grabbed his halter, and rubbed Filibuster's nose to distract him.

After a moment, the trainer stood up. "What's your name, son?"

"Arden, sir."

"You've got good hands, Arden." He nodded, his face pulled into concentration. "There's heat and a bump near that joint."

"So, there is something wrong with him?"

"Likely one of two things. At times, a horse will grow a knob on its leg. Right out of the blue. We call these a splint. The horse will have a leg that is hot and tender as the splint forms. They recover from this condition after a few weeks with rest and good care."

"And the other?"

"It could be an abscess. That's an infection under the skin. They're usually caused by a puncture or cut."

Arden studied Filibuster for a moment. "Is there anything we can do to help him? To ease his discomfort? He seems to favor that leg."

"You'll need to make a poultice. If it's an abscess, the poultice will draw the infection to the surface, possibly making the skin open and let the infection out."

"And if it's a splint?"

"The poultice won't hurt a splint, so I've decided we'll start with that."

"I'm sorry, sir, but I don't know how to make any kind of poultice. My mama is the only one at home who has made one."

The trainer gave him a sideways grin. "Then I'll have to teach you."

Arden smiled. "Thank you, sir."

Do you think you can stay in the barn tonight?"

"I can if'n I tell my mama I'm staying."

He patted Arden's shoulder. "We'll get this potion made and applied. Then you can run home and explain you'll be staying here for a day or two to help this horse."

"Thank you, sir."

"I'm going to put you in charge of Filibuster until this problem is fixed. It's probably an abscess and will be drawn out and ruptured in a day or two. You can be in charge of taking take care of him. Got it?"

"What about Slim? Won't he be upset?"

"I'll talk to Slim. He'll be fine with this when I explain I'm training you."

With a nod at Mr. Tate's reasoning, "Yes, sir. Thank you."

"Arden, you've done something exceptional here. For you to spot a problem so early is to be commended."

Arden's face flushed. He wasn't used to compliments directed toward him.

Mr. Tate revolved to leave, then turned back. "If you take care of Filibuster and get him past this issue, I'll recommend you for a promotion to groom."

"Oh, my. Thank you, sir."

"Thank you, son, for bringing this to my attention. Now you need to follow me. I'll show you how to make that poultice."

Arden puffed up with delight. He'd done a good job.

He reached for Filibuster's lead, and they followed the trainer.

One horse slightly limping, one boy walking on sunshine.

Chapter Nineteen

Arden
Fall 1920

Mr. Tate gathered the ingredients for the poultice explaining the need for each one, while Arden held Filibuster.

"Did you notice Filibuster has a puncture wound at the top of his fetlock on that sore leg?"

"Above the joint at the fetlock? No." Arden glanced down at his boots. "I'm sorry. I felt that heat and went to find Slim. Next time, I'll try to figure out the problem."

"It's fine. Just something to think about for next time."

Arden watched the trainer mix the poultice and did his best to memorize the ingredients and the proportions. The mixture smelled awful, and Filibuster danced around, obviously not pleased to have it smeared on him. Arden petted, rubbed, and made soft noises to keep the horse calm.

Mr. Tate explained as he applied the treatment, "This

poultice is to draw the infection to the wound's surface. If it's an abscess, the heat is from the infection."

He patted the last of the mixture onto the area and wrapped a bandage around the leg. "I believe this is most likely an abscess. If we can get a wound like that to burst, we can clean it out. Then we let it heal. They are quite painful if allowed to grow."

Arden hesitated to speak. After a moment, he found the nerve. "I've had to cut open an abscess on a pig before."

"We have to be more patient with an abscess on a show horse. We can't mar their hide. This should rise to the surface in a day or two. Once we can see the problem, we can make a slight cut to keep it from bursting, then clean it out and watch it."

"I promise to do that, sir."

"Any visible blemish on this horse could disqualify him from being a show horse. That would make him not worth anything to a breeder or a trainer since he's a gelding.

Arden looked into the horse's eyes. He admired the bright intelligence shining there. He ran his hands down the regal neck. "Filibuster will always have value for me. He's beautiful."

Mr. Tate shook his head. "We're in this business to make money. As much as you love horses, never forget that it's about money and developing a sterling reputation. Loving the horses comes third."

Arden would not argue with Mr. Tate, but in his mind, he reckoned Mr. Bass believed the love of horses should come first.

Mr. Tate finished wrapping the leg and stood. "Take him down to the end of the aisle and back. I want to watch him walk with that wrapping. If it's too loose, it won't be effective. If it's too tight, it will cause the leg to swell and possibly do more damage."

Arden walked the horse, watching for any downward thrust of Filibuster's head as he walked. Years ago, his father had taught him that was a telltale sign of pain. He didn't see anything that made him worry.

The trainer nodded as they returned. "It's good. A new poultice needs to be made in the morning. Think you can do that, Arden? Make the poultice? Wrap the leg?"

"I'm willing to make the poultice. Could you check the leg when I re-wrap it? I don't want to cause additional problems for Filibuster. I've done no bandaging before."

"That is wise, young man. You're confident in your skills but not so confident that you'd put your horse at risk. I'll come find you in the morning and make sure the poultice is correct and the leg's wrapped right."

"I'd appreciate that."

Without another word or backward glance, Mr. Tate hurried off.

Arden took Filibuster to his stall, which he'd cleaned out earlier in the day. He hesitated once he was sure the chestnut was comfortable. He felt an almost overwhelming feeling of dread associated to talking to the barn manager. With Mr. Tate giving him duties, the barn manager might not appreciate losing time from his usual duties for the next few days.

With a deep inhale of breath, Arden set out to find the manager and suffer through whatever type of heat Mr. Rawlson might have for him.

He found the manager deep in conversation with Mr. Tate.

Mr. Rawlson turned to him. "Best run home and tell your mama you'll be staying here a few days. I assume Filibuster is in his stall and has water?"

"Yes, sir. Thank you, sir."

"Good work, son. Catching that abscess so early might have saved Filibuster's show career."

Arden all but ran home. He was eager to tell them the good news about his find and the rare praise he'd received from two of those in charge at the stables.

When he returned to the stables, Arden made a bed for himself in the aisle, at the front of Filibuster's stall. He wanted to be close enough to hear any distress from Filibuster during the night.

Most of the night, the horses had been calm. There was an occasional blow of air from a horse or the clang of a hoof hitting a water bucket, but that was music to his ears.

Several of the barn cats prowled outside for varmints, but a few were deep in the hayloft's straw. Jess curled up beside him, snoring as loud as a grown man.

Arden grinned in the darkness. There was no other place he would rather be.

Before daylight, Jess bolted upright, which startled Arden. He couldn't tell how long he'd been asleep, but had no doubt the dog's reaction woke him.

Jess now stood beside him, tense, swinging his head from side to side, as if the dog was locating the source of the sound that awakened him.

Arden squinted through the murky darkness. He saw nothing unusual and he couldn't hear anything that caused him concern. What had Jess heard?

The dog stiffened and began a low growl. The sound sent gooseflesh up Arden's arms. Jess sounded like he was warning someone or something about his presence.

Arden's stomach churned. Probably a rat or mouse. Everyone at the stables fought to keep vermin away from the grain storage and the loose grains scattered by accident throughout the structure. Those little devils could wreak havoc with the feed.

Arden placed a hand on Jess to calm him and found Jess's

hair was standing up along his back. The tension in Jess was a warning to Arden, accelerating a scramble to his feet.

At the squeak of a hinge, Arden turned toward the noise, his heart pounding. Someone from the outside was sliding open the side door near the west track. Arden could see a crack of light winking through the opening.

No one locked the stable at night. Such a thing was too risky if there was an emergency, like a fire. The horses would have to be evacuated quickly. A bolt or bar across the entrance could cost a horse its life.

That instant, Jess darted toward the door, barking like mad.

Arden nearly jumped out of his skin. He wished he could see who was entering the barn, but he also didn't want to leave his horse. If Filibuster reacted poorly to the disturbance, he might hurt his leg.

Arden decided to slide inside Filibuster's stall once he realized the fellow was shuffling in there. Blowing air. Nervous.

Once inside the stall, Arden tried to calm the horse as he also listened to determine who was in the barn. Jess had stopped barking, so he must have recognized the intruder.

Had Mr. Tate or Mr. Rawlson come to check on Filibuster?

In the middle of the night?

There was a murmur of voices. Arden strained to make out what they were saying but failed. The whispers grew nearer. He listened as they crossed in front of the stall, then the whispered voices decreased after they passed by.

There were at least two of them. Must be up to no good. Neither were doing any of the daily chores. What were they doing here?

He remembered his bedroll was lying outside the stall.

131

They must not have seen it in the darkness. Either that or they hadn't recognized it. Thankfully.

After a moment, his tension grew as the unknown visitors made their way toward the expensive, special horses.

How could he stop them?

He ensured Filibuster was back to being calm, then took a deep breath, held it, and stepped out of the stall without making a sound.

There was no place to hide along the open aisle of the stable. He hunched over and crab-walked toward the men, praying he could get a description of them or recognize their voices before they discovered him.

God or an angel must have been with him, as the men never turned around to see they were being followed. Normally, the stable was void of humans at this time. Thus, they expected nothing else.

Arden inched close enough to catch pieces of their conversation.

"... Not too much. We don't want anyone to think this was on purpose ..."

"... No one is gonna suspect nothing. Bunch of fools here ..."

"... Watch out. He's swinging around for a bite out of your shoulder ..."

"... If'n you held him right, that wouldn't happen ... If he bites me, I'll have your head, Frank."

Arden sucked in air when he heard the name.

Had they heard him react? He grimaced and prayed they hadn't.

He'd been suspicious that Toby was up to something. Now, one voice had been identified as Frank. He was Toby's friend, leaving Arden positive the other voice belonged to Toby.

Did this mean Toby and his gang were acting out whatever

plan he'd devised? Was this the event needed to put money in their pocket?

Arden scurried back to Filibuster's stall as fast and as silently as he could. They'd beat him, or worse, if they caught him here.

Once hidden again in the stall, Arden worked through logical reasons he thought the other man was Toby. Frank was the groom who always did Toby's bidding. Toby always had a bossy tone to his speech, and Frank wasn't smart enough to resist Toby's orders. The other man had a bossy tone and was condescending, like Toby. He must be Toby.

What were they up to? He should have counted the number of stalls between his horse and their stall. He could guess, but guessing wasn't good enough.

Arden hid in Filibuster's stall for what seemed like an eternity. He wanted to make sure the men had left but couldn't risk being seen. When Jess came whining to the stall door, Arden took this as a sign they'd cleared out.

He opened the stall door cautiously, then stepped out and froze.

Nothing.

No sounds, no movement he could attribute to humans instead of horses and cats. With a few tentative steps, he let out a sigh and slumped down onto his bedroll.

Jess spun in a circle three times, then nestled in beside him. Arden patted him while he calmed his own nerves.

After a few minutes of gathering his own courage, Arden rose to investigate which horse the men were trying to hurt. He checked all the stalls and narrowed his suspicions down to two. The new horses brought in earlier today were Rascal and Dancing Doll, both owned by the Lee brothers and were among the best Saddlebred horses in the country.

What kind of scheme could Toby have related to one of these fine beasts?

Although he couldn't tell which one had been Toby's target, both horses showed signs of nervousness. Pain could leave a horse anxious. The hijinks tonight could have caused the other horse to act up in sympathy.

Because of the darkness, he used his hands to search for blood or a sign of a wound. Nothing felt wet. He ran his hands over both horses, but neither reacted with any distress in all the areas he touched.

Eventually, he gave up. There was no point trying to examine their hooves in this darkness. He could wait until tomorrow to check their hooves in the daylight.

Should he mention to Mr. Tate about the night visitors?

He tossed ideas around and concluded he'd wait another day since he was scheduled to be in the barn another night. Would they be back? Perhaps tomorrow night, he could mark the stalls to identify which one was being opened.

Right now, all Arden could do was get some sleep. Tomorrow, he'd check the horses again as best he could. It wasn't right to accuse someone of wrongdoing until he had proof.

He would also need a plan for some protection. They would hurt him, maybe even kill him, if they discovered he was spying on them.

Chapter Twenty

The Angel of Justice

I sat by the window at Ralph's doughnut shop the morning after the fire. My mission was to enjoy my time watching and hearing people talk as they learned about the blaze.

Thanks to my planning, I showed no outward sign of being near a fire. My cap, gloves, boots, and a fire-resistant jumpsuit were hidden in the woods. Once the firefighters and law enforcement left the area, I would return and dispose of them. Permanently. These were the only items tying me to the fire, besides my memories.

Ralph's had a drive-through window, and it was the busiest part of the store. However, there was spacious indoor seating for patrons to enjoy a leisurely morning. Townsfolk gathered to gossip with other patrons while they sipped their coffee and munched on food.

These indoor people interested me today—the busybodies

from town. My plan was to eavesdrop on these conversations without appearing to hang onto every word.

Last night, I'd delivered vengeance on someone who'd earned her fiery death a hundred times over. I felt unexpectedly powerful.

Today, I wanted to bask in that power. I was an acting hammer of God and owed the opportunity to listen to what people had to say about it. Without them being aware, I was the reason for the fire and Katherine's death.

Just thinking about it made my skin tingle.

They'll know about the fire first. Tongues will wag even more once they realize she's dead.

I recognized Liesl Schroeder when she walked in and ordered. She chose a table in the center of the store, so it was unlikely I'd overhear her conversation if someone joined her.

My guess would be she's meeting her friend Nicole. Although they wouldn't qualify themselves as such, they were as guilty of gossiping as anyone in town, and it might benefit me to sit nearer to them.

I took a moment to consider relocating and decided against it. Such a move might draw attention to me, and that's the *last* thing I wanted to do.

Within minutes, Nicole Smith walked into the shop. She joined Liesl at her table and they had a lively conversation. If only I could hear what they were saying. The subject might be the fire, but I couldn't be sure.

As I tried to eavesdrop, I waved and nodded at a few passing patrons. Then I spotted Margaret Sterling push through the doorway. Her arrival made me smile. From her posture and expression, one could tell she had news and wanted to spread it to anyone who would listen. Would she come to me?

She spoke to the occupants of the table next to mine. That

disappointed me, but I could eavesdrop on their conversation. I watched them while casually sipping my coffee.

Margaret's opening greeting was, "Did you hear the news about the fire at Katherine Mull's house last night?"

The women at the table reacted with stunned looks, and then a passionate exchange of information ensued. Excitement coursed through me as they reacted to the information. There was also the gloating countenance of Margaret, who lived for passing along such gossip.

Margaret was a milder version of Katherine. She always had something spiteful to say but camouflaged her venom by cloaking her remarks as concern. Unlike Katherine, her spiteful ways ended with the spreading of hurtful words.

When Margaret squeezed every bit of delight from that conversation, she moved on to Liesl's table. Her arrival displeased Nicole and Liesl. Their conversation grew animated, and then, moments later, Margaret stalked away in anger. What had caused Margaret's nose to be out of joint? I was sorry I couldn't hear.

After this, Liesl received a brief call. When she hung up, she appeared confused. She turned to Nicole, and they had another conversation. Their faces provided proof they were talking about something serious.

Then, a look of disgust crossed Liesl's face. They were discussing something gruesome because revulsion and shock painted Liesl's facial features. When she shared whatever this was with Nicole, she also reacted in horror.

Was her cop boyfriend involved in working the fire? Or was he involved in Katherine's death investigation? If I read the reactions of their earlier conversation correctly, the girls were aware of the fire.

Yet, the expression on their faces went beyond news of the fire.

My stomach turned. Was it possible Liesl heard Katherine was dead? If Liesl had figured it out, then it wouldn't be long before the whole town would know Katherine was dead.

Liesl and Nicole have a reputation for sticking their nose into investigations. They had a history of working with the police to solve murders.

The unwelcome realization they might collaborate with detectives sucked away all of my fun. I pushed away the last quarter of my doughnut and walked out of the store with my coffee.

They had to stay out of Katherine's death investigation. I could no longer waste time eavesdropping. Time for me to act again. It was necessary to keep Liesl and Nicole from meddling in this matter.

The risk of them discovering more than I wanted anyone to know was huge.

I had to stop them. I'd kill again to keep them from interfering.

Chapter Twenty-One

Kurt

At the fire scene, Kurt and Hector checked in with an exhausted Assistant Chief Goodgame. "I'm calling in the Missouri Division of Fire Safety Investigators to help us. It's just too much for us. So, I can't let you wander around in this mess yet."

Hector nodded. "We understand, sir. Is it possible for us to view the body?"

"You'll have to get with the coroner or the medical examiner for that." Goodgame gestured to a group in the middle of the ruins. "The Medical Examiner and team are planning to take the deceased right now. Our coroner is helping them. You'll probably have to wait for viewing at the autopsy."

Hector turned to Kurt. "I see Tony with that group. I doubt he has time to talk to us, either."

Kurt raised his eyebrows at Hector. Translation: They were powerless to do anything. "So on to Plan B?"

Hector nodded. "Canvas the neighbors?"

"Perfect. Hopefully, they've seen things pertinent to our investigation."

"We can dream, can't we? With a probable victim who had nothing but enemies, how can we find a killer hidden in all the dislike?"

They walked to the closest dwelling to Katherine's house, a beautiful home across the street from the scene. Although this structure was less than half the size of Katherine's, Kurt considered it an extensive property. It was a relatively new home with a brick exterior, a full two-story design, and an attached three-car garage.

Hector rang the doorbell several times, to no response. Then he pounded on the wooden door with his fist. No one appeared. Eventually, he peered into the glass upper half of the door. "I don't see any movement."

Kurt pointed to a security camera tucked into a corner of the porch. "We may have video from this home. I think it belongs to Becky Poindexter. We'll need to verify that."

"Okay." Hector scribbled down the house number and a note about the camera. "Let's move on."

They walked to the modern home situated next door and rang the doorbell.

A middle-aged woman dressed in a robe with mussed brown hair opened the door. She invited them inside with a smile. "I figured you'd come talk to me today. Just didn't expect you quite so early. Please excuse my attire."

Kurt inhaled the aroma of sausage, and his stomach growled.

Hector apologized for the early hour on a Saturday, but she waved away his apology.

"I'm Melissa Nettleton. Follow me. Would you like coffee?"

Both men accepted her offer.

Mrs. Nettleton's kitchen connected to a small den where a red-haired girl about six years old sat watching cartoons.

"That's my daughter, Amanda, in front of the magical babysitter called television."

Kurt waved at her. "My son, Ross, is younger than your daughter." He felt a pang about Ross's current absence. He missed his mini-me even though the frequent calls to his parents assured him Ross was enjoying his time at the lake.

"I have two older boys, I should say teenagers, still sacked out upstairs. No idea when we might see them. My husband is walking the dog, but he should be back shortly."

Mrs. Nettleton turned off the burner under the sausages and opened a cabinet to gather two coffee mugs. "Please sit down." She gestured at chairs lining the large kitchen island. "Anyone take cream or sugar?"

Both men indicated they did not.

She set two steaming mugs of coffee in front of them. "What do you want to know?"

Hector pulled out his notebook and pen. "When did you first notice the fire, Mrs. Nettleton?"

"When I heard the fire trucks. Can't miss those horns when they're blasting. Amanda wanted to see what was happening, so we went out and watched from our porch."

"When did you go outside?"

"My husband was home, and we'd already eaten dinner That would have been about seven." She paused. "My teenagers left between nine or nine thirty."

Hector nodded and wrote in his notebook.

Mrs. Nettleton smiled. "You must think it's strange for me to tell time related to activities here."

Kurt shrugged. "Whatever works is fine."

Hector asked, "Did you go any closer to the fire?"

"No. I didn't want Amanda to get anywhere near it. My

141

husband joined us on the porch for a bit. Then we went inside when more trucks arrived." In a lower voice, she added, "Such excitement is a draw to Amanda. I didn't want her trying to sneak off and run closer."

Kurt nodded. "I understand completely. I have an seven-year-old."

Hector asked Mrs. Nettleton, "Did you see anyone arrive or leave the area? Either before or during the fire?"

She hesitated and then replied, "No. Just fire trucks and police cars. I didn't see anyone on foot who wasn't in a uniform of some sort."

Hector asked, "Do you have security cameras for the outside of your home?"

She nodded. "One camera in the front. Two others in the back, facing the pool. It's more of a way to keep anyone from jumping in our pool when we're gone than to provide security. This neighborhood is safe."

"You always leave the cameras on?"

"Yes. We get mad at the boys when they turn off the cameras. We know they're up to no good."

Kurt asked, "When did the boys return?"

"I made them come back close to eleven. More trucks pulled in to fight that fire. I didn't think the fire would come over here, but I wanted all my chicks safe in the nest. They could have been blocked off from the neighborhood."

"In the future," Kurt said, "if they show their driver's license to any law enforcement officer working an emergency or crime perimeter, they'll try to get them back to their home, if possible."

She smiled. "Good to know."

"Did the boys go over to the fire or the trucks?"

"No. They wanted to, but my husband wanted all of us to watch from upstairs. Our guest bedroom faces the front, so we stood at those windows for a while. Those firefighters worked so hard. We were impressed by their efforts."

Kurt and Hector exchanged a glance.

Kurt said, "We were part of that."

"I should have realized it would be all-hands-on-deck."

"As a public safety department, we're trained in law enforcement and firefighting. We specialize in either police work or fire safety, but pitch in to help either department when needed."

Hector flipped a page in his notebook. "Back to your security system. Any idea how big its memory is? How long are your recordings available? Twenty-four hours? A week?"

"My husband can tell you. He's an engineer. Gadgets are like toys to him. I leave all that stuff to him."

She chuckled and continued, "I only understand the basics. I can review what recorded, but all the rest I leave for the guys. My boys are experts with the security system too."

"We'll take that up with your husband, then. If you both agree, we'd like to have a copy of the footage from your cameras."

With a shrug from Mrs. Nettleton, she said, "No problem with that, other than I can't help you copy it. But why would you want that?"

"We'd check if your cameras picked up anything associated with the fire at the Mull residence. A pedestrian walking nearby or a car driving past frequently, that type of thing."

"We have a lot of people who walk in our neighborhood. With the Green Estate Park nearby, people walk up Teal Lake Road to Huntingfield Road or catch Apple Tree Lane within the park. Dog walkers and joggers. Mostly during the day but sometimes at night."

Kurt shifted in his chair. "Before we go, Hector and I tried

143

to talk to someone at the house next door, but no one answered. Do you know those neighbors?"

"That's Becky Poindexter's house."

Kurt nodded. He'd thought that was her house. Mrs. Poindexter attended his church.

Hector asked, "Is she in town?"

"Actually, she's out of state."

"Does she live alone?"

"She's a widow. One of her friends had surgery and needed someone to take care of her while she recuperated. Becky packed up her dog and headed to Michigan on Thursday."

"Do you have her cell phone number?"

Mrs. Nettleton grinned. "Yes, her phone number, a key to her house, and the code to her security system. Want me to call her?"

Kurt nodded. "I'd like to talk to her about accessing her security system."

"Sure."

Mrs. Nettleton called and spoke with her neighbor, then hung up and gave Kurt Mrs. Poindexter's number. "She's expecting your call."

Kurt excused himself and walked to the dining room, where the television wasn't so loud. When he returned, he said to Hector, "She agreed to let us make a copy of her security system. She even suggested having Mrs. Nettleton's older boy go over and make a copy for us right now."

Mrs. Nettleton nodded. "She knows the boys are great with electronics. They help her when she has a problem."

Kurt said, "She made me promise her I'd order you to call her and fill her in on everything that's happened when our business is finished."

She laughed. "I'm sure she's curious about the fire and you." As she refilled their coffee, she said, "Give me a minute to get one of the boys awake. Waking up a teenager can be dangerous. I try to do it gently. Self-preservation, you know."

At that moment, an enormous but friendly-looking Mastiff bounded in through the back door, followed by a short man with a shock of red hair streaked with gray.

Mrs. Nettleton said, "Introduce yourself to my husband while I go wake up our sixteen-year-old. Between John here and our eldest, we'll have all the technical stuff to you in a flash."

Kurt and Hector had John Nettleton up to speed by the time Mrs. Nettleton returned. She was accompanied by a teenage boy with red hair sticking out in several directions. This verified the teen was roused straight from his bed.

"This is our son, Grant."

Grant shook Kurt's offered hand.

"Hey, man," Kurt said. "Sorry to bother you on a Saturday morning, but your mom says you may be able to help us with the security system at the Poindexter house."

The young man nodded. "She's right. I can help."

"Do you know her surveillance memory?"

"Yeah. It's two weeks before it over-writes itself. I think hers is backed up at the security system office, like ours." He glanced at his mom.

She pulled a face. "Don't look at me."

Mr. Nettleton confirmed. "That's correct."

Hector and Kurt exchanged a look, then turned to Grant. "If we gave you a thumb drive, would you be able to copy what was recorded on the Poindexter system?"

"Sure. If she's okay with that."

Kurt smiled. "Thanks to your mom. We've talked to her and have her permission."

Hector asked, "Will you need more than one thumb drive?"

"Doubtful. It's a motion-activated system like ours. I can probably get our footage and her footage on one drive."

"Let's keep them separate, if you don't mind." Hector stood. "I'll get the drives from my car."

"Give me one of your drives for our system," Mr. Nettleton said. "Grant can do Becky's."

The teenager glanced down at his pajamas and robe. "I'll throw on some clothes. Be right back."

Kurt finished his coffee and took their mugs to the sink. "Thank you for the coffee and for answering our questions."

Mrs. Nettleton nodded. "Glad we could help."

After securing the security recordings from both houses, they crossed to the house on the opposite side of the Nettleton home.

A short, round woman with swirling gray hair and a kind smile answered the doorbell.

Hector introduced them and offered her a brief description of their mission.

"I'm Genna Salazar. That was a big fire last night." She stepped back to admit them into the large entry. "Please come in. May I get you coffee or tea?"

"No, thank you, ma'am," Hector replied. "Were you here when the fire started?"

"Yes. We returned home after seven. We were at the Simmons Stable fundraiser before that. I made Roger drive to our favorite Mexican restaurant and pick up some carry-out. I didn't feel like cooking after standing at the fundraiser. We'd finished eating and were watching television when the fire trucks arrived."

"Did you see anyone in the neighborhood? Anything unusual?"

"Not at all. This morning I've been wondering about Katherine. I haven't seen her since the fundraiser. It's not like her to go unnoticed, especially with her house going up in flames. You'd think she'd be standing around yelling at everyone."

"Do you know her family?"

Mrs. Salazar turned toward a rotund man who approached from the hallway behind her. "This is my husband, Roger."

Roger held out his hand. After they exchanged greetings, Roger asked, "Do amphibians have family?"

Mrs. Salazar gasped. "Hush, Roger."

Hector turned toward Mr. Salazar with a frown. "What do you mean 'amphibian'?"

"I mean, the Mull woman is a toad. Aren't toads hatched or something? She's not human."

"Roger!" Mrs. Salazar's face flamed red. "Stop it now. Can't you see these gentlemen are with the police? They don't appreciate your jokes."

Mr. Salazar pulled a face. "I'm not joking. The woman is not human. She's a cold-blooded toad. I believe that makes her an amphibian."

Mrs. Salazar said, "I apologize for my husband's outrageous behavior."

She turned to him. "You need to go away. I'll answer the questions these men have." She gave her husband a slight shove and then turned to Kurt and Hector. "What was the question again?"

Hector placed his full attention on Mrs. Salazar. "I asked if you were acquainted with Katherine's family."

"She doesn't have any."

"Any close friends?"

Mrs. Salazar put her hand to her lips. "The only people at her house were workers. Cleaning help, men who mowed the yard." She glanced at Mr. Salazar. "Why haven't you left yet?"

"I may know more than you."

Mrs. Salazar rolled her eyes at the detectives and then turned back to Roger. "Did you ever see her with any friends there?"

He shook his head. "Never. The woman doesn't know how to be a friend, so she doesn't have any."

Hector asked more questions. Mr. and Mrs. Salazar confirmed they had seen no one unusual in their neighborhood prior to the fire, and they had no security system. With that information, Hector caught Kurt's eye and gestured toward the door with his head.

"Thank you for your time, Mr. and Mrs. Salazar." Kurt moved toward the door. "We'd best continue our rounds."

Outside, Hector allowed a sufficient distance from the house before turning to Kurt. "Toad, is it? That's rather harsh, but the man's not wrong."

They crossed the street to talk to Mr. Colby, Katherine's neighbor, immediately to the right of her property.

Before they could climb the stairs to the front porch, the door opened. A tall, middle-aged man with hair so black it had to be enhanced by hair dye said, "Tell me she's dead."

Kurt frowned. "Excuse me?"

The man shouted this time. "I said, 'Tell me she's dead.' Katherine. Make my day."

Hector stepped up to the porch. "You realize we are the police?"

The man stepped down onto the porch to join him. "I do. You realize I live next door to that horrible person? I hope the fire might have knocked her off."

Hector pushed his face closer to the man. "Did you set the fire?"

Mr. Colby snorted. "I'm not brave enough to do that. She'd sue me for every dime I have. Using my constitutional right to free speech, I expressed my hope her life was lost when the house burned. I don't actually know whether or not she was there."

Kurt climbed to the top of the steps and stepped on the porch. "That's a harsh statement."

Mr. Colby turned toward Kurt, his lip curled. "Do you know her? You wouldn't say that if you did. The woman is a monster. Describing her with lessor terms would be dishonest."

Kurt and Hector exchanged glances. Kurt understood Hector wanted to take charge of the questioning.

"Why would you want her dead?"

"I built this house before she built that monstrosity next door. My family was happy here until she moved in. She made us all miserable."

Mr. Colby pointed to the side of his property. "See that enormous fence? I spent thousands of dollars building that to block her view of my house, my wife, and my kids. People joke about her being like the devil, but it's nothing to joke about. She's evil."

Chapter Twenty-Two

Kurt

Kurt was relieved to move on from Mr. Colby and walk to the next house. The anger emanating from the man was overwhelming. Hector and Kurt walked in silence until they reached the adjacent home, a splendid version of modern design with large glass windows, clean lines, and mixed metals.

When Hector rang the doorbell, a cacophony of barking erupted from the other side. Both men grinned at the voice of a man yelling, trying to herd the dogs away. The sound of barking faded from inside but transferred to the backyard.

A dark-skinned man answered the door with a body that exhibited extensive gym workouts. He appeared to be about Hector's age and sported a trim beard.

Hector smiled. "Hello, David. When did you buy this house?"

"I wish." David waved them inside. "This is a house-sitting gig for Dr. and Mrs. Johnson. They're on a medical mission trip to Panama. Whenever they leave town, I stay here and take care of their dogs."

With a glance at Kurt, David stuck out his hand. "David Whittier."

Kurt shook the offered hand. "Kurt Hunter."

David grinned at Kurt, then gestured his head toward Hector. "Why are you hanging out with this guy?"

"We're investigating the fire at the Mull residence."

With a nod, David said, "Better come in."

David led them to a cozy den area at the back of the home that provided expansive views of the rolling hills and beautiful landscaping that ended with a large fence. "You can see that house-sitting here is a pleasant job."

He gestured toward a comfortable couch. "The dogs aren't allowed on the furniture, so no dog hairs or odors there. Would you like bottled water? Or I can look for some coffee or tea. I don't drink it but could make it."

Kurt answered for both of them. "Water is fine for us. We've had our fill of coffee this morning." He glanced at his watch. "Rather, I should say afternoon."

David turned to Hector. "Working on a Saturday. This is why you never have time for some hoops."

Hector smiled. "Even if I had the time, do I look stupid?" He turned to Kurt. "David was a college ball player and could have made it in the pros if he hadn't injured himself."

Kurt eyed David with new respect. "I played football but wasn't any good at basketball."

When David left to get their water, Hector asked, "You don't mind if I ask the questions, do you?"

"He's your friend. He'll be more open with you."

"That's my hope."

Once David returned with the water, Kurt pulled out his

notebook and pen but sat back to give Hector center stage. David settled in a recliner across from them.

Hector pulled out his own notebook and pen. He flipped to a new page and scribbled a couple of notes. "Were you here last night?"

"Later in the evening. I arrived around ... I guess it was just after nine o'clock." He focused on Hector. "I'm working with the track coach. One of his students has great potential for discus and shot put, and I tutor him during their summer practices."

Hector turned to Kurt. "David and I were on Mexico's track team back in the day. He was a star in track, basketball, and wrestling. I was just there to look cool for the girls."

Kurt laughed.

"Hector was more than a pretty face," David said. "He was an amazing runner. I've always been a big guy, so I concentrated on areas that required strength, not speed."

"Kurt and I are talking to the neighbors about the Mull fire."

"What do you need to know?"

"Tell us what you might have noticed when you got back here"

"It was dark when I turned off the Boulevard and onto Teal Lake Road. I saw the red sky when I got close. When I was driving down Teal Lake Road, I had to stop to let a fire truck pass. After I got here, I pulled into the garage and the dogs were going crazy inside the house."

Kurt asked, "Crazy due to the sirens? Or something else?"

David shrugged. "I assumed it was the sirens, but it could have been something else. They don't like anyone crossing behind the back fence."

Hector asked, "Did you see anyone walking or running nearby?"

"Not that I recall, but people walk along here all the time. I don't know that seeing anyone would have registered. It's normal for people to be out day and night."

Hector asked, "Even though this isn't your regular residence, did you have any contact with Katherine Mull?"

"The owners warned me to stay away from her the last time I kept the dogs. They had a run-in with her when the German Shepherd escaped. She called the police, and they had to pay a fine."

Kurt made another note. "Any idea when this happened?"

"No. Sorry. It was before Christmas. I stayed here with the dogs while they left over the holidays. They warned me about her then."

Hector asked, "Does this house have security cameras?"

"They do, but I think they're only on the inside. It's for viewing the dogs while Dr. and Mrs. Johnson are working."

The lack of an exterior camera show disappointed Kurt. External cameras might make or break this investigation.

Hector nodded. "Where is the system stored in the house?"

"In the mudroom. Want me to show you?"

"If you don't mind," Hector stood. "Kurt, could you reach out to Mexico Security? Ask Donnie if he has a backup for this system. If he doesn't and we confirm the cameras are only interior, we won't need to bother the owners while they're in a third-world country."

While Hector and David checked out the system, Kurt called Donnie, but it went straight to voicemail. He left a message and then walked to the wall of windows. A German Shepherd, a Rottweiler, and a small foo-foo dog lay collapsed on a concrete pad near the back door. He surmised the small dog was the boss of the pack.

Before Hector and David returned, Kurt received a return call from Donnie Davis. Although Donnie had been Kurt's long-standing high school nemesis, as adults, they'd made peace. Kurt considered him a friend now.

Donnie was aware of the Johnsons' system information even though he wasn't in the office. He explained the Johnsons were the only people in town who had an interior camera system solely for their dogs.

When Hector and David returned, Kurt reported the system was interior only and not backed up at Donnie's business.

"David showed me the monitors for the cameras. Everything on them was interior footage." Then Hector turned to David. "We'll get out of your hair now. Great to see you, and thanks for cooperating."

"Good to see you too. Anytime you want to come watch track practice, you're welcome to join us. You should help coach sometime."

Hector smiled. "I'd enjoy watching you guys work with the students, but I'd be no help myself. My work is the only reason I try to stay in a reasonable shape."

Kurt remembered all those windows looking out toward the backyard. He turned to David. "Do the dogs ever go crazy at night? Like they hear something in the woods?"

"They went nuts about a week ago. I attributed it to a deer or other wild creature getting close to the house. Why?"

Kurt shrugged. "Just curious. A well-prepared criminal stakes out the area for things to avoid."

David nodded. "Like barking dogs?"

"Exactly."

At their car, Kurt turned to Hector. "What is David's occupation? We never discussed that."

"He teaches computer science at the high school."

Kurt nodded. "If I were looking for a route in and out of this neighborhood, I'd avoid this house and the Nettleton's house.

The dogs around here are like alarms. Ready to go off at any time."

"Point taken," Hector said. "When we map out the neighborhood, let's mark the homes with dogs. Maybe it will clue us to a route the possible arsonist used." Hector started the car and turned the air conditioner on high. "Let's get some food. I'm starving."

Chapter Twenty-Three

Arden
Fall 1920

The following morning, Arden performed all his stall duties with speed. He wanted to squeeze in time to check the two horses he suspected Toby and Frank had targeted last night.

Their actions haunted him since he'd overheard their whispering. What were they doing? Was someone bribing them to injure a likely winner? Who would stoop so low just to make their own horse worth more?

Could they want the horse injured so it would sell for less at the next sale? Then miraculously recuperate to sell at a large profit?

At Arden's turn to rotate for breakfast, he hung back to examine the two horses that could have been Toby's target. Neither appeared upset nor hurt. Neither of them minded him pulling up their hooves for a close inspection in the daylight.

Nothing.

After each inspection, Arden patted the neck of the high-strung dynamo. Who could purposely hurt one of these beautiful creatures?

Toby. Arden trusted his instant dislike for Toby. Since Toby had hurt him for the fun of it, then he wouldn't hesitate to hurt an innocent creature.

Arden wished he could get Bert involved, but resolved it was best to keep looking for clues alone. He didn't want to expose Bert to injury and ridicule from Toby. The horses deserved protection, and he would give it to them. He could handle it.

After he finished a quick breakfast, Arden was grateful Mr. Tate hadn't asked him anything about his overnight stay. Arden didn't lie. If Mr. Tate had inquired about events last night, he'd have to say someone came into the stables. However, with the trainer distracted by other conversations at the table, Arden was able to return to work in peace.

Arden unwrapped the poultice from Filibuster and found the wound had opened. He filled a bucket with water and then washed the wound. At a loss for what to do next, Arden left the stall to search for Slim or Mr. Tate.

He couldn't find Slim but spotted Mr. Tate on Rascal, running him through their high school maneuvers. Top-tier events, such as the American Royal and the St. Louis Horse Show, were the intended competition level for this horse. Arden paused, taking a moment to admire the fancy steps.

Bert walked up and joined him, a bridle in his hands. "Admiring the training?"

Arden grinned at him. "I've learned these horses have three gaits. They naturally walk, trot, and canter. What are they doing with him now?"

"To make a five-gated horse, they're taught two additional gaits if the horse has the strength and inclination to learn them. The additional gates are called slow gait and rack."

"How do they know which horses stay three-gaited and which are trained for five gaits?"

Bert shrugged. "The animal decides, according to Mr. Tate. Seems it depends on their basic walking and trotting skills. Do they show they're suitable to learn the other two classes?"

"How do they do that?"

"Five-gaited horses are bolder with power behind their moves. They're more heavily muscled and have a naturally quick trot. With both slow gait and rack, horses only have one hoof on the ground at a time, which takes strength. The larger, stronger horses are chosen for five-gaited training since it's harder."

"Are five-gaited horses better?"

"Nah." Bert fiddled with the bridle in his hands. "Three-gaited horses are cherished too. They're judged for their elegant look and the action shown as they change gaits."

Arden was so caught up in talking to Bert and watching Mr. Tate, he didn't realize Mr. George had joined them at the fence rail. Mr. George Lee was shorter than Mr. Will but took the care and training of the horses and mules as seriously as his brother.

"Oh, Mr. George. I didn't see you there."

"I was torn between watching Rascal do his work and watching you boys admire him." He chuckled. "When I was a boy, the prettiest sight in the world was one of these horses."

Arden nodded. "I'm grateful every day that you and Mr. Will gave me a job. Thank you for paying me to take care of these beauties."

Bert said, "I'm thankful too."

"These horses are the joy in my life," Mr. George said. "It eases my mind to have workers surrounding these beautiful beasts who appreciate and care for them."

"That would be us." Arden smiled at Bert.

Arden ran a hand through his hair. "I actually came out here to find Slim or Mr. Tate. The abscess on Filibuster has just broken open. I've washed the wound but don't know what to do next."

"I'll send Mr. Tate to you as soon as he finishes the paces with this one." Mr. George turned to Bert. "Do you need something from me?"

Bert's face reddened. "I need to get back to work." He shuffled off, the bridle still twisting in his hands.

Arden paused for a moment. "I'm heading back to my duties, sir, but I wanted to thank you. I promise to take the best care of your horses as I can. Thanks again for the chance to work with them."

"I know, son." Then Mr. George turned his attention back to the track.

About an hour later, Arden walked one of the horses up and down the aisle in a cool down. The aisle of the stable was the only shaded area outside of the stalls.

While they walked, Arden eavesdropped on the conversation of two guys working at a table, repairing tack. Gossip was always circulating among the men in the barn. This discussion was between a middle-aged, lanky red-headed groom named Nate, who was bragging to Clyde, a heavyset, brown-skinned young man a few years older than Arden.

"We can credit all the trainers in town for Mexico being called 'The Saddlehorse Capital of the World.' It began with Mr. Bass. He left here when he got famous and moved to Kansas City. There, he became even more famous. Then moved back here."

Clyde asked, "What made Mr. Bass famous? Just showing horses?"

"President Grover Cleveland was an admirer of Mr. Bass. Witnessed him riding at the Columbian Exposition. That was many years ago. In the Eighteen-nineties. President Cleveland even came here to town."

"Here? In Mexico?"

"Sure did. He and Mr. Bass stayed friends until Cleveland died."

"A President of the United States?" Clyde asked. "In Mexico, Missouri? You're joking."

Nate shook his head. "No sir. Honest truth. Mr. Bass was friends with another President too."

"Are you kidding?"

"Nope. That one was Theodore Roosevelt. Roosevelt commissioned Mr. Bass to find him a horse to use when he was living in New York City. Roosevelt came to Kansas City intending to meet Mr. Bass and either buy a horse Mr. Bass had trained or have him locate a suitable horse."

Clyde smiled. "It's hard for me to believe someone my color would meet a President of the United States. Here you're telling me he was friends with *more* than one."

Arden took delight in being acquainted with someone who had been befriended by presidents. Imagine!

"He's met lots of famous people 'cause he's famous himself. Famous people run into each other at horse shows and exhibitions. He's sold a horse to Buffalo Bill Cody, Will Rogers, and the Anheuser-Busch fellows, the beer men. Heard tell Queen Victoria of England invited him to England to show his horses, but he turned her down."

Clyde's head bobbed up. "He told the Queen of England 'no'?"

"That's what they say. Seems he didn't think the horses

would do well on an ocean liner for weeks. I've never had the courage to ask Mr. Bass about it."

"Did other trainers move here because of Mr. Bass?"

Nate shrugged. "Don't know for sure, but Mr. Clark, Mr. Potts, the Lee Brothers, and other famous trainers being here helped the town build a great reputation."

At that moment, Mr. Tate walked up. He glanced over at Clyde. "Hey, can you walk this horse for a minute? I need Arden to go with me to check a wound on Filibuster."

Clyde straightened. "Yes, sir." He strode to Arden and took the lead.

Arden trailed behind the trainer as they headed toward Filibuster's stall.

Once inside, Mr. Tate kneeled down and examined the leg. He paid special attention to the area above the fetlock where the wound had been festering.

"This looks good, actually. Not much skin was damaged in the rupture. I think this will heal with no scar."

Arden was pleased to bursting to hear this news. Filibuster was a beautiful beast and should get his chance to compete in the show ring.

Mr. Tate stood. "Follow me. I'm going to mix up some ointment. Apply it to that area about four times a day until it heals. It won't be necessary for you to stay over tonight."

With shuffling feet, Arden said, "But I'd like to. Just one more night. I want to make sure he's comfortable. I believe he was calmer last night, knowing I was near."

Mr. Tate stared at him for a moment. "There's no reason for you to be here tonight. Is something else going on you're not telling me?"

Arden's face flamed. "I don't want to make trouble for anyone. But I also don't want horses hurt for any reason."

"Horses hurt? Son, you better tell me what you know. Now."

"Can we talk in private? I'll explain everything, but not here. Not in the stable where so many people can overhear me."

"Follow me."

Mr. Tate took off at a brisk pace. Arden struggled to keep up with his stride.

Mr. Tate opened the door of the tack room and peered around inside. "Mr. Will? Would you come to the farrier's shed?"

"Why?"

"There is some information we need to discuss, and it's best to not discuss it here. Is Mr. George around?"

"No. He went into town."

Wood scraped against stone as Mr. Will pushed back his stool.

"Lead the way, Mr. Tate."

When they reached the shed, the farrier was nowhere to be found. The men and Arden entered and stood in a circle.

Mr. Tate said, "You and I need to listen to what Arden has to say."

Arden shifted from foot to foot, unsure where to start.

Mr. Tate skewered him with a look. "Arden, tell us why you think horses might be targeted. I want every detail."

Under the growing concern of Mr. Will and Mr. Tate, Arden explained the nighttime disturbance. When he described how the two men appeared to be doing something that caused the horse to bite them, anger painted their faces.

Mr. Tate exploded. "Why didn't you tell me about this first thing this morning?"

Arden slumped. "I had no proof of wrongdoing. Only their conversation that came to me in bits and pieces."

"What makes you think it was our men and not someone else's guys?"

"Jess. He growled the minute someone opened the door. Then he darted over there, barking like crazy. But he stopped as soon as he recognized whoever it was."

Mr. Tate stiffened. "Should have come to me first thing today."

With those words, Arden hung his head. "I'm sorry, sir."

Mr. Will put a hand on the trainer's arm. "Now, Murry. This isn't the boy's fault. We're lucky he was there. Let him finish."

Arden straightened and then continued. "The leader called the other guy Frank. The leader, the other man, I never laid eyes on."

The men traded a glance, then Mr. Will asked, "Any idea who it was?"

"I believe it was Toby. It sounded like him and he has a bossy way about him. They only went into one stall. In the dark. I couldn't tell if it was Dancing Doll's or Rascal's."

Mr. Tate slapped his leg. "I'll kill them if they hurt either of them."

Arden rushed to add, "I couldn't spot anything wrong with either of them this morning, but I am just learning about horse ailments."

Mr. Tate threw up his hands. "I'll look at both of them and see if I can find anything."

"Hold on, Murry. We need a plan. I want you to check both horses for any kind of injury, but you're going to have to do it on the sly. Not when you're angry like this."

Mr. Tate turned to Mr. Will. "What are they up to? They need to be fired. Right now."

"With the American Royal coming up, someone may have

bribed them to take either one of those horses out of contention. Who would benefit from that circumstance?"

They discussed various owners and trainers who might profit from these horses being lame. Arden didn't know any of these people, but didn't leave or interrupt. After much discussion, Mr. Will turned to him.

"Son, are you brave enough to stay in the stable tonight? I trust you, and we might need a kid who can run faster than three old men. Mr. George is going to want to be involved in this too."

Arden nodded.

Mr. Tate spun toward Mr. Will. "What are you thinking?"

"I think you, me, and George must be inside the stalls of the two horses he thinks they messed with. Maybe they'll be back tonight doing more mischief."

"What if they don't?"

"Then we'll be out there every night until they come back, so we can catch them."

The trainer took off his cap and ran his hands through his thick, curly hair. "Are they trying to lame them temporarily? Permanently? Or something else? Maybe make them skittish about something?"

Mr. Will shrugged. "Could be any of those things. I'm going to hitch up my buggy. I'll hunt down George, wherever he is in town, and then we'll go have a chat with Sheriff Ford."

"What do you think the Sheriff will do?"

"I want him to know what we suspect. He needs to be available to arrest them. But we're going to have to catch 'em in the act, using whatever tool or method they're using to mess with my horses."

Mr. Tate focused on Arden. "Thank you for telling us. Why don't you and I go make that liniment for your horse? Then we casually go check out Rascal and Dancing Doll."

"Yes, sir." Arden followed him out the door and then hesitated. "If you think they're going to run when we catch them, why don't we rig a rope across the aisle I pull from my stall? If you, Mr. Will, and Mr. George are at that end of the barn, they'll likely run my way to escape."

The trainer grinned. "We could cover it with plenty of straw. They won't see it in the barn's darkness, and you'll hear them running toward you. Good thinking, Arden."

Chapter Twenty-Four

Kurt

The remnants of his delayed but appreciated lunch dotted the top of Kurt's desk. He felt better after a burger and fries. Kurt *cleaned* by making a game of tossing the wrappers into a nearby trashcan.

He picked up Katherine's dental records from Dr. King, who had opened his office after hours, and dropped the records at the coroner's office. Tony was assisting the medical examiner, who had scheduled the autopsy. These records should either verify the body was Katherine or eliminate her.

If the body wasn't Katherine, where was she? No one had reported seeing her since the Simmons Stable fundraiser. Her normal behavior would have had her confronting those fighting the fire. So why hadn't she been there?

All her vehicles were victims of the fire. If she hadn't been home when the fire began, someone either picked her up or she walked from her house. If she left, then why hadn't she made an appearance?

Hector and Kurt planned to conduct round two in Katherine's neighborhood as soon as they finished the necessary paperwork and calls. Kurt dreaded the inevitable interviews with more neighbors complaining about Katherine, but they had to do it.

Kurt ended his call with the crime lab and turned to Hector. "They agreed to review all the surveillance footage we've got. Said it will take a week before they can completely analyze it."

Hector frowned at this news. "I suspected that. We need information now, not in a week."

"Good thing I made copies before I put the drives in outgoing mail." He grinned at Hector. "I'll review them in my spare time."

Hector nodded his appreciation of Kurt's offer. "How about we divide the videos and both review them? It would be faster."

"Awesome." Kurt tapped on his computer for a moment. "I've put the Nettleton footage in your secure drop box. I'll review the Poindexter and Colby recordings. Then we can swap."

"Sounds good. I should be able to view them tonight. Keep in mind the videos are just one tool in this investigation."

"I'm aware." Kurt glanced at the clock. "Three o'clock. I'd better call Liesl and cancel our date tonight."

"She won't be surprised."

Kurt used his personal phone to call Liesl. Recently, their chief had suggested they carry a personal cell phone and use their issued work cell for only police work. Some defense attorney had obtained a subpoena for the cell phone of a neighboring county's deputy and embarrassed the department by publicizing his personal texts.

Hector's prediction was accurate. Liesl expected he'd be too busy for a date. She had not had any nomadic visitors, which made him happy, and she told him she was happy for a night home to recover from the fundraiser. He promised to make it up to her. When he hung up, he wondered what they could do for a special night out.

Kurt turned his attention back to Hector. "What's our motive for this killing? Assuming, of course, the body is Katherine, and this fire was arson?"

"Whatever motivated this killer is no small thing. My guess would be absolute fury about something. Money? Revenge? Blackmail?"

"I don't see how money comes into play. We have found no heirs. She didn't have a will. By law, her estate passes to her immediate family. We haven't identified any."

"There are relatives out there somewhere. Whoever they are, they'll inherit millions. That's motive in my book. We'll find them. Eventually." Hector folded his arms across his chest and leaned back in his chair. "Moving on from money. What about a spurned lover?"

Kurt chuckled. "Are you kidding? The revenge angle? She didn't have any boyfriends. She didn't have any friends. Period. If it was revenge, it's for something outside of love or romance."

"But she could have kept someone under wraps. In a town like this, it's hard to do, but not impossible. She could be dating someone from out of town. Meeting them outside of Mexico."

Kurt considered this. "True. So, how would we discover something like that?"

Hector shrugged. "We don't have access to her credit cards and bank statements yet. The best sources for information are family and close friends. Since she has none of those, let's start with her employees. A housekeeper, house cleaning service, or something. Also, a gardener or a lawn service."

"Liesl might know who worked for Katherine. I'll reach out to see what she knows." He tapped out a text to Liesl. "What about revenge?"

"Plenty of people despised her. Murder is the best revenge against someone who has done you wrong."

Kurt ran his fingers through his hair. "You have more experience with this. I have trouble understanding how someone could move from hate to murder."

"Reasons vary. She could have ruined someone's life or taken all their money. If a person was ready to crack and Katherine pushed them over the edge, killing would be possible."

"I'm going to make a spreadsheet. We can adjust the information so many ways, like plausible motives, means, opportunity, etc."

"It wouldn't hurt."

"Okay. I'll get on that. That negative neighbor, Mr. Colby, is going on my list. He might not be a strong suspect, but his first words to us were, 'Tell me she's dead,' and that's highly suspicious."

Hector popped up his head from the map he was spreading across his desk to glance at Kurt. "Don't forget the man who called her a toad. That was Mr. Salazar. He should be on the list."

Kurt nodded.

After a pause, Hector added, "Let's do the interviewing on their turf as much as possible. We can get an impression from their surroundings as much as their words."

Kurt nodded. "Makes sense. What about her bank accounts? Someone meddled with those."

With a shrug, Hector said, "I put the bank mischief to someone who has technical skills. Or, maybe someone broke into her house and accessed the banking apps on her phone."

With an intake of breath, Kurt shook his head. "If someone actually did that from her phone, they probably got into Katherine's house at night. While she was sleeping. While her alarm was set."

Hector reached for his phone. "I'm calling Donnie Davis again. We need documentation from him as her alarm provider for the fire investigation. I'm sure he can run a report on the activity times for that house. For weeks, not just a few days."

"You think someone was sending her a message? Or a warning? Or maybe just messing with her? To scare her?"

"She was unscrupulous. With her love of money, she might have been blackmailing someone, and they stopped her. Or, maybe she was the blackmailer, and whoever she was blackmailing stopped her. Her banking breach is hard to understand. They didn't steal the money. They just moved it to a charity."

"They were just messing with her." Kurt sighed. "But my gut tells me the banking deal is connected to her death."

"I can't argue with your gut," Hector said. "My senses have been tingling about whether this was a vigilante killing. Seeking justice. A vigilante is both judge and jury. They decide who deserves to die, and then they kill them."

"What kind of man could do that?"

"Don't sell a woman short. A vigilante can be a man or a woman. They're motivated by their twisted sense of justice. Either gender could have overtaken Katherine and set the fire."

Hector pushed the map to the side of his desk and stood. "Since you're dateless tonight, do you feel like going back to Katherine's neighborhood and trying to catch the Bass family at home?"

"Sure, but I want time to review the videos tonight. Since Ross is with his grandparents, I have time to do it."

"You got it. Do you miss the little guy?"

"You bet I do."

Within ten minutes, Kurt parked their car in front of the Bass residence. It was on the opposite side of the Colby house, which made it two houses down from Katherine's place. The Bass property had an expansive front and side yard of beautiful wooden rail fences and rolling grass-covered hills.

Kurt spotted a well-built black man, his shaved head shining in the fading sunlight, leading a fabulous-looking horse into a small barn. He gestured to Hector, and they walked over to the stable, skirting the rail fence surrounding the pasture.

"Sir?" Hector called. "Mr. Bass?"

The man turned, his surprise at their presence reflected on his face. He stopped but didn't move toward them.

Hector approached the man cautiously. "Sorry to disturb you, sir. I'm Hector Vega, and this is my partner, Kurt Hunter." He held up his badge to Mr. Bass.

In a resonate voice, the man said, "I'm George Bass. How can I help you?"

The horse danced beside Mr. Bass, causing Hector to eye him with suspicion.

Kurt admired the enormous horse. He had a red sheen to his shiny coat, was well muscled, and showed some spirit.

"We're investigating the circumstances of the fire at the Mull property last night. Were you home when the fire occurred?"

"I was. My whole family was here."

"Did you see anyone or anything out of the ordinary? Either before or after you were aware the house was on fire?"

Mr. Bass shook his head. "I was in this barn. My best horse was showing signs of colic, which is an extremely serious condition. I was out here trying to doctor her, walking her in circles. Those fire engine sirens didn't help her relax, but we got through that."

Kurt interrupted. "So, this fella isn't your best horse?"

Mr. Bass grinned. "Not by a long shot."

"But he's amazing."

Hector shot Kurt a look that meant, 'Shut up, you're veering off the point of the interview,' but Kurt ignored it. This creature fascinated him.

With a nod, Mr. Bass said, "He is amazing, isn't he? Zeus is from a fine bloodline, but Lilac Ridge is twice the show horse he is. Come on in and see for yourselves."

Kurt rushed to follow Mr. Bass while Hector tossed him a glance cold enough to freeze running water.

Mr. Bass proudly walked them to every horse in the small stable, regaling them with descriptions of their features, personality, and rows of ribbons, silver trays, bowls, and cups that were prizes they'd won in shows.

Kurt asked, "Are you related to the famous Tom Bass?"

Mr. Bass nodded. "I'm a distant cousin."

Hector didn't hide his annoyance at Kurt for this sideshow, but Kurt wasn't deterred. Once the tour was finished, Mr. Bass pulled out a currycomb and brushed the horse he'd been leading to the barn.

"Have you noticed anyone on foot that caught your attention in the last week or so?"

"Can't say that I have."

"Do you have surveillance cameras?"

"Never could justify the expense of that. These horses cost us enough. Besides, there is always someone here. My mother-

173

in-law lives with us. She doesn't go to the horse shows anymore."

"Did anyone in your family notice anything different?"

Mr. Bass hesitated. "Best thing is to ask them." He put down the comb. "Follow me. I'll introduce you to my wife and kids."

Hector shot Kurt a look of relief.

This made Kurt smile. Was his brave partner afraid of horses?

"My family'll tell you everything you want to know and more. None of them ever stops talking. Even when they're asleep."

Kurt chuckled.

"I'm not kidding. You'll see."

Mr. Bass led them to the back door of the house. Three children were side by side at the kitchen table, a puzzle spread out in front of them.

"Shelly? The police are here."

The three children stared at them, mouths gaping open.

Kurt and Hector glanced toward each other, then away, trying not to laugh.

Mr. Bass turned to Kurt. "I didn't realize it would take law enforcement to render my family speechless."

When they'd finished questioning all the residents of the Bass household, dusk had dissolved into a night with a beautiful harvest moon rising.

Back in their car, Kurt started the engine. "You want to head home? Or are you game to talk to one more neighbor?"

"Who's left for us to see?"

Kurt grimaced and pointed to the acreage next to the Bass property.

Hector sighed. "Oh, no. The Overton residence. I'm not sure I have the stomach for them."

"No one has the stomach for them when they're fighting. However, we aren't answering a domestic disturbance call there now, are we? I say we get it over with. We've got to talk to them sometime."

Hector sighed. "Let's make this quick."

"You better believe it."

Chapter Twenty-Five

Kurt

Kurt parked on the circle drive of the Overton property. When Hector made no move to get out of the car, Kurt said, "We don't have to do this tonight."

"Let's be as fast as possible." Hector opened the car door. "We don't want to start a fight between them."

They approached the front door, but before they could ring the doorbell, a dog barked and snarled from the inside.

Kurt turned to Hector with raised eyebrows. "The fight might be with their dog and involve our ankles, instead of between them."

"You'd better pray that doesn't happen. I might be older than you, but I can outrun you."

"You think?"

An enormous man who filled the doorframe opened the door. Tall and wide, he was on the older side of middle age. His wore a T-shirt, shorts, and bare feet, and held a cocktail in his paw-sized hand.

His dog, a medium-sized schnauzer, stood panting in a gesture of welcome that belied his response when they'd approached. The dog gave each of them a 'Who, me?' glance, as if they'd imagined his earlier reaction.

Mr. Overton blinked with recognition. Then shouted over his shoulder, "Did you call the police on me again?"

A female voice shouted from another room. "Not yet, but I can if I need to."

"No need. They're already here."

Mr. Overton shouted over his shoulder again. "That's it!" The man shouted. "I can't put up with you for one more minute. I'm moving out!"

"Great. I'll help you pack as soon as I finish with these dishes."

Kurt fought off a grin.

Before the man could shout any further reply, Hector held up his hand. "Mr. Overton, we're here to ask some questions about the fire. That's all."

The man pursed his lips for a moment. "That was an enormous blaze, wasn't it?" Mr. Overton stepped back and opened the door wider. "Come on in. Nice to have you here for something besides some fight we're having."

Hector and Kurt followed Mr. Overton to a study that was outfitted as a man cave with testosterone its decorating design. A built-in bar contained bottles, glasses, shakers, and all other equipment necessary for cocktails. A television blasted a baseball game. A worn brown leather couch and two recliners completed the furniture.

Mr. Overton gestured them toward the recliners while he sat on the couch. Then, he muted the television. The dog curled up beside him and promptly snored.

"Would you like a drink, fellows?"

Hector shook his head. "Thanks, but we're still on duty. We're contacting neighbors of Katherine Mull to inquire about you seeing anything unusual before or after the fire. Did you see anything that seemed odd? Or did you see someone who appeared out of place or loitering?"

"The fire spread quicker than a home fire should have, in my opinion. The first truck arrived about an hour after I got home. Never noticed any signs of a fire when I drove past the house."

Hector reached into his jacket pocket and began taking notes. "What time did you pass her home?"

"Must have been eight-thirty or so."

"Was a garage door open?"

"Everything was buttoned up like normal. No cars in her driveway. There's rarely any movement there, you know. Just landscaping workers, and her inside help comes during the week. All of them are usually gone when I get home."

"Anything else you can tell us?"

"I had no contact with that woman. I'd sooner sock her in the mouth than put up with her attitude. Good thing she has nothing to do with the trucking business." Mr. Overton frowned. "You know, you'd be better off talking to Nancy Jo about this."

Hector nodded. "We'd be happy to talk with her."

Mr. Overton said, "Better you than me. She works from home, and she's nosey, so she might be of help to you."

When Mr. Overton said nothing else, Kurt stood. "Okay then, we'll talk with Mrs. Overton. Could you point us in the right direction?"

Hector rose beside him with an unbridled enthusiasm Kurt hoped Mr. Overton didn't notice.

Instead of giving directions, Mr. Overton shouted, "Get in here, Nancy Jo. These guys want to talk to you."

A female voice responded, "Send them to the kitchen. I'm busy in here."

Mr. Overton smiled. "You heard her. Kitchen's on the other side of the house." Then, he unmuted the volume of the television.

Kurt and Hector rushed from the room and made their way through the maze of hallways until they reached the kitchen.

A petite, blonde woman dressed in stylish Capri pants with a colorful top stood in the kitchen, loading the dishwasher. She glanced up at them and smiled. Her pretty face lit up when she did.

Hector visibly relaxed. "Good evening, Mrs. Overton. I'm sorry to disturb your routine. I'm Hector Vega, and my partner is Kurt Hunter. We're here asking questions about the fire at the Mull property. Did you see anything unusual any time prior to the fire?"

Mrs. Overton ignored the question. She turned to Kurt, who stood on the opposite side of the kitchen island. "Isn't your mother Jennifer Joy Hunter?"

"Yes, ma'am."

She nodded. "I've been playing bridge with her for years. You look like your father, don't you?"

Kurt reddened. "I've been told I do."

Mrs. Overton turned to Hector. "It's nice to talk to you when I'm not asking you to arrest that creature who occupies the bat cave."

Hector dropped his head. "I agree, Mrs. Overton."

The discomfort in the room surrounded Kurt. He cleared his throat and changed the subject. "Mr. Overton suggested since you work from home, you might have seen someone or something unusual."

Mrs. Overton raised her brows at Kurt. "I'm sure he didn't describe my assistance that nicely. I'm not aware of anything usual recently. Since we're close to the Green Estate, there's a steady stream of people walking or jogging all the time."

"Could you give us the names of those who do?" Kurt pulled out his notebook and pen and set them on the kitchen island.

"Sure. Probably the most frequent walker is James Kellar. James is a former athlete standout in high school. I think he also had a college career. Now that he's back home, he competes in five-K runs and bike tournaments. Lives off of South Boulevard." Mrs. Overton gestured toward Hector. "Hector likely knows him."

Kurt glanced up from his notes to see Hector nod.

"Mr. and Mrs. Nettleton walk at night when the weather's good. Their huge lug of a dog is usually dragging them down the lane." She shrugged. "I don't understand the appeal of a dog walking you, instead of you walking a dog. But that's not my business."

She put a glass on the top shelf of the dishwasher. After she closed it, she turned it on, and the quiet motor began to hum. "There's the fella who house sits for the Johnsons. I see him jogging by on the days he's house-sitting."

"David Whittier. We've talked to him," Kurt said. "Anyone else?"

"There's a guy …" she frowned and shook her head. "His name escapes me right now, but he works at some homes around here during the summer. He's a young guy. Around mid-thirties, I'd guess. He mows. Part-time, filling in for homeowners when they're out of town, or helping with spring planting or fall leaf raking."

"Is he one of the regular walkers in the neighborhood?"

"Yes. You'd think his lawn work would get him enough

exercise to satisfy himself, but apparently not. I've seen him almost every evening for months now. He may be burning off steam and killing time. His wife died about six months ago. I understand he was devastated about her death."

Kurt wasn't sure who she meant, but he took down all the details. If Hector didn't know the name, he could look up obituaries and find the death of a younger woman. Not a common thing around here.

"Are these walkers and joggers always at the front of your house? Never in the back of your property?"

"I've never seen anyone cut through our yard. I'm not sure our dog would welcome anyone coming into what he considers his territory. Plus, the Bass's fence runs along the west edge of our property. Between that fence and his high-spirited horses, it should keep anyone from coming through their back property. If someone startled those horses, they could hurt an intruder."

Hector nodded. "Do you have any exterior surveillance cameras?"

"Not here. We do at the concrete business across town."

Kurt traded a glance with Hector and shut his notebook. "Thanks for your help. If you think of anything unusual, please give me a call." He walked to her and handed her his business card.

She perused his card for a moment. "You know your mother is very proud of you."

Kurt felt his face flush. "Yes, ma'am. I hope to continue to make her proud."

"We'll, now that you're back to dating Liesl, try not to ruin it for the second time."

Hector turned, hiding his grin.

Kurt replied, "Yes, ma'am."

Once outside, Kurt asked, "Does everyone know everyone's business in this town?"

Hector clapped him on the shoulder and laughed. "Well, it appears everyone knows *your* business."

Chapter Twenty-Six

Kurt

Kurt was running on fumes. No doubt Hector felt the same way. He'd grabbed a few hours of sleep after reviewing some of the video from the neighbors. He'd set it aside after about an hour, afraid he'd nod off and miss something important.

Now, it was Sunday. He'd called Liesl before she left for church. In their rushed conversation, she'd known the name of Katherine's housekeeper. When he arrived at the station, he'd discussed the situation with Hector.

They decided to interview Janet Cross as soon as possible. She appeared to be the only human who had regular contact with Katherine. Even though it was Sunday morning, Kurt made a call to Ms. Cross, and she confirmed her willingness to talk with them later this morning. She attended early church services, so they arranged to meet at her home afterward.

When they pulled to the curb at Ms. Cross's house, both men stared at the decrepit structure.

Hector asked, "Any chance we're in the wrong place?"

Kurt pointed to the house number. "It's the address she gave me. The street name is correct." He unbuckled his seat belt but remained seated. "What a terrible-looking place. The roof over the front door looks like it could collapse at any moment."

"I'm going to speculate this is one of the rental houses owned by Katherine Mull. She has a reputation of never doing proper maintenance on her properties." He swung open the car door. "Let's go find out."

As they picked their way along the crumbling sidewalk, Janet Cross came to the door of her home and held the tattered screen door for them. "Please use care. The walkway is treacherous."

Though it had been months since Kurt had seen Janet in town, he knew her. She was a few years older, making her in her early thirties. She had dark brown skin, curly black hair cut short, with deep brown eyes. Her jeans and T-shirt were worn, but clean.

Hector introduced himself. "Thank you for talking to us."

When Hector gestured toward Kurt to introduce him, Janet said, "I know Kurt. His mother was my Sunday School teacher when I was young."

She stepped back to allow them into her house. "I figured the most pleasant place for us to talk is my kitchen. I have a table and chairs there. Would you like some coffee or tea?"

"Thank you. I'd love some coffee," Kurt said. "I take it straight up."

"Same for me, Ms. Cross. Thank you."

"Please call me Janet." She led them down a narrow hallway. Then she turned left into a kitchen created in the 1950s or 1960s and never remolded. The metal cabinets were worn, but the surfaces polished to a gleam.

Kurt and Hector sat at the metal table, which was from the same era as the cabinets. These retro styles were making a comeback with interior designers, but this furniture, cabinets, and linoleum were all original.

Hector gave Kurt a slight head nod, indicating Kurt was to take the lead on this interview. Either Hector wanted to observe Janet while she answered the questions or felt the past association between Kurt's mother and Janet would serve them better today.

Kurt pulled out his notebook and pen from his sport coat pocket and also removed his cell phones. He turned his personal cell to silent, but his work cell had to keep its audible ring. He laid that one on the table. "Janet, we thank you for meeting with us today."

She brought them steaming coffee mugs. "Better let those cool for a moment." Then she took a seat. "How can I help you?"

Kurt flipped open his notebook. "Let's establish your employment, Janet. Would you tell us about that?"

"I'm Katherine Mull's housekeeper."

"When did you start there?"

"It's been nearly two years."

"Do you work there full time?"

"I began working one day a week. But eventually Katherine wanted me five days a week. Although she never said, I think she was impressed with my work ethic and my cleaning skills. She didn't want to pay me very well, so I told her I couldn't afford to work for her daily with the wages she was willing to pay."

Kurt nodded. "So, how did you come to an agreement?"

Janet gestured with both hands. "She said I could live here, rent free, for as long as I worked for her."

Kurt resisted the urge to eye the aging kitchen. *Not much of a bargain.* "Does she also pay you a wage?"

"She does. Just the minimum wage rate." Janet pulled her lips into a wry smile. "I take side jobs on the weekends to help pay my bills. Katherine doesn't know about those. Please don't tell her."

Kurt blinked. "There's no reason for us to do that."

Janet didn't appear to be worried about Katherine. He'd address that issue in a moment. "Would she object to your side work? Even when it's on your own time?"

"She is selfish. The world revolves around her. It's not her nature to share me with anyone. So, I don't tell her. I make sure those I work for won't tell her either."

"Do you know where Katherine is? Right now?"

It was Janet's turn to blink. "No. Am I supposed to?"

Kurt ignored her question. "When did you last see her?"

"Friday morning. She was upset about something and yelled at me before she left the house."

"She was mad at you?"

"No. She's the type of person who yells at those in her path when she's angry. Something had set her off."

"Do you know what it was?"

"I assumed it was a business problem. She slammed the door of her office and came stomping down the stairs. Yelled that the fireplace hearth was dirty."

Kurt considered this for a moment. He planned to scour Katherine's home office, no matter what shape it was in, as soon as the fire department allowed them access. Her bank issue happened around that time.

On Friday, after he and Hector had investigated the issue at the bank, Mr. Barnaby was able to redeposit all of Katherine's money that had been transferred to the Butterfly House. She had huffed out of the office, saying she would take her business to a different bank. Kurt noted Mr. Barnaby appeared neutral at that remark.

Katherine denied making the money transfers. Yet, the bank's records showed the transfers occurred through the banking application on her personal phone. She assumed the bank's app was faulty or had suffered a glitch. Mr. Barnaby researched the issue on his side, and his technical group denied any problems on their end. Everything the techies verified the transfer came directly from Katherine's phone.

Now, they would need to consider whether or not someone made the allocation from her actual phone. That meant someone accessed the interior of her home.

"Tell me the name of anyone who had access to Katherine's home."

"Access, like the alarm codes?"

"Yes."

"I'm the only one who has the code besides Katherine. As far as I know."

"What about the prior housekeepers?"

"I was her first weeklong housekeeper. The others came on certain days of the week. I don't know about codes for them. You'll have to ask Katherine about that."

"Do you have access to her office?"

"By myself? Never."

Hector turned to Janet. "Does Katherine have an office in town? Anything related to her rental house business?"

Janet shook her head. "Not that I know anything about. She called her office that big room at the top of the stairs on the east wing. She keeps it locked when she isn't using it."

Kurt leaned back and let Hector handle this line of questioning.

"Do you clean that room?"

"Every six weeks or so. I clean the floors and dust the built-in bookshelves. Katherine unlocks the door and stands there, watching me. For some reason, she feels a need to watch me."

Hector furrowed his brow. "You said floors and bookshelves? You don't clean anything else?"

"I never touch anything on her desk, computers, monitors, or file cabinets. Those are off-limits. Same with her trash can. She dumps the trashcan herself. It's the only trash she personally handles."

Kurt jumped back in with questions. "Who is normally working around the house?"

She counted with her fingers. "I'm the only daily inside person. Katherine has a service that comes once a quarter to steam clean her upholstered furniture, rugs, and her curtains. They make their arrangements with her, and then she tells me what day to expect them."

With finger two, she said, "Phil Woolfolk does the landscaping. I've only seen him doing the work, but he could have employees. Phil would know best about that."

"What about pest control or HVAC maintenance?"

Janet bit her lip. "I'm so sorry. I forgot about them. She has a quarterly pest service, and she does a semi-annual HVAC service for her heat and air. With that enormous house, there are three air conditioning units and three heaters. The service people are there for hours."

Kurt requested for the company names and added them to his notes. "What about her security system? Do you know who installed it?"

"No idea."

"Cameras?"

She shook her head. "Not that I know of. I just know how much time I have to enter the code."

"Did she have visitors?"

"Katherine?" Surprised radiated from Janet. "Not that I'm

aware of. I've heard she and her father used to host parties there, but she's never had a party or even dinner guests since I've worked for her."

"A boyfriend or love interest?"

A smile tugged at Janet's lips. "No. At least, not to my knowledge."

Kurt tried not to let his own amusement show. "Who are her friends and relatives?"

Janet studied her hands folded on the table. "I'm unaware of any friends. As far as relatives, she made one comment once about having several worthless cousins but never named them."

"What brought up the cousin comment?"

"She came in one afternoon and was angry. When she's angry, she takes it out on everyone and everything in her path. Toddlers are the same way." A guilty look crossed her face. "I'm sorry. It's not my place to talk like that about her."

Kurt gestured toward Hector. "We will not tell anyone your personal comments unless they apply to our investigation."

"She'd bumped into one of her cousins in town. She didn't say where. She said she despises them, and one almost ran her down in his truck, which made her mad."

"On purpose?"

"I highly doubt that. Katherine always makes drama out of nothing."

"Okay, then." He turned the page in his notebook. "On Friday, after she left the house ..."

"Yes?"

"Did she tell you what made her mad?"

"She mumbled about the bank being incompetent. Mr. Barnaby too. That's why I didn't take offense at her yelling at me. If she thinks Mr. Barnaby is incapable, she's mistaken."

"Have you noticed anything unusual at her house lately?

Like the alarm not being set when it should have been? Or things out of place?"

She paused for a moment, then shook her head. "No."

Janet held up a hand. "Wait. It was unusual for Katherine to have plastic gas cans in the garage."

Kurt jerked his head upwards. "Gas cans?"

"The cans were in the garage's corner about a week ago. Katherine would *never* touch or mess with gas cans, so I assumed Phil Woolfolk put them there. Her grounds are extensive, and he refills his mower frequently."

"Do you remember what day you first spotted the gas cans?"

Janet pondered the question. "The first two cans were there on Monday." She paused. "No, it was Tuesday because I spotted them when I took the trash to the big trash container."

After staring into space, she said, "When I leave on Tuesdays, I fill the big can with the bags and pull it to the curb. They pick it up on Wednesday."

Hector straightened. "You said, 'the first two cans.' Did you see more?"

Janet nodded. "There were two more cans there on Wednesday, lined up beside the first two. I noticed them when I dragged the big garbage can back inside. After I washed it out, of course." She paused. "Must have been Friday before I went out to the garage again. There were even more cans."

"This past Friday? Two days ago?"

She nodded. "That's right."

"How many total by then?"

"At least five. Maybe six or seven, I didn't count."

"How did you know they were gas cans?"

"I didn't. They were those red plastic cans. I just assumed they had gas in them. There was a gasoline smell." She shrugged. "Could have been anything in them. Or nothing, for that matter."

Kurt asked, "You never went over to them to check them out?"

"No." A look of concern crossed her face. "Should I have done something about them?"

"No, Janet," Kurt reassured her. "You've helped us tremendously with this information. We'll get with Phil and find out more about those cans from him. Thank you."

After a few more questions, Kurt closed his notebook. One glance at Hector relayed he was satisfied with what they'd accomplished here.

They thanked Janet for her time and her hospitality, then headed out. In their vehicle, Kurt turned to Hector. "Do you agree Janet had nothing to do with Katherine's fire and probable death? I just don't get that vibe from her."

"She has multiple reasons to hold a deadly grudge against Katherine." He turned to glance at the house. "This *home* needs to be condemned, but like you, nothing bothered me about Janet. She appeared honest, trying to help our investigation as much as possible. She also never referred to Katherine in a past tense. To her, Katherine is still alive."

Kurt scrunched his face. "Do you think she has mice in that hovel? Or cockroaches?"

"I'm sure there are unwanted creatures in the attic, but her living room and kitchen were immaculate. She must work hard to keep it that clean. Even with the place falling down around her ears, she takes pride in it."

"I suspect she has no health insurance or social security paid on her behalf."

Hector sighed. "There are times I wish I could right every wrong in the world."

"Poor woman. She's doing the best she can." Kurt paused.

"I wish she'd work at my house. Her cleaning skills are obviously amazing."

"My bachelor pad could use a hard worker like her too. Maybe we approach her together. When all this is over?"

Kurt turned on the car. "Maybe she could give you some fashion advice while she's handling your laundry. Your Hawaiian shirts need to go."

"What? I'm being insulted by someone who wears a golf tee with a sports coat."

Their playful banter lasted several minutes. Eventually, Kurt asked a serious question. "Would you try to track down Phil Woolfolk? Maybe we can catch him and ask about those gas cans. Or, I should say, those cans. We don't know if they held gasoline."

Hector fished for his work cell. "Everything we know right now indicates the fire was arson. Until the experts finish, we have to rely on their instincts, and they think the fire was set."

"If I were a smart arsonist, delivering the accelerant to my target house *before* the fire is genius. Filling one can at a time, at gas stations all over town, would not catch anyone's interest."

"I don't believe Phil or his guys put them there," Hector said. "What client would want cans in their garage? They're a hazard if they are full of gasoline. If Phil uses them for his landscaping business, then why wouldn't he bring them along with his equipment? It doesn't make sense to store it at a client's house."

"Any reason Katherine would have them?"

Hector shrugged. "Not that I can think of." He punched buttons on his phone. "I need you to find Phil Woolfolk for me. I need a location rather than a phone number. We want to pay him a visit."

While waiting for the weekend desk Sergeant to do his

magic, they decided lunch was in order and drove through for burgers. They pulled into a parking space and let the air conditioner run while they sated their appetites.

The Sergeant phoned with a location on Phil. Seems he was working on a Sunday afternoon to catch up on projects.

When Hector read off the address, Kurt said, "That's only a few blocks from Katherine's neighborhood."

"We'll check in with the fire investigators too. Maybe they're ready to let us pick through the site."

"When we've finished with Phil?"

"Yes. We need to catch him quickly. Those cans bother me."

"They bother me too."

"After we talk to Phil, we'll tell the fire investigators about them."

At the given address, they pulled in behind a dually pickup truck and an even larger flatbed trailer with its ramp down. Both men exclaimed when they spotted a red gas can strapped to the trailer.

They followed the sound of Phil's large John Deere riding lawnmower around the side of the house. He was a fireplug of a man, not too tall but wide in the shoulders, with arms like a bodybuilder. Kurt wished his own yardwork would work that same magic on his frame.

Phil registered surprise to see them. He stopped his mower and turned it off. "What can I do for you fellas?" He reached into his back pocket, pulled out a blue bandana, and wiped the sweat from his face.

Hector held up his badge. "We have a couple of questions for you. Sorry to interrupt your work, but this is about the Mull fire."

Phil put away his bandana as he stepped down from his mower. "Can we talk in your car? With the air conditioner running?"

Hector waved him toward the car. "You better believe it."

Once Phil was settled in the back seat and the air conditioning was on full blast, they asked him general questions about his work for Katherine.

Phil revealed Katherine's father hired him. Once Mr. Mull passed away, Katherine kept the same arrangement with him, at the same pay. "To be honest with you fellas, I'm resigning at the end of this summer."

The guys exchanged a glance.

Hector asked, "Why?"

"She refused to pay me more than her father paid. With inflation, I'm barely clearing my costs. I told her I needed more money, but she refused."

"Did you tell her you were leaving?"

Phil's eyebrows rose. "Do I look stupid? She would have pitched a fit. Jumped all over me. I wanted none of that."

"How were you going to tell her?"

"Every time I mow her place, I think about it. I'd landed on sending her a letter once mowing season is over. There's no way I'd do that face to face."

Kurt nodded. "We understand." He scratched a note in his notebook, then asked, "How did she pay you?"

"I send her monthly invoices through a payment app, and she sends me the money. A lot of my clients use them."

"Did you have access to her house?"

He stared from Kurt to Hector. "You mean like a key or something?" He shook his head. "Absolutely not."

Hector clarified, "So you had no access to her garage? Or house?"

"Nope. Wouldn't want it. You know how she is. If I had access, and something was out of place or broken or something, she'd blame me."

Kurt frowned. "So, you've never been inside her house?"

He shook his head. "Her old man hired me when I bumped into him at the hardware store. I've never set one of my grass-covered boots on that interior."

Hector shot a look at Kurt. "Never been in the garage?"

"Not once. Those garage doors are closed when I arrive and stay closed until I leave." He paused. "Except when Janet is dragging out the trash. The doors are up, then. If I'm not mowing, I'll drag the container down that long driveway for her. It's a long way from the garage to the street."

"Any of your crew have access to the house or garage?"

Phil chuckled. "I wouldn't trust them."

"So, how do you transport gasoline to and from a job site?"

"I've got a five-gallon gas can strapped in my trailer. I refill every day after I finish. Saves me from having to leave a job site."

Chapter Twenty-Seven

Arden
Fall 1920

Arden busied himself with his chores and kept his eyes down so no one would talk to him today. He had too much churning in his mind for interaction with others.

Would the Lees be able to catch Toby and Frank in the act? What if they didn't come tonight? Would Mr. Tate and the Lee brothers think he made up the whole thing?

The Lee brothers went around taking care of their everyday work.

Mr. Tate worked horses and then later turned to watching the gaits of other horses as they trained. Arden was grateful Mr. Tate barked no orders at him. He feared his face, his reaction to anything the trainer might say, might act as a tipoff to Toby and Frank about their plot.

Arden also carried a burden with him as he worked. If he was right about Toby and Frank misbehaving, they would hurt him or get back at him for snitching on them. That's how they were. It scared him to think of what they might do to him.

Mr. Will returned from town in his buggy, followed closely by Mr. George and his buggy. Arden studied them as carefully as they could. Were they mad at him for not telling them about this earlier?

Both Lee brothers appeared more concerned than angry as they barked orders to nearby grooms. Neither indicated to Arden of the results of their meeting with the sheriff.

Once Arden finished his own duties for the day, he helped Bert complete his chores. As much as he wanted to share with Bert what was supposed to happen tonight, Arden figured the Lee brothers and Mr. Tate didn't want his mouth running on about what they suspected was going on. A leak about anything negative could hurt the stable's reputation.

Bert was happy to have help. He showed no curiosity as to why Arden was helping him. When they'd finished everything, Arden watched Bert head home, then returned to Filibuster's stall.

Arden was unsure what he needed to do for supper. Yesterday, he'd been invited to the kitchen to eat due to his plan to stay overnight. Today, after the emotional discussion they'd had, Arden didn't want to be seen with Mr. Tate or either of the Lee brothers, even if it meant missing food. Until everyone left for the night, Arden would stay in the stall with Filibuster as if he was still tending the wound.

When the stall door opened, Arden tensed until he recognized Mr. Tate.

"Thought I'd find you out here." The trainer handed him something wrapped in a cloth napkin. "Everyone else has gone for the day. We can talk without concern."

"Thank you." Arden took the bundle. He smiled when he unwrapped the sandwich and apple. "This looks good."

Mr. Tate nodded. "Bacon and tomato sandwich made special by Mrs. Tate. She wanted to express her appreciation for what you're doing. We figured you'd need something in your belly to keep it quiet tonight."

Arden smiled through a mouthful of sandwich.

"Any idea what time those guys came in last night? Early? Late, as in near dawn?"

Arden mulled over this question as he chewed and swallowed. "My guess would be it was near midnight or one o'clock. There was no light. It could've been near dawn, but I doubt it."

"Finish that sandwich. Then let's get that trip rope lined up while we have enough light of day to get it settled."

Arden polished off his sandwich and put the apple in his pocket.

They worked quickly. They tied the rope to the opposite stall, ran the rope down the door, across the aisle, and into Filibuster's stall. Arden would wait for the men to run his way while he remained hidden inside the stall. When they came close, he'd pull the rope as hard as he could and hang onto it, hoping to trip or entangle them.

Arden didn't believe he could see well enough through the slats of the stall door in the dark to know when to pull the rope. He'd have to listen and rely upon his ears.

On his way out, Mr. Tate said, "I'll be back with Mr. Wil and Mr. George later this evening. We're going to hide near the horses you suspect they're targeting." He moved to open the stall door, then turned back. "Did you sleep in the stall last night?"

"I was sleeping in the aisle. I slid into the stall when they opened the stable door. Jess was barking at them, so they didn't pay any attention to anything but him."

"You're sure they didn't see you?"

201

"If they had, they'd have said or bullied me today. Last night, Filibuster got restless at their disturbance, so I hid in there and calmed him."

"It's best if you stay inside the stall tonight." He eyed Filibuster. "This wicked devil seems fond of you. He's normally a feisty boy who would crush most people, but he has taken a shine to you."

Arden patted Filibuster. "He knows I made his leg feel better. That's why he tolerates me."

"To be honest, Arden, I questioned why Mr. Bass came in and convinced Mr. Will to hire you. We always have a need for barn boys and hard workers. But a stable with this fine reputation can have its pick of cream. And you're so young."

Arden deflated at this comment.

Mr. Tate held up a hand. "Hold on. I'm not trying to hurt your feelings, son. I'm giving you and Mr. Bass a compliment. Mr. Bass spotted something in you. Something that I either missed or wasn't looking for."

Arden straightened.

"Mr. Bass makes all his decisions by asking, 'What is the best decision for the horses?' He was right about you. Whatever he spotted in you, it was best for the horses."

Arden didn't know how to respond. "Mr. Bass caught me watching you work a horse that day. He came and stood beside me, and we both watched you work 'em. I didn't know what horse at the time, but you were putting Samson through his paces. I'd never seen anything so beautiful."

"One of the best things about working for famous owners and trainers is you get to help train champions. The longer I work for them, the more the Lee brothers allow me to do more training. One day, they'll be too old to ride them at shows, and I'll get to do that too."

Arden dropped his head. "I've never been to a horse show.

Even with the fairgrounds nearby, we never could afford the entry fee."

The trainer patted him on his shoulder. "Don't worry. You'll have your chance to work hundreds of shows. We're busy on an average day here, but just wait until you see all the work at a show."

"I'd love to do that one day."

"Those who go to the shows work as a team to help the Lee brothers hop off one horse and hop on another. The work is even harder than the work here."

Arden grinned at Mr. Tate. "But it's more exciting."

"Son, we're going to have plenty of excitement either tonight or one night soon. Now try to get some sleep."

"Yes, sir."

"I'll be back with Mr. Will and Mr. George in a couple of hours. Let's hope we can catch those fools tonight. I don't know how long I can keep a neutral face around them. All day, I've been wanting to knock 'em flat."

Mr. Tate grumbled as he walked away.

Arden resisted the urge to tell him he felt the same way.

It took Arden a long time to fall asleep. He dreaded what might happen tonight and tossed and turned, but this night, he was inside Filibuster's stall. He made himself as comfortable as possible and prayed things would work out with no person or animal being hurt.

Jess wasn't pleased about being forced to sleep outside in the aisle of the stable, but Arden needed Jess to hear any intruder and run toward them, like before.

A low-pitched growl from Jess woke him. Arden held his breath and remained still.

Jess ran off but stopped growling as soon as he determined who had entered. This again meant he recognized the person.

Arden prayed the visitors would be Mr. Tate and the Lee

brothers, instead of Toby and Frank. Until he identified them, he had to stay hidden.

Shuffling boot sounds grew louder as they neared Arden's hideaway. His stomach tightened. If this was Mr. Clark and the Lees, they would have said something by now.

Filibuster stomped around the stall, echoing the noises other horses were making. Arden soundlessly rose and stepped toward him. He ran a hand along his neck. The agitated blowing. strained whinnies and hoof stamping from the horses multiplied. Why were the horses reacting like this?

Something must have gone wrong. If he read the reactions from the horses correctly, the nocturnal visitors were back, and Mr. Tate and the Lee brothers had not yet come in.

Arden would have to face them alone.

Although icy fear snaked through his limbs, Arden worked hard to quiet his breathing and listen to the intruders.

Should he try sneaking out to overhear them?

No. If they caught him, it would be two against one. He had a better chance of catching them as they left. Could he tie one up in the trip rope? His chances of catching two of them were slim.

The men passed Filibuster's stall without hesitation.

He stood, trying to remain frozen in position. Seconds dragged until the squeak of a stall door being opened reached his ears. Were those footsteps from men? They were so faint.

Then, the groan of an injured horse echoed through the stable. What were they doing to the poor animal? Filibuster danced around in the stall. Other horses reacted the same way to the suffering of their stable mate. At least one horse kicked inside its stall.

Arden took a deep breath and gathered his courage. He was going to put a stop to this, no matter what the men would do to him.

He moved silently to the stall door and reached over the top to unlatch it from the outside. Suddenly, the barn lights went on.

He drew back his arm, then blinked, his eyes reacting to the sudden light. He stood motionless for a second, trying to figure out what was happening.

The sound of angry men's voices filled his ears.

When he heard approaching footsteps, he moved into action.

Arden peered over the stall door and spotted Frank and Toby running toward him. He *knew* Toby was involved! They were only a few yards away.

He dropped down and felt along the straw for the rope they'd hidden earlier. When he wrapped his fingers around the rope, he quickly looped the rope around his hands and pulled on it so hard, he tumbled backward. The force of the men running into the rope yanked him upright again.

With the rope still in his hands, Arden ran out of the stall. He jumped to avoid stepping on Toby and Frank. They were on the ground in front of the stall, tangled in the rope.

Mr. Tate ran up and jumped on Toby as he squirmed. "Oh, no, you don't."

Arden turned to Frank, who appeared to have been injured. The man was sitting on his knees, rocking back and forth, his right arm cradled in his left arm.

"It's broken," Frank said. "You broke my arm!"

Arden shifted over to stand in front of Frank as Mr. George and the sheriff ran toward the melee. Two deputies followed them, and they leaped to secure Frank and Toby in handcuffs.

Waddling in behind everyone else was portly Mr. Will, walking slowly and breathing hard.

Frank screamed when they twisted his injured arm behind him.

There was not a speck of sympathy for him from anyone in the stable.

Mr. Will huffed to catch his breath as he stared at the captured men for a moment. "What were you doing to our horses?"

Toby grunted from the ground as the deputy pushed him to respond. "Nothing, Mr. Will. This is all a misunderstanding."

Mr. Will spoke to the deputy holding Toby. "Let him up. I want to see what he has to say for himself."

The deputy yanked Toby to his feet. "Talk!"

Toby's face flamed. "We were just checking to make sure Dancing Doll was doing all right. She was limping earlier today."

Mr. Will seared him with a look. "So, you reported that limp to me? To Mr. George? Or to Mr. Tate here? Who'd you tell?"

Toby dropped his head.

After a search in Dancing Doll's stall, the deputies discovered a knife filed down to a slender pick. The tip was wet with a red substance.

Sheriff Ford approached Toby and Frank with the pick. "Care to explain why there is fresh blood on this instrument? You boys wouldn't be hurting this horse for any reason, now would you?"

Both men stared at him in stony silence.

Sheriff Ford turned to Mr. Will. "These men your employees?"

"Not anymore."

"Do you wish to press charges for trespassing or damaging your property?"

Mr. Will eyed the men. "Yes, I'd like to charge them for both trespassing and damage to our property."

The sheriff studied Mr. Will. "That all?"

Mr. George pushed his way in front of the sheriff. "As for our former employees, we want them banned from our property forever. We'll make sure every trainer or owner in the United States is aware of what they have done here. Neither one should ever be allowed near any animal again."

The deputies grabbed Toby to lead him away.

Toby turned to Arden as they pulled him toward the entrance. "You." He tried spitting on him, but the spittle landed in the dirt at Arden's feet. "You had something to do with this. Better look over your shoulder. I'm gonna get you for this. I promise."

Arden straightened. "God will make you pay for this, Toby."

"God won't be able to help you." Toby's malicious laughter echoed throughout the stable.

As Arden watched the deputies escort Frank and Toby away, he silently prayed he'd never see either of them again—especially Toby.

Chapter Twenty-Eight

Kurt

W hile they drove back to the police station, Hector asked, "Who would know details about Katherine Mull's cousin or cousins?"

"Liesl might. We need someone who has knowledge of old family history." Kurt realized Mrs. Sizemore would be more likely to know this information than anyone. He groaned.

Hector chuckled. "You're thinking about Mrs. Sizemore, aren't you?"

"What gave me away? The groan or the sick expression on my face?"

Hector threw back his head and laughed.

"Hector, Mrs. Sizemore can be as mean as Katherine Mull. Don't make me go face-to-face with her again. I took it for the team last time when we needed her help. It's your turn."

Hector pierced him with a glance. "That lady hates me for some reason. She'll barely nod in my direction. No, thank you."

"Mrs. Sizemore is one of the *Grande Dames* in town. Even

though she's in her eighties, her mind is still sharp. And her attitude has the same sharpness."

"Prickly, you mean. She shouldn't treat me like that. I've done nothing to her to deserve it."

"It's not just you, Hector. She treats everyone the same awful way. Don't take it personally. The way she treated me when I broke Liesl's heart, well ... I was a leper to her. She's better now that we're dating again."

Kurt pulled up to the station.

"Good. Then you should be the one to talk to her." Hector opened the door. "Count me out."

Kurt frowned at Hector's back as he walked away. If only he could say no to a conversation with Mrs. Sizemore. Now he was taking 'One for the Team' a second time. Hector owed him *big*.

Mrs. Sizemore was judgmental, rich, and could keep a secret. Interacting with her would expose him to two things— the knowledge she innately has from being a busybody her whole life, and the crabbiness and possible treachery she freely exhibited in her golden years. Any filter she might have had in her youth was gone.

Inside the office, after doing everything he could to delay his conversation with Mrs. Sizemore, Kurt picked up his phone and called her.

Her housekeeper answered.

"This is Detective Kurt Hunter with the Mexico Public Safety Department. I'm calling to schedule a time with Mrs. Sizemore to ask her for help with a police matter."

"When would you like the appointment?"

"As soon as possible."

"Hold, please."

He held for an age before the housekeeper returned. "She can see you at five p.m. today for tea. Does that suit?"

Tea? Did she say tea? "Ma'am, excuse me, but did you say something about tea?"

"Yes. Mrs. Sizemore has invited you for tea. She will also serve coffee, sandwiches, and some cakes."

He hesitated but eventually said, "Please thank her for me and tell her I'll be there at five."

When the call ended, he wrestled with his feelings. She was going to see him. That was good. But tea? What would that entail?

He was already groveling for her assistance and would have to compliment her into cooperating with his inquiries. Now he had to endure teatime? Why wasn't anything easy with Mrs. Sizemore?

He would have to make a list of questions and put them in order of importance. Whenever Mrs. Sizemore grew tired of him and his questions, she'd cut him off and send him away. That was just what he expected from her.

Tea? Oh, my. He would talk to Liesl about *taking tea* with Mrs. Sizemore.

With only a moment to wallow in his misery, he called Liesl.

After exchanging a few pleasantries, Kurt rolled into begging mode. "I need to ask a favor."

"Is it something where I can see you?"

"Sure. I'll stop by and talk to you about this in person."

"Good. Then I'm happy. What's the favor?"

"I have an appointment with Mrs. Sizemore. She invited me for tea."

Liesl's muffled giggle reached through the phone lines.

"I can hear you laughing."

"Sorry." Laughter erupted again. "It's just imagining you sitting down and trying to have tea with Mrs. Sizemore. Forgive me, but the idea is hilarious. I wish I could watch."

"Why do you say that? There should be nothing unusual about the meeting other than my goal to sip tea without spilling it."

"Have you ever had tea with anyone?"

"No."

She smothered another laugh.

"Would you stop that?"

"If you've never sat down for a proper tea, then you'll be surprised. It involves teapots, sugar bowls, tea sandwiches, tea cakes, silver utensils, and cloth napkins."

Kurt groaned.

"I'll stop laughing, and I'll help you have tea while not making a fool of yourself. But you have to come here and practice."

"Practice? That's ridiculous. I already know how to eat and drink."

"Not this way. You have to get comfortable having tea, which is a whole different animal."

He sighed. "Even though I can't see you, I'm fully aware you're over there smirking."

"I *am* smirking. But I don't get a chance to laugh at you very often. That said, I promise to help you impress Mrs. Sizemore. It will translate into more warmth from her in the future."

"Ha. Her 'warmth' is still ice cold, but I get your meaning. Speaking of cold, Hector is forcing me to conduct this interview with her alone. Again."

Liesl giggled again. "I can't help your situation with Hector, but I can help you prepare for tea. Come early. I'll drag out all the items for a proper tea. You know Aunt Suzanne's grandmother was a British citizen, right?"

"I'd forgotten that."

"Well, she brought all of her tea things from England."

After a pause, Kurt said, "All right, you can train me. But you'd better not do more laughing today. My manly ego can't take it."

"I promise."

"Thank you."

"Whatever information you need from Mrs. Sizemore must be important."

"We hope she has knowledge of the background information we need."

"Regarding Katherine Mull?"

"None of your business, Liesl."

"You know I'm drawn to mysteries."

"Drawn to mysteries? You mean you've always been nosey."

"I'm just curious. I'm a puzzle solver."

Kurt harrumphed. "Tomato, to-mah-to. No matter how you look at it, you're sticking your nose in someone else's business."

"Friends and associates are my business."

"Isn't it my business? After all, I'm the cop. You're an innocent bystander."

"Then you'd better do your job and put a stop to all this."

Kurt laughed instead of losing his temper. "I'm trying. Your help to impress Mrs. Sizemore is appreciated. Ultimately, I hope it helps the investigation."

"When you don't need my help, you accuse me of nosing in on your investigation. When you *do* need my assistance, then suddenly, I'm *assisting with* your investigation. As you say, 'tomato, to-mah-to.'"

Kurt admitted she had him there. "Okay, I give up."

"Good. Oh, and regarding that invitation for tea? It means Mrs. Sizemore likes you again."

213

"She's held a grudge against me for breaking your heart as long as or longer than you did."

"See? Getting back with me is a bonus for your relationship with her."

He smiled. "Getting back with you has been a bonus in many ways."

"While you count the ways, Mr. Poet, I have to run. Joey and I went to church this morning. Nicole invited us to her house for lunch, but Joey prefers to stay home and have KFC. I need to grab his food now or else I'll be late to Nicole's house."

"Okay. See you later this afternoon."

* * *

Kurt's stomach flipped when Liesl opened the door wearing a pair of jean shorts and a cotton shirt with flowers. Both she and her outfit were adorable. Would she always have this effect on him?

Her eyes widened when she noticed the suit he wore. Good. That means she approves. Maybe it will impress Mrs. Sizemore too.

Liesl invited him inside.

Kurt walked to her and pulled her into his arms. "It seems like it's been forever since I've seen you." Then he gave her a long kiss.

When they broke the embrace, Liesl smiled up at him. "If you're going to kiss me like that, I'm never going to let you out of my sight again."

With his arms still wrapped around her, he picked her up and swirled her around the living room area of her Victorian home to the sound of her laughter. "I'd love never being out of your sight. Sadly, the bad guys might flourish while I'm hanging around with you all the time."

When he set her down, she held onto his arms. "I need Mrs. Sizemore to ask you to tea more often. You look handsome in a suit and tie."

He rolled his eyes. "Seemed best to dress up for her *Ladies Tea*."

"Hey. Men do formal tea in Great Britain."

"Well, this is Missouri, and I'm not British. Men hunt and fish here. I dread this, but let's get rolling."

They strolled hand in hand into the library, where there was a small locking cabinet along an upper bookshelf. Anytime Kurt came to the house with his service weapon, he locked it inside the cabinet for safety.

After he'd hidden the key behind books on an upper shelf, they went to the dining room, where Liesl's table was covered in a massive amount of silver and china. An enormous silver tray sat with two silver pots on it, one larger than the other, plus dishes, silverware, and bowls. The setting included raised cake platters and several three-tiered serving dishes.

Kurt stared at the assortment. "What's all this?"

Liesl sat down and gestured for him to sit across the table from her. "*Tea*." She winked at him.

"I feel like I've just walked into the dining room of Downton Abbey."

Liesl laughed. "They would have actual food and tea. We're just going to pretend."

He frowned. "Pretend? I thought you were just going to talk me through this."

"Please, sit down."

"Why are there two pots?"

Liesl waved her hand toward the two silver pots near her right arm. "Mrs. Sizemore will have two pots on her tray. The taller, thinner pot is for boiling water and the smaller, wider pot is for brewing tea."

"This is ridiculous."

Liesl flattened her hands upon the cotton tablecloth and grimaced. "Are you trying to vex me? Because it's working."

"I just want to know what I'm supposed to do. Maybe you could give me the Cliff's Notes version?"

She picked up a cup and saucer and placed it in front of her, then picked up the smaller pot and pretended to pour tea into the cup. "Sit down, already."

"No. This is not what I thought you meant when you said you'd help me. What are you doing?"

"I'm being *Mother*, which means I'm serving you."

"Good. I don't touch any pots. What's next?"

"Once your tea is poured, she'll ask you if you prefer cream, sugar, lemon, or any combination of the above."

He sighed. "I'll take it straight up."

Liesl offered the cup and saucer to him. "This works better when you're sitting."

He refused the items. "I'm not playing tea party with you. Just walk me through it."

Liesl pursed her lips, then set down the offered cup and saucer. She reached for another cup and saucer and pretended to pour tea into that cup. Then, she pretended to pluck an invisible cube of sugar from the sugar bowl using silver tongs, *dropping* it into the cup. She picked up a spoon, stirred, then placed the spoon beside the cup. "I'm taking one lump."

"Stop it. I've had enough of this game." He ignored the look of hurt on Liesl's face caused by his outburst as he stalked out of the room.

She called after him, "You're going to be sorry."

It took all his patience to retrieve his weapon and leave the house without shouting a response to her or slamming the door behind him.

That was a ridiculous waste of my time!
Then he scurried to his car.

Chapter Twenty-Nine

Kurt

On his drive to Mrs. Sizemore's home, Kurt regretted he'd lost his temper with Liesl. She'd only been trying to help him. He'd acted childish and now owed her a giant apology.

When Kurt reached Mrs. Sizemore's house, he tapped out an apologetic text to Liesl. It wasn't enough to make up for his behavior, but it was a start.

Between treating Liesl unfairly and having to deal with the icy Mrs. Sizemore, his nerves were stretched thin. He wiped his sweaty palms on a blanket Ross had left in his sedan, then prayed his hands would remain dry as he made his way to the front door.

Although he was well aware a domestic worker would open the door, if Mrs. Sizemore was waiting just inside, he would have to shake her hand. Kurt ascended the massive front steps and rang the bell. As expected, the domestic, wearing a white apron over a black shirt and pants, welcomed him in.

"Afternoon, Detective. Mrs. Sizemore is expecting you. Please follow me."

She led him through the house and past the formal living room, where Mrs. Sizemore had spoken to him several months ago. They went through French doors to an all-weather room completely encased in glass. Thankfully, the room was air-conditioned.

The sunroom faced Mrs. Sizemore's back gardens, which were extensive and beautifully maintained. The bushes, trees, and flowering plants were neatly trimmed and ornate but not ostentatious.

"Please make yourself comfortable. Mrs. Sizemore will join you in a moment."

The table in front of him was covered with a crisp white linen tablecloth and dotted with the same cutlery, plates, and serving pots Liesl had gathered at her house. He regretted his loss of temper with Liesl's offer to practice with her tea set.

He remained standing while he waited for Mrs. Sizemore. After a few minutes, the lady of the house appeared. She wore a frilly floral dress with sleeves extending to her elbows.

Remembering how Mrs. Sizemore appreciated compliments, Kurt walked toward her and praised his hostess for inviting him and mentioned her good taste in a beautiful summer outfit.

Mrs. Sizemore appraised his suit and tie, then eyed the rest of him from the top of his head to the tips of his shoes.

He was thankful for Liesl's compliment about his suit, which gave him the courage to flash his white teeth at Mrs. Sizemore.

He stood until Mrs. Sizemore took a seat at the table, then sat in the chair she indicated. "Thank you for seeing me. I appreciate your time. I believe you are the only person who'll know the answers to our questions."

Mrs. Sizemore's expression relayed her agreement with his assessment. He placed his hands to his sides and waited patiently for Mrs. Sizemore to proceed with the tea ritual. He'd do his best to resist questions until the tea was finished or nearly finished.

"Tea?"

Kurt spied the two pots on the tea tray. Liesl had correctly predicted them. "Yes, please."

"How do you take it?" She shifted her hands to the teapot with a smile.

"Just plain, ma'am."

She passed the cup and saucer to him.

The moment his hand touched the saucer, he wobbled it. The cup continued to rattle on the saucer until he set it on the table in front of him. His face flushed with embarrassment.

For her own cup of tea, Mrs. Sizemore grasped the silver sugar tongs and dropped two cubes in the dainty cup. Then she stirred her drink with one of the silver spoons.

Hiding his hands under the table, he wiped his sweaty palms on his pants, then grasped his cup and held it as steadily as possible. He took a sip and replaced the cup in the saucer without shaking. His success made him feel as if he'd passed a test. Never would he have imagined he'd do this as part of offical police work.

Mrs. Sizemore waved her hand in a theatrical gesture toward the tiny sandwiches. These delicacies filled plates beside the tea tray. "May I interest you in a sandwich?"

"Yes, ma'am."

She passed the sandwich plates to him, one at a time. In a quick examination, Kurt guessed one plate was ham or tuna salad. The other two had white and creamy filling. He didn't care if these turned out to be chopped liver. He would smile and be grateful this woman agreed to talk to him.

When they'd finished the selected sandwiches and tea, he declared the sandwiches delicious. This seemed to please Mrs. Sizemore. She refilled his tea while he pulled out his pocket notebook and pen.

"Mrs. Sizemore, my imposition upon you today is to discover the next of kin of Katherine Mull."

Mrs. Sizemore's face transformed from playing tea party to reflecting a serious event. "Oh, that means she's dead."

"Although we believe this is true, we must await scientific identification of the remains found. We have released no information about this to the public. I ask you to keep what we discuss private, for now."

Mrs. Sizemore pulled her lips together and nodded. "Continue."

"We must notify the victim's next of kin once identification is verified. If the deceased is Katherine, her attorney has no record of any legal relations. We could not find any other source of her probable next of kin, including her father's obituary. This brings me to you, with the hope you know enough to help."

Mrs. Sizemore wiped the corner of her mouth with her dainty lace napkin and stared out at the beautiful garden.

Kurt waited to let her respond when she was ready. He put down his pen and paper and took another sip of tea.

Eventually, Mrs. Sizemore turned to face him. "You see, being from a small town, I know you and your immediate family, and I'm also knowable regarding the roots of your family. Both sides, actually, thanks to the long history your family has here."

"Yes, ma'am." He said nothing further as he awaited more pearls of wisdom from her.

"My parents associated with Katherine's mother's parents. The Findley side of her family was deeply entrenched in this town. I was acquainted with Katherine's father when he was a young man. He was not from here. In fact, he was from Hannibal."

Kurt tried not to react to this information. Neither he nor Hector had previously uncovered any connection to Hannibal.

"It wasn't common for people to move from a river town like Hannibal to Mexico, which was known for general farming and stock animals, Saddlebred horse training, and brick refractories. I was introduced to Mr. Mull, Katherine's father, when her grandfather moved here to manage a large farm holding. Her grandfather was a clever man. He bought land and properties when he could."

"Was Mexico booming at the time?"

"Not really. It was during the Depression. Land was cheap, if you had money to buy it."

Kurt nodded. "Please continue."

"Instead of sending Katherine's father to college, her grandfather put him to work collecting rent for the buildings and homes he rented. Katherine's dad sent her to college. Thankfully, as he was aware, she needed an education to run the family business. I also speculate that he resented never getting the chance."

"So, her grandfather originated the business? I understood it had been her father."

"Her grandfather originated the business. When Katherine's mother and father dated, her mother's family, the Findleys, did everything they could to divide the couple. They even threatened to take away her mother's inheritance if she married this *lowly* man outside of high society."

"How did the business end up with her father?"

"Katherine's mother was an only child. Her parents

withheld their money until they died, and then she inherited all their wealth. Katherine's father used it to buy more properties. Then, Katherine's mother, Francis, died soon after Katherine was born."

Kurt scratched in his notepad. "Do you think there are any Findley relatives left?"

Mrs. Sizemore shook her head. "Doubtful. But Katherine's father had a sister who married a man from Hannibal named Palmer. They bought a farm near Martinsburg. She and her husband had several children."

"Why doesn't anyone else know about this association?"

Mrs. Sizemore smiled, but the smile didn't reach her eyes. "I'm going to surmise the Palmer family distanced themselves from Mr. and Mrs. Mull as a result of the greedy, slum lord reputation Mr. Mull developed over the years. They separated themselves from the Mull family long before Katherine was born."

"That long?"

"Gossip indicates the split has lasted for decades, but as you know, *I* never gossip."

He fought back a smile. "Of course not. Thank you, Mrs. Sizemore. This is great information. Any idea of documents that would show the family connection?"

"Perhaps the marriage license for Francis Findley and Mr. Mull. Mr. Mull's sister was a witness to their marriage. She should be listed on their marriage license."

"Were they married in Mexico?"

Mrs. Sizemore shook her head. "Hannibal. Her parents wouldn't acknowledge the wedding and wouldn't pay for it either. His family paid for the wedding, so it was held in their town."

"Again, great information. Thank you. Did you know Katherine well?"

"I avoided her at any opportunity. Her mother passed when she was quite young. Her father raised her and never remarried. She learned the property business from him, and he was much more responsible toward his tenants. Once her father passed, Katherine focused on squeezing every penny out of her tenants."

He took a final sip from his cup and thanked Mrs. Sizemore for her help.

She rose and wished him well in his investigation.

Once he reached his car, he checked his personal phone for a response from Liesl. She hadn't answered.

Chapter Thirty

Arden
Winter 1929

Everyone at the Lee Brothers' Stables was afraid.

The fall stock sale had gone well. But at the end of October, the United States stock market had plunged. After another month of misery and worry, the market reached its lowest point.

Now, all eyes focused on the New Year—1930. Would anyone have enough money to buy Saddlebred horses and high-quality mules? Winter was upon them. The immediate past had been bleak, and the future was unknown. But the horses they still owned needed to be fed and trained.

The Lees held two sales a year. The next would be in the spring. Everyone prayed that the economy would improve by spring.

Arden had no investments in the stock market, so he'd officially lost nothing in the crash. Over the past few years, his older brother had grown into a competent farmer. This left

Arden contributing a smaller amount of his earnings to support his mother and his youngest sister, still at home.

In fact, he and his brother had split the cost of additional acreage that connected to their father's original homestead. God had protected their family. They both had withdrawn their savings from the bank to buy this property two months before the bank closed its doors.

The rising prices of life's necessities hurt Arden's pocketbook, but his needs were simple. He all but lived at the Lee Brothers' Stables, and they provided most of his meals. But how long could they last if there were no buyers of trained horses? How long could Mr. Will and Mr. George pay their workers if no one could afford to board their horses for training?

Thanks to the economy, everyone repaired equipment as much as possible. Arden was working on a training bridle that had seen better days. He had faith that the old girl had more life left. All she needed was someone to give her some new leather straps, and he was the one willing to try.

Bert found Arden on a bench in the tack room, hard at work on the bridle.

"I figured I'd find you here, warming up to the stove."

Arden grinned. "You take me for a dolt? On this cold day, there's no place I'd rather be." He scooted down the bench. "Come rest a moment and get warm."

Bert moved with lightning quickness to sit on the bench. He held his arms out to the stove and pushed his booted feet close.

Day and night, the wood stove burned steadily, no matter the weather. The heated atmosphere kept the workers warm in addition to chasing away mold and mildew from the tack.

Arden eyed Bert's clean appearance. Bert had changed in the past years, but his black hair was still straight. Now that he was busy courting a girl, Bert kept his hair and mustache neatly trimmed.

Bert shifted on the bench. "Mr. Samuelson says Mr. Hamilton is sending some lads over with a horse from the Blue Grass Stock Farm this afternoon. We're supposed to help them get him settled. He's going into Fireball's former stall."

"Why the transfer?"

"You know how Mr. Samuelson is—tight-lipped. He'll tell us when we need to do something with the horse."

"Or we can ask one of the Blue Grass stable lads about it." Arden winked. "I'll bet they know the reason. Mr. Hamilton isn't the type to keep everything secret, like Mr. Samuelson."

The horse arrived while Bert and Arden were walking back from lunch.

Arden elbowed Bert. "Look there. A groom coming down the Boulevard on a winner. A bay." He gestured toward the Saddlebred horse.

Bert whistled. "What a beauty!"

They rushed to meet the horse and rider at the main entrance.

The rider was thin but appeared well-built. When he slid off the horse and handed the reins to Bert, he walked around in front of the half-circle stained-glass window above the door of the stable. "This is a mighty fine stable. And that window! I've never seen the like."

Arden walked over, hand extended. "I'm Arden Rahn. Welcome to the Lee Brothers' Stables."

The young man shook his offered hand. "Art Simmons. Nice to meet you."

Bert extended his hand. "Bert Graham. Same here."

After they shook hands, Art stepped back. His head swiveled as he took in the majesty of the huge stable and fenced tracks abutting each long side.

Bert held the lead of the horse. "I'm taking this fellow inside. Can't let him get cold."

"Thank you. I'll check on him in a second. His name is Hudson Bay. We call him Bay. He's a good sort most of the time."

When Bert turned and led Bay toward the stables, Arden called after him, "We'll catch up in a minute."

Arden studied Art while the new arrival admired the stables. This guy was new around here. The Saddlebred horse world was small. The local horse community knew each other very well.

The nature of the business required people to constantly change stables to move up to a higher-skilled job. A steady stream of new people replaced those who left. Luckily, they'd bump into former acquaintances at horse shows and exhibitions, allowing them to renew their friendships.

Bert and Arden remained in their stables, a fact for which they thanked the Lee Brothers. The Lees liked to keep their workers and moved them up in their duties whenever an opportunity presented itself.

After a moment, Art gave up his gawking and moved toward the stables. "Guess I'd better catch up with Bay. Mr. Hamilton will kill me if anything happens to him during the transfer."

Arden fell in alongside Art, their discussion turning to the animals they loved.

Once inside, Art said, "I'm amazed at this place. You're lucky to work here."

"I agree. Been here nine years. You'll have to see all the property before you go. We have a maternity stable, a farrier's shed, and grain bins."

"How old were you when you started working here?"

"Twelve," Arden said. "Follow me, and I'll lead you to a

stove if you promise to tell Bert and me why this horse has been moved here."

Art chuckled. "It's a deal."

As Arden showed Art around, they chatted about local famous horses and trainers and their conversation turned to the King of Trainers, Mr. Tom Bass.

Art paused at the tack room and pointed to some bridle bits hanging there. "You all use the Bass curb bit regularly?"

"Sure do. It's much more humane that most bits. Plus, we enjoy making Mr. Bass happy when he stops by. It brings a smile to his face to see us using his bit."

Art drew his eyebrows together. "Is it true that Mr. Bass didn't patent that bit?"

"He was afraid patenting it would make the price too expensive for most farmers and trainers to use. He wanted a comfortable bit to be affordable for every horse."

"I hope to see him while I'm working in Mexico."

"It won't be hard to do. He is a favorite of all the stables around here. When they have a horse hard to train or an injury they can't heal, they bring in Mr. Bass."

"Did you ever see him on Rex McDonald?"

"The most famous Saddlebred horse in the world?" With a downward glance, Arden shook his head. "Nope. I've only seen him stuffed."

"Didn't he burn up when the Ringo Hotel burned down a while back?"

"No, he didn't burn, but he was slightly singed and smoky-smelling from the fire. They brought him back to Mr. Bass, who has him on display in his stables now. You should stop by there before you head back. It's just around the corner."

When Bert caught up to them in the tack room, Art explained he understood Bay was being brought here for breeding purposes. "He's getting older, so maybe they think he has a future at stud."

Bert whistled. "He has a fine head and a beautiful neck. I can see why they think he could improve our stock."

After more conversation, Art announced he would check on Bay one more time, then head back on foot.

At Bay's stall, the three of them admired him for a moment. The stallion was tucked in, calm and cool, not upset to be in a new place.

"Bay's going to do fine here. He's been a show horse for so long, he's used to going to unknown places." Art ran his hands down Bay's ears. "I'll miss you, fella."

Art glanced at them, the sorrow at leaving Bay behind displayed on his face. "Time for me to get back."

"Don't envy you there, Art," Bert said. "It's such a chilly day."

Art shrugged. "That's our life, and I love it." He tossed another sad look at Bay. "Even when you have sad days, it's the best job in the world. You guys might laugh at me, but one day, I'm going to buy a stable like this."

Bert chuckled, but Arden took him for his word. "When you do, I want you to hire me. I can tell you love horses as much as I do. I always want to work for our kind of people."

Art smiled and offered his hand. "It's a deal."

As Arden watched Art walk down the Boulevard, he noticed a Model T bumping along the dirt road, a tall man in a bowler hat at the wheel. Black and white fur from a blanket enveloped a teenage girl.

The girl was in the back of the motor car, under the canvas hood, wearing a white fur hat tied under her chin. Her features were dainty. There was no doubt this girl would be a beauty when grown.

He shivered as the girl turned her head in his direction and spotted him.

Caught staring, he turned back toward the stables.

Who was that girl? She resembled a princess bundled in all that fur.

Who had any money in these times? It appeared her family did. The value of the vehicle and furs grounded him, dashing any hope of an introduction. She was a rich girl.

There would be no place for him in her life.

Chapter Thirty-One

Kurt

Kurt tried to call Liesl several times last night, but she hadn't answered his calls or responded to his apology text. Although he deserved her silence, what could he do to make up for his wrong against her?

Between Liesl's silence and the absence of Ross, he had plenty of time to review the surveillance video from the Poindexter house. As much as he dreaded showing it to Hector, a jogger on the street in front of Katherine's house around noon the day of the fire looked like David Whittier. Hector was going to be devastated if his friend turned out to be an arsonist and killer.

At work, it was an unbelievably busy Monday. Kurt put off talking to Hector about his friend. He started by calling the local coroner to get a status on the autopsy.

When Tony answered, he put him on speakerphone while he and Hector readied to take notes.

"Sorry to bother you, Tony, but we'll be heading to the

scene a little later. We've been cleared to go into part of the house—the areas not so badly burned. Anything we need to look for possibly related to the death?"

Tony sighed. "We don't know if there was forced entry. Too much fire damage. The chief said they checked with the alarm company. The last time the alarm was deactivated, the code was used within the acceptable time limit. No alarm was triggered."

Hector and Kurt exchanged a glance.

"Before you ask what time the deactivation occurred, I didn't ask the chief about that, so I don't know. What I know is the chief said the heat sensors installed in the lower level didn't trigger the alarm. A heat sensor from a room upstairs did."

Hector shifted in his chair. "So, the killer takes out the heat sensors on the first floor. Obviously well planned. This killer is organized."

Tony's response was clipped. "You're assuming this was a murder? I never said that."

"True," Kurt said. "But if this was an accidental death, it's unlikely the victim disabled the heat sensors before accidentally causing a fire. Someone, possibly Katherine herself, could have disabled the sensors to burn down her house and got trapped in it."

Hector shook his head. "We'll keep an open mind, Tony, I promise. However, whoever took out the heat sensors was a planner."

"I agree, but that's just my opinion," Tony said.

"We'll take guesses," Kurt said.

"I will not give you speculation. The victim's clothing was mostly incinerated. Minute particles were found in protected areas, like between the pelvic cradle and the charred wooden seat of what appeared to be a chair. The victim is a female."

Kurt made a fist. "More reason to believe it's Katherine."

"The victim might have been tied to a chair, possibly with zip ties, due to the consistency of what remained after the blaze. The state lab will make that determination. We don't know if they were standard zip ties, with a standard thickness and color similar to household ties, or specialty ties."

Kurt made a note to search for zip ties in the debris.

Hector asked, "Cause of death?"

"Undetermined. No bullets or shell casings were recovered. The skull had cracks, suspected to be heat fractures, but a forensic pathologist will make that call."

Hector frowned. "How many experts will be involved?"

"Plenty. They might make your case for you. You'll have to wait and see."

Under his breath, Hector mumbled to Kurt, "Or they'll complicate the issues, and we won't get a jury to understand what happened."

Kurt asked, "Any fingerprints found?"

"None on the remains," Tony said. "You'll have to ask Assistant Chief Goodgame about fingerprints at the residence. Doubtful they recovered any in the seriously burned areas."

"If they find any, we'll need fingerprints from the housekeeper," Hector said.

Tony continued. "Fingerprints from the recovered victim were a no-go. Thus, the dental records were needed."

Kurt leaned toward the phone. "Any report on that yet?"

"No. The ME called in a forensic dental expert to compare Katherine's records with what was recovered from the victim's partial mandible and maxilla. No idea how long that'll take. I'll let you know when I know the results."

Kurt leaned back, disappointed. "We appreciate that."

"I need to run. That's all I can tell you right now."

Kurt thanked Tony and ended the call.

To Hector, he said, "Give me a minute. I want to write down everything Tony said."

Hector stood, shifting from foot to foot, as Kurt scribbled in his notebook. "What I want is to get inside that house."

Kurt's stomach knotted when he turned to Hector. "Last night I found something on that video from the Poindexter house."

"Your face is signaling I'm not going to appreciate this discovery."

"Not a bit. Just don't kill the messenger."

Chapter Thirty-Two

Liesl

On Monday morning, Mrs. Zimmerman arrived for duty while Liesl was having her second cup of coffee at the kitchen table. Liesl was glad for the diversion of Mrs. Zimmerman. She'd stewed enough about Kurt's behavior since yesterday. Time to let it go.

Liesl called out, "Please join me for a cup of coffee, Mrs. Zimmerman. I'm in the kitchen."

"Be right there. I have to hang up my raincoat in the sunroom and let it drip dry."

Liesl watched Mrs. Zimmerman carry the damp coat out to the porch area to give it a shake on the slate floors. Then she spread it over a sunroom chair to dry, fluffed her graying red hair, and entered the kitchen.

"Good morning, Liesl. How are you today?"

"Aggravated at Kurt, but I don't want to talk about him. How are you doing?"

"I'm loving the slightly cooler temperatures. Soon, we'll have full-blown fall."

Liesl gave Mrs. Zimmerman a grin. "Almost Mizzou football time."

Excitement flashed in Mrs. Zimmerman's eyes. "I can't wait."

"This morning, I'm taking Joey to his physical therapy appointment, which is at nine."

While Mrs. Zimmerman busied herself with pouring a steaming cup, she asked, "Will you both be back for lunch?"

"We should be. Thank you, Mrs. Z, for always keeping us well fed."

Mrs. Zimmerman brought her coffee to the table and sat down.

"We had some unexpected visitors on Friday." Liesl explained the events.

"They scared Joey. Since I wasn't here, I pulled the surveillance video, and they made me uncomfortable too. Kurt watched the tape and believes they might be part of a nomadic group of traveling storm chasers. The chief of police should be issuing a warning to the public about them."

"Oh, my. Poor Joey. I'm sorry they upset him."

"He didn't call me or anyone else. He hid in his apartment and didn't answer the door. I talked to him about calling nine-one-one, but he said it wasn't an emergency. That explains why the back fence is locked."

"That's fine. We'll keep it locked until they've left town."

Liesl sipped her coffee. "Thank you for understanding. Now, for a happier topic, we need to discuss redecorating my favorite room in the house."

"The library?"

"Yes, ma'am. When Kurt's son, Ross, pointed out the furniture needed to be updated several months ago, I agreed with his assessment but haven't done a thing to make that happen."

They discussed donating the old furniture to the Butterfly House. Liesl served on the board. Although her furniture was worn, it was sturdy and could serve a long life at the Butterfly House.

Mrs. Zimmerman asked, "If we could time it so the room is empty for a few days before any new furniture arrives, I can do a deep cleaning in there."

"Great idea. And how about we go one step further? What do you think about having the wood floors re-stained and polished?"

"I'm sure they would benefit from some tender loving care. Want me to call some flooring contractors to see what they suggest?"

"Yes, please. The guys who repaired the main entrance and living room from the fire damage would be my first choice. But get bids from several, if you can. Also, why don't we have the music room floors repaired simultaneously? Then all the wood floors on the ground level would be redone."

The housekeeper smiled. "Excellent idea. And some new rugs wouldn't hurt."

Liesl nodded. "I'll add those to the spreadsheet for Nicole. She's my main designer girl and is eager to shop with me." Liesl smiled. "She excels at spending other people's money."

"You ought to give her a gift for helping you do this redesign."

"Another good idea. If you have suggestions, let me know."

Mrs. Zimmerman nodded. "We'll need to clear out all the books and knickknacks in those rooms before the floor work begins. Do you have time to start packing today?"

"Yes. We can start after Joey's appointment."

"While you're out with Joey, I'll fix a casserole for the two of you to eat tonight. Then, when once you're back, we'll knock out a big part of packing those rooms. I'll bring up some boxes from the basement."

"Do you think we could stack the packed boxes in the dining room?"

"Suits me, but are you planning on having any guests?"

Liesl laughed. "No guests that would use the formal dining room. The only guests I'm likely to have would rather sit at the kitchenette and play games, anyway."

"When is Ross returning?"

"His grandparents are bringing him home next week. I've missed him. He'll be the first fellow I'll invite over when the remodeling is complete." Liesl drained her cup and stood. "That reminds me. I'm going to need a temporary desk while the library is under construction. If we use the dining room floor for stacking boxes, I'll put the protective covers on the table and use it as my desk."

It didn't take long for the two of them to get the dining table set up as her office area. After cleaning up enough to be seen in public, Liesl swung by the kitchen where Mrs. Zimmerman was cooking something that smelled delicious.

"I'm off to take Joey. Need me to pick up anything while we're out and about?"

Mrs. Zimmerman stirred a pan. "Can't think of a thing."

"Okay. We should be back in about an hour."

Barney followed Liesl to the front door and watched her as she grabbed her raincoat and purse. She noted his sad eyes and patted his head. "Sorry, but you're going to have to stay home."

Once outside, she crossed the lawn to Joey's garage apartment. He opened his door before she could knock.

He wore nice pants, a plaid shirt, and held a raincoat in his hand. His expression was neutral, but his voice relayed surprise, "You're three minutes early."

She smiled. "I know you don't like being late."

While Liesl opened the double door of the garage, Joey slipped into the passenger seat of her SUV. She joined him and was backing down her driveway when a white pickup truck pulled into the driveway, blocking her exit.

Liesl braked and studied the white truck. It didn't move out of her way, so she put her car in park and hopped out.

An older man with graying red hair dressed in overalls exited from the driver's door of the truck. The passenger door opened and a tall, younger man climbed out. He also wore work clothes.

She didn't recognize either of them for a moment. Then it hit her. These were two of the three men who'd trespassed the other day. Anger pulsed through her veins and she approached them with quick strides. "I'm leaving and you're blocking my driveway."

The older man gave her an insincere smile and held out his hand. "We've had a hard time catching you at home."

She ignored his offered hand and crossed her arms. "I have no business with you. Get out of my driveway."

The older gentlemen let his hand drop but remained in place.

The younger, tall man moved closer. "We need to talk to you. Just a few minutes of your time."

The older man said, "We're here to offer you some special services. We can remove trees, repair your roof, and do repairs to other storm related damage you've suffered."

She straightened and stared from one to the other. "I recognize both of you." She pointed to a camera on her front porch. "Although I wasn't here when you trespassed on my property, I've reported it to the police and gave them proof of the crime."

"We didn't trespass," the tall man said. "We just inspected your property."

"It became trespassing when you opened the gate and entered my backyard. For the last time, leave."

The tall man took a step closer. "Now listen here, little lady …"

She held up a finger. "First, I'm not a 'little lady.' I've asked you to leave, and you've ignored me." She pulled her cell phone out of her raincoat pocket, flipped to her favorite contacts list, and found the contact she wanted.

"Roxy? I have two men in my driveway and they've refused repeated requests to leave." After a pause, she said, "Thank you." She put the phone back in her pocket.

The older man frowned. "Who was that?"

"The police."

The tall man turned to the older man. "We'd better go."

The wail of a siren reached them, bringing a smile to Liesl's face. Living in a *five-minute town* had its advantages. It only took five minutes to cross from one side of town to the other. Even less for a nearby patrol car to be rerouted.

"I asked you nicely, and you ignored me. Now I'm going to press charges."

"Press charges? For what?"

"Trespassing. I have the proof you did it the other day. Today, you're back and have refused to leave. Your vehicle is detaining us from an appointment. I wonder if that's false imprisonment?"

The men exchanged a glance and turned toward their truck when a cop car screeched around the corner from the Boulevard to South Jefferson. It pulled up behind their truck parked. Patrolman Dennis Bates climbed out of the sedan.

"You okay, Liesl?"

She nodded. "I want to press charges against these men,

Patrolman Bates. This is the second time they've been here. The first time, they trespassed into my fenced back yard. Kurt already has the video of them trespassing."

"Good for you," Bates said.

Liesl waved an arm in the direction of their truck. "Today they've blocked my driveway and refused to leave. I'm trying to take Joey to physical therapy. I feel we're being held captive."

Bates walked to the men's truck and peered inside. With lightning speed, he opened the door, reached inside and pulled out their keys. He held them aloft so everyone could see what he did.

The men stammered, but Bates silenced them with a look.

Bates turned to Liesl. "I'll move my car and their truck, so you can drop off Joey. Come back once you do that. We'll get all the paperwork done on these guys. I'll need your statement about this and about the first incident."

"No problem. Thank you, Dennis." She turned to the men, who were red-faced with anger. "Next time someone asks you to leave, do it."

Dennis handcuffed both men and placed them in the back of his squad car. Then he moved his car and their truck to the street.

Liesl returned to her still-running car, worried about how Joey had reacted to the situation.

When she opened the door, she realized she shouldn't have worried. He was smiling.

"Patrolman Bates sure got here fast."

"Those guys scared me. They're intimidating."

"I couldn't tell. I'm glad you caught them. They made me uncomfortable the last time."

As they headed toward the physical therapy clinic, Liesl was thankful to get those men under police scrutiny. They were up to no good. She felt it in her bones.

When she returned home after dropping off Joey, she was surprised to find Kurt and Hector's assigned vehicle in front of her house. They were standing by the patrol car.

At the sight of Kurt, she bristled. The way he'd walked out of her house yesterday had been childish. Even though he'd immediately apologized by text and tried repeatedly to call her, she wasn't having any of his grins and puppy dog eyes today.

She parked on the street. Kurt approached her side of the car and she gave him a death stare as her window rolled down. "How did you find out about this?"

"Dennis called to tell me he was arresting your visitors. Figured I wanted to be involved. We were on our way to the fire scene, so just swung by here."

"I think Dennis has this handled."

Kurt furrowed his brow. "More has happened since you left. Good thing we were already here. There was a third man of this group who jumped your backyard fence while these two kept you busy in the front."

She gasped, "Are you kidding?"

The look on his face told her this was no joke.

"Mrs. Zimmerman's here. Is she okay?"

"Barney alerted her to the man in the backyard. She ran over and locked the back door before he could get in. He jumped back over the fence when he'd been spotted."

"Mrs. Zimmerman must be a mess."

"She called nine-one-one without realizing there was an officer already in the front yard."

"I should have called her and told her what happened after we left." Liesl turned off her car and got out.

Kurt reached his arm around her shoulders but she brushed it off.

"I'm sorry I lost my temper yesterday."

"You should be."

He sighed. "Moving on. We have a BOLO out for the third man. He's probably heading out of town. Hopefully, the highway patrol or sheriff's office will catch him."

"BOLO is cop-speak for what?"

"Be on the lookout. Law enforcement is on alert for a white truck with out-of-state plates."

"Guess you'll need me to pull this morning's video too."

He nodded. "I'm counting on using it to prosecute them. They can't deny anything documented by your system. It's a good thing you have it."

Liesl spotted the circles under his eyes and noted his general fatigue. She felt pity for him. "You're worn out. Now this has added to your problems."

"Arresting these guys will help chase them out of town." He lowered his voice to a whisper. "The minute they make bail, they'll be lost to the wind. These nomadic contractors won't be coming back to Mexico again if we have an outstanding warrant on them. That's a good thing."

"Their arrest protects the population from fraudsters."

Kurt nodded. "We've received several complaints similar to yours, but you're the only one who had video proof of their actions. I'm glad they came back *and* that you called for help."

Liesl put her hands on her hips. "They refused to leave. I had Joey in my car counting down the seconds until his physical therapy appointment. Calling Roxy was my only option of shifting them from my driveway. They were intimidating too."

"They're well-practiced con men." Kurt ran his hand through his hair. "We'll do our best to identify them with fingerprints. Likely they'll give us an alias at the station."

Liesl glanced at her watch. "I have about thirty minutes

before I need to pick up Joey. Want me to pull the video? I can do that and give it to you before I leave."

"That would be great." Kurt shifted his weight and ran a hand through his hair. "At least this video won't make Hector mad at me."

"What?"

"It's something I'll explain later."

"Give me a hint."

"Something recorded by Katherine's neighbor may point a finger to who started the fire."

"Wouldn't that be a good thing?"

"Not when it appears to be a friend of Hector."

"Oh, no!"

"Mere speculation at this point. The film is so grainy, it's hard to tell." Kurt waved an arm at the pickup truck in the street. "Right now, we're towing this truck to the station. We'll verify whether it was legally purchased, legally registered in their state, and that it's equipped with original parts."

"Why do all that?"

"These nomadic groups sometimes do vehicle identification number switches or use chop shops to put together pieces of stolen vehicles."

Liesl shook her head. "Is nothing legitimate with them?"

"Let's put it this way. We're proving everything is aboveboard. We've got them for trespassing and now attempted burglary. What we don't know is what else they'd planned."

Liesl stiffened.

"I'm not trying to scare you, but your house is large and filled with expensive furniture and knickknacks. They set up this situation today to steal your stuff."

A shudder ran through Liesl. "How can we protect ourselves from such crooks?"

"Exactly what you've done. By having cameras and a security system, reporting their behavior to law enforcement, and alerting others."

He waved toward the house. "Go get that video. When you pick up Joey, drop him off here, and then come to the station to do the paperwork. We should have the fellows booked by then. Once these guys are processed, we're heading back to the fire scene."

"Fair enough. One more thing. I'm missing Ross. When he's back in town, I'd like to see him."

"He would love time with you." He held her gaze. "His father would love some time too."

Her resistance melted. "Same here. But no temper outbursts allowed."

"I promise."

Chapter Thirty-Three

Kurt

The smoky stench of the burned hulk of the former mansion remained strong. After three days, the fire department still had not relinquished the scene. The chief had set up perimeter guards to maintain full control of the area but was finishing today. The only obstacle that kept them from entering the house was a dog trained in sniffing for accelerants.

Hector had a general search warrant signed off by a local judge as a precaution for the suspected crime or crimes. Although they still had no solid proof, there was a high probability of arson, and a human life had been lost in the blaze.

When they'd approached Assistant Chief Goodgame, he said, "Sorry, fellas. We've got to bring in the dog before the rain hits. Then it's all yours."

The three men scanned the darkening skies.

"You'll be in there soon. The state fire investigators have

been working all morning. Now they're ready for the dog. You're welcome to watch it work, if you like."

Hector and Kurt stood off to the side. As they waited, Hector pointed to the standing two-story wing. "That wing appears sturdy. It'll have heat and water damage but appears strong enough for us to look around."

Within moments, the K-9 officer of Boone County arrived and unloaded his Belgian Malinois. Another deputy from Boone County unloaded a glimmering black Labrador Retriever.

As soon as it hit the ground, the retriever pulled the leash with the deputy loping behind to a grassy area. The dog pointed his nose down and sat.

Hector turned to Kurt. "Was that a signal? In the grass?"

"I think it was."

The handler called over to Assistant Chief Goodgame, and they had an animated conversation while the dog remained in a seated position. After a moment, Goodgame left, returning with one of the fire experts with an unlabeled paint can and a shovel in his gloved hands.

The expert placed a small flag where the dog indicated. Then, he motioned for the deputy to move the dog out of the way. He placed the can near the flag, pulled a digital camera from his pocket, and took a picture. With his shovel, he gathered dirt and grass from the area and placed it inside the can. He took a picture of the can filled with dirt and grass, then placed the lid on the can.

After donning a new pair of plastic gloves, the expert hammered the lid shut with his fist and marked the lid with a permanent marker. Before he removed it, he took another photo.

When the deputy walked the dog closer to the structure, the dog repeated the signal again within another two feet.

Kurt watched in fascination. Why was the dog signaling before he'd even entered the house?

Hector turned to him with confusion on his face.

The entire process of sample-taking was repeated.

The expert waved Goodgame over again for another discussion. After a moment, Goodgame motioned to Kurt and Hector.

Hector asked, "What's going on?"

"The dog appears to be reacting to an accelerant that transferred onto the grass. Best guess is it came from the bottom of the shoes of someone inside the house. Someone who walked in an accelerant and then escaped the fire."

He held up his hand to Hector's eager face. "I've seen dogs do this before. The arsonist walked through the accelerant and left you a trail to follow."

"Us?"

"Not you exactly. A hound. A scent dog trained in tracking. It's possible, but not probable, that between substance on the grass and a good scent dog, you might be led to the home of an arsonist."

"I can't believe this." Hector turned to Kurt. "The sheriff's office has a couple of bloodhounds."

Kurt smiled. "Get 'em here."

They both perused the sky. Kurt prayed God would keep the rain at bay long enough for them to catch the arsonist.

* * *

When the bloodhound arrived, the guys were ready. They had their flashlights, overalls, booties, water bottles, and gloves packed in their backpacks. Running shoes were strapped to their feet.

It was muggy, but there was no active rain. The clouds appeared ominous. They had little time.

The sheriff's deputy took a slow-moving bloodhound out of the back seat of his sedan. The animal stood motionless, showing no interest in the area crawling with vehicles and firefighters.

Kurt's hopes fell. This dog gave the impression he was the laziest dog in the world. How would he help them?

Hector shook the deputy's hand. "Thanks for doing this, Chuck."

The tall deputy pointed to the bloodhound. "Thank Buddy here. He's the one with the nose. Ready to run?"

"Yes, sir." Kurt remained doubtful such a dog could run.

"Are those flags where the accelerant was identified?" He pointed to a line of orange flags, each about two feet apart and leading to the structure.

"Yes."

Kurt pulled out his police phone, opened the video camera, and began recording. "We're rolling."

The handler gave the dog what he called his "call to action." Then, he led the dog to the area dotted with flags where the scent was marked, but no sample had been taken.

When the hound drew close, he bolted toward the back of the house. The three men ran behind. The hound led them behind the house, along the backyard, and then to the brush area that ran beside the gravel road. They followed the dog beside the gravel road, passing plowed areas used for farming.

Ten minutes later, all the humans were wet with sweat, panting, and the dog was tugging on the long lead, desiring to go faster. Kurt and Hester traded a glance, unable to speak due to lack of oxygen.

Kurt remained filming with his phone, wishing it had been

Hector doing the recording. His shoulder hurt. Although cleared for regular duty, his muscles were telling him his injured shoulder wasn't back to normal.

Eventually, the dog shifted left into a deeply wooded area. Buddy circled one tree, sat down for a moment, and then circled the tree again. On the third trip around the tree, he pointed toward the ground with his nose and sat, remaining still this time.

The deputy said, "That's the signal. The trail ends here." He unwound the lead from around the tree.

Hector and Kurt caught their breath while examining the ground. The dog was lying on top of an area that appeared freshly moved, as if someone had been digging there.

Hector pointed to the overturned dirt. "Let's see what he found."

With Kurt continuing to film, Hector put on a plastic glove from his backpack and slowly moved dirt away from the upturned area with his hand until something could be seen. It appeared to be the outside edge of a boot sole.

He glanced at Kurt and grinned. "Time to call forensics."

* * *

It was hard for Kurt and Hector to walk away from the woods but forensics had to do their magic. They'd beaten the rain but still needed to get inside the Mull residence.

When they reached the property, they drank water and caught their breath. Then, they changed into firefighting overalls, fire boots, and gloves. Each carried a container that held supplies they might need to gather evidence.

When they were steps from entering, they donned ventilators to avoid inhaling smoke and toxic fumes.

Communication was limited with the use of this equipment, but their focus was to find any business and personal paperwork not destroyed by the fire.

With a thumbs-up signal from Hector, Kurt followed behind as they made their way up a back staircase to the second level of the only wing structurally sound. The floor was hard to traverse. The hardwood had curled from the water used in fire suppression efforts.

Every door was open along the hallway. Thanks to the doors being open when they'd extinguished the fire, the curling wood floors held them in place. They passed bedroom after bedroom, each checked, but none appeared to be belonging to Katherine.

At the far end of the structure near the front staircase, the floor showed little water damage. It was here they identified an office with a massive wooden desk in the center of the room. The desk was a high-quality hardwood desk with little damage. A layer of smoke discolored the desktop, and the varnish showed crazing from the heat.

Hector strode to a locked file cabinet. He pried it open and loaded paperwork into evidence bags.

Kurt opened drawers of the desk, finding paper inside was smoky but intact. He began bagging all the paperwork drawer by drawer.

One typed letter caught his eye. Then he realized there were several in the drawer. Each had a brief message. The threatening words took him by surprise.

These letters were threats to stop Katherine's actions by suing her, incapacitating her, even threats to kill her. She'd never reported these to the police.

It was possible the state forensics people could get information from them. Katherine had saved the envelopes with them, so Kurt gathered them too.

With a grunt, Hector captured Kurt's attention and signaled it was time to go. Neither of them located any zip ties in their search.

Chapter Thirty-Four

The Angel of Justice

As the wind blew against my back, and the telltale scent associated with the misty rain permeated my nostrils, I crunched my way through the dried stalks of harvested corn with a happy heart.

Everything was going to plan.

Katherine was dead. No one noticed me leaving her house as the fire began. In the woods, I transformed into a *jogger*. No one paid any attention to joggers around here. Nor did I appear to be anything but a jogger as I traveled behind Teal Lake to my horrid little shack.

I had gotten away with murder.

The police conducted door-to-door canvassing immediately after the fire. Nothing unexpected. I'd watched them finish their interviews with the closest neighbors.

Now, there was a window of opportunity to retrieve my hidden clothes and boots before they broadened their scope to the surrounding area. I'd buried my outerwear in a pre-dug pit when I planned Katherine's murder. It gave me a drop zone for my crime scene clothes so I could walk or jog back to my neighborhood without any gasoline or smoke smell.

The night of the murder, I stripped off my boots, socks, overalls, and shirt when I reached the pit and changed into a pair of jeans, sandals, a T-shirt, and a baseball cap.

I made my way home with no one paying attention to me.

Tonight, I'd set off with my military shovel hidden in my backpack. My shovel was perfect to conceal in my backpack without arousing suspicion because it was a collapsible military-issue entrenching tool. Even though it folded to a small size, when assembled, it was strong.

My return to the pit was cautious. I walked slowly, ensuring no one was near after dusk had settled. The night sky was dark, thanks to a storm blowing in that brought heavy cloud cover.

I'd walked about a mile and had nearly reached the pit when I noticed a light or some sort of bright area ahead. Had someone rigged lights on the tree-lined side of the adjoining cornfield?

This was not good. I halted abruptly, then stood motionless, trying not to breathe. My brain scrambled to figure out why the area was lit.

Where did the light come from? A car that ran off the road, headlights still glowing? Or a broken-down tractor? Maybe a farmer was using headlights from a car or truck to make repairs? Perhaps a crash between vehicles?

It was none of those.

In silence, I crept closer to the lighted area. My heart galloped when I spotted people in dark clothing with 'Crime Lab' written across the back of their coveralls. The realization that cops surrounded my pit was the most frightening thing I've experienced since my wife died.

Men and women were painstakingly uncovering each item I'd buried. They took pictures of every find from various angles. Then they used a yardstick or a ruler and took pictures of the measurements. All pieces carefully placed in evidence bags.

I wanted to howl. To scream. To cry. To put my fist through their faces. To take a baseball bat to their heads. Instead, I watched their movements with dread, my chest heaving with unspent emotion.

My luck had run out.

They were uncovering my DNA with every item they pulled from the pit, and I couldn't stop them.

Anger bubbled inside me like a witch's cauldron. I considered grabbing my shotgun from the house and returning to mow down these stinking pigs. How many could I take down before someone took me out? There was pride in dying like Bonnie and Clyde.

With my DNA in their possession, I'd have only a few weeks before they figured out I killed Katherine. Since the military has my DNA, it won't take them long to match the DNA they recovered from the pit to me.

I backed away as silently as possible to give myself time to plan. To act.

How had they found my stash? What possible clue led them here? Maybe someone spotted me after the fire and followed me here? How could I have missed being followed?

As I worked to increase the distance from their operation, I considered skipping town. Running away.

Why would I run? Where? I had no place to go and had no money to pay for the trip.

The only person I'd loved in the entire world was dead. Dead by Katherine's hand. I'd gotten justice for my wife's premature demise, but it would cost my freedom.

Or would it?

I had two or three weeks at the most to strategize before they identified my DNA. I would go down fighting. No cowardly flight for me. I was a warrior.

The police had done nothing to stop my wife from dying. If I was going to get revenge against them, I needed a plan. A good plan.

When I reached the jogging path, I headed toward my shack.

I'd take down those responsible for identifying me—the two detectives on my case and Kurt's busybody girlfriend. Take them out before they turned on me with guns blazing.

Chapter Thirty-Five

Arden
Fall, 1932

Arden had uncovered the identity of the girl riding in the Model T, wrapped up in all the fur. He'd dreamed about her for weeks. God brought him her name to him through her father.

When a tall man wearing a bowler hat came to the stables seeking Mr. George Lee, Arden had been polite and led the man to him. Then Arden scrambled to make his way out the front door to see if he'd arrived in a Model T.

He had! *Could this be the father of the girl of my dreams?*

Later in the day, it took little prodding to entice Mr. George to talk about the gentleman who'd stopped by earlier. By the end of their conversation, Arden had the answers to all his questions.

She was a local girl. Family entrenched in the town. Wealthy.

Now that Arden knew she lived in town, he watched for her

whenever he was away from the stables. He searched for her at his school and at church functions. Yet he'd never spotted her.

Three years later, Arden was now twenty-four and was the head groom for the Lee Brothers. Mr. George had ordered him to pull one of his horses to show to a potential buyer. With the fall sale coming up, the customer sought a gentle mare and wanted to preview their best stock.

Before the customer arrived, Mr. George asked Arden his opinion of Dolly and Star Dance. Both were gentile mares, both well trained.

Arden spoke in favor of Dolly. "Star Dance can be temperamental. Just the other day, she was fighting getting new shoes."

Mr. George nodded. "I think you know best here, Arden. Grab Dolly. Polish her up and put on her show saddle and bridle."

With those orders, Arden pulled his charge from her stall and gave her a quick brush so her coat might shine in the limited light of the fall day. His thick fingers flew to braid her mane and tail.

As he walked Dolly through the stable, there was the smell of bootblack, saddle soap, and Balsam of Myrrh, a horse liniment that smelled to Heaven. Grooms were brushing, wiping, braiding, and polishing every animal.

The scent of pine tar also permeated the air. Grooms and stable boys were polishing the horses' hooves with pine tar to impress the buyers at the approaching sale.

He led the liver chestnut mare to the east track without realizing today would be the second time Arden laid eyes upon Olivia Knightly.

When he spotted her, he gasped. It had been three long years, but he recognized her. She'd transformed from a beautiful, gangly teenager to a blooming girl on the brink of womanhood. At that moment, in that tiny space of time, his heart belonged to her.

She stood next to her father, a tall man wearing his trademark bowler perched on his head. But Arden only had an interest in her. She must be about eighteen years old now. Her eyes, the bluest he'd ever seen, were focused on Dolly, rather than him.

Those beautiful eyes never strayed toward him, and he shrugged away the disappointment. Why would she look at him when such magnificent horseflesh was on display? Those eyes appraised the horse and shone with approval.

A smile came to his lips. He couldn't argue with Olivia's assessment of his charge. Dolly was an amazing creature and had an unusually sweet temperament for a Saddlebred horse.

Her father stood rigidly next to her. He did not appear to appreciate Dolly.

Mr. George Lee, noting the hesitation of Mr. Knightly, launched into a discussion of Dolly's many virtues. He extolled the hours of training she'd had and complimented her accomplishments to this point. With a gesture behind his back, he signaled for Arden to move.

Arden pulled himself away from Olivia and walked the horse around the track. Whenever he could, he'd steal a glance at her.

Her dark brown hair was such a contrast to those blue eyes. There was color in her cheeks, likely due to the chill of the morning. Olivia paid no attention to his interest in her. She was focused on assessing Dolly's movements.

His interest in Olivia left him fighting to concentrate on what he was supposed to do for Mr. George. Dolly, being her usual good-natured self, made the best of her time in the fresh air.

When those blue eyes eventually shifted from Dolly to him,

excitement shot through his veins. He gave her a quick grin, then averted his gaze, his own cheeks blazing with embarrassment at being caught staring.

The quality of her black wool jacket and the shining leather of her riding boots stood out to him. These were regal riding clothes. No store within a radius of hundreds of miles of Mexico, Missouri, sold anything of similar worth. He remembered her furs from years ago.

How wealthy was this girl? How could she find and then afford such fine riding gear?

Arden noted her father was engaged in conversation with Mr. George. With both of them distracted, he took the opportunity to walk Dolly nearer to Olivia.

As they approached, Olivia walked forward to meet them.

When they met halfway, he halted Dolly, who shook her head in greeting and danced sideways.

"She is a beautiful beast."

He chuckled. "Yes, ma'am, and she knows it."

"Please, call me Olivia."

"My name is Arden."

"Pleased to meet you, Arden." Olivia dipped her hand in her pocket and pulled out two lumps of sugar. "Would it be acceptable to feed these to her?"

Her voice was timid at first, her enunciation cultured. Was she from out of state? Or out of the country? Her words had a lilted and clipped quality, like someone from Britain. Because the stable had buyers from all over the world, he was familiar with some foreign accents.

"Yes, ma'am. She'd love them. She's a gentle soul. We call her Dolly, but her registered name is Delilah Queen."

"That's a big name for a beautiful horse."

"Some owners feel a name will impact the personality of the horse." He shrugged. "I've never had the chance to name any. Regardless of what she's called, I like her enormous eyes and nice temperament."

"Yes, she seems calm."

Arden reached over and rubbed one of her ears. "Her attitude is the best of any we're training. Dolly's the only horse in the stable that is truly gentle. Yet, she possesses the spirit all trainers want to find in a show horse."

The girl glanced over at the men, then turned to him. "Are you involved in her actual training?"

"One day, I hope to be an official trainer. Currently, I've worked my way up to Head Groom. I help with training when I can. Becoming a trainer is my next goal."

"I'm sure you'll do a good job once you're a trainer. I can see how Dolly's nuzzling you. She's partial to you." She grabbed more cubes from her pocket, which she offered to the horse.

Dolly stretched out her neck and lipped the sugar off her flat hand. This must have tickled Olivia because she laughed.

The sound of her laughter was musical.

"Olivia!"

The girl stiffened and turned toward the man. "Yes, Papa?"

"Get away from that beast. She might bite or kick you."

In a whisper, Olivia said, "Dolly wouldn't do that, would she?"

He grinned at her and whispered in return, "Not this sweet girl."

"What about your other horses?"

"They range from those who are occasionally gentle to the crazy types who are constantly jumping out of their skin. Beautiful, but deadly."

She gave him a full smile, displaying a line of straight white teeth. "It's easy to tell Dolly is both striking and gentle."

His stomach somersaulted. Her smile was like a ray of

sunshine. How could someone he'd just officially met make him feel like this?

Olivia walked back to her father as a surge of joy filled his heart. He'd never experienced an instant attraction with anyone before. Though he might never see her again, he'd enjoy every second of her eyes and her smile.

Mr. George signaled for him to walk the fence, which he did for the second time, with renewed energy. Eventually, Mr. George ordered him to assist Olivia into the saddle.

He shot a grin at Olivia as he rushed to do his employer's bidding. She smiled back, sharing the delight at the prospect of riding Dolly.

Arden gave Olivia a leg up into the saddle, then handed her the reins.

"Dolly has been schooled for walk, trot, and canter so far. Our trainer thinks she can be five-gaited due to her size and strength, but she'll need more training for that."

With another smile, Olivia nodded and squeezed her knees gently against Dolly's side, and they rode around the fence. She led her through all of Dolly's motions with grace.

Arden could see Olivia was an excellent rider. She sat in the saddle confidently, held her heels down like an expert, and smoothly handled the transitions to every gait.

Olivia's smile widened, and her eyes flashed. Her face broadcast she was doing something she loved. She appeared one with Dolly, and Dolly gave her everything she could. The two worked well together.

When her father called out for her to stop, Olivia slowed Dolly to a walk and came back to him. The second she reached him, she slid off the saddle, right in front of him. Too fast for Arden to offer help.

"What did you think of my girl?"

"Absolute Heaven."

Hours later, when he could pin down Mr. George, Arden quizzed him about their visit.

"Did the people like Dolly this afternoon?"

"Mr. Knightly is seeking a gentle horse his daughter can show. They passed on Dolly because they're not interested in a horse in the process of being schooled."

"They want a five-gaited horse for the girl?"

"I told them Dolly was a good candidate for training in five gaits. She just needs more time for that." Mr. George shrugged. "He refused."

Two days later, Arden overheard Mr. George tell the stable manager that Dolly was to be pulled from consideration for the October sale. This surprised him. Dolly would fetch a hefty sum, thanks to both her beauty and gentle personality. Why was Mr. George pulling Dolly?

Arden stewed on this until he cornered Mr. George.

"I'm sorry to interrupt, sir, but I've been handling Dolly. I hear you've pulled from the sale. Is she injured?"

Horses frequently injure themselves, and it could happen anytime, whether during a workout or while tucked away in their stall. A step in a gopher hole could break a leg or tear a tendon. Inside, they can cut themselves on a nail or a splintered board.

Mr. George turned to him, somewhat distracted. "Nothing like that, son. She's been sold."

Arden's shoulders dropped. He'd hoped to have another chance to see Olivia again. With Dolly gone, there was no other horse at the stable suited for her. It meant Olivia wouldn't be coming around anymore.

His face must have telegraphed his feelings.

Mr. George smacked the top of his shoulder. "If you're worried about losing Dolly, she's been sold, but the new owner will leave her here for training until his daughter can show her."

"Daughter?" Arden's stomach flipped. "Was she purchased by the Knightly family?"

He frowned. "Yes. They're from town. The well-to-do sort, you know. Wasn't it you that showed the horse to them the other day?"

"Yes, sir."

Arden prayed he could discover more about her, even though their stations in life would keep them separated forever.

This was the second time he'd been told she was from Mexico. But her riding habit was foreign, which showed she could be an out-of-towner. Which was true? How could he find out?

He spent the rest of the day walking on air. They were going to train Dolly as a five-gated horse. This was his opportunity to admire the new owner, the blue-eyed beauty, for days and weeks to come. Although their social stations in life could not be more different, that had no effect on his feelings for her.

Her feelings for him? He was nothing to her. As a groom, he was a laborer, even though as Head Groom, he was a skilled laborer. He had to accept that he was someone who crossed her mind when she needed to order him about.

Her father also saw him as a mere laborer, which was exactly what he was today. This placed him many levels below their station, making him unsuitable for his beautiful daughter. It was heartbreaking.

Olivia was accustomed to a privileged life. Arden had to scramble for every penny. He still helped to support his mother and his youngest sister still at home, plus save for his own future.

Why had God allowed his heart to go out to this girl? Was God playing a cruel trick on him?

Could they even be friends? Would her family tolerate such a thing between them? Would she be interested in such a friendship?

God, I know I'm not enough for her, but you put her in my path. I pray you will show me why in Your own time.

Chapter Thirty-Six

Arden
Fall, 1932

Dolly began her training to learn the additional two gaits associated with a five-gaited Saddlebred horse. Rack and slow gait, especially slow gait, took strength from the horse and Dolly had it. Although three gaits were natural gaits, rack and slow gait were manmade by training.

Rack was a four-beat gait, with each hoof hitting the ground at equal intervals. The timing of the rack was part of the judging criteria for show horses. Slow gait, sometimes called "the stepping pace," was a slower four-beat gait. This gait required extra strength from the horse.

Arden and Bert were carrying buckets of grain to feed the horses their evening feed when Arden spotted Dolly training in slow gait. Olivia watched outside the track, standing behind the fence with her father.

"Look at her, Bert. She's an amazing creature."

Bert's brown eyes twinkled. "Are you talking about Dolly or the girl who bought her?"

"Both." Arden chuckled. "Am I that obvious?"

The grin slid off Bert's face. "I know you're fond of the Knightly girl, but you and I both know there's no chance for a future with her. I say this as a friend. You're going to get hurt."

Arden kicked at the dirt. "I know. At least, my head knows this. Everyday logic tells me I have no chance with her. Then I see her, and my heart pounds, my hands turn sweaty, and I'm carried away."

Bert moved on with his buckets, shaking his head as he walked.

Arden caught up to him. "I appreciate you looking out for me."

"I can talk about you getting hurt all day, but that doesn't mean you're listening to me or taking my advice."

Thanks to Dolly being in his care, he was aware when they scheduled her for training. When his duties allowed, Arden watched the trainer work with her. He wanted to watch Dolly train, but he also wanted a chance to see Olivia.

Olivia and her father visited to watch Dolly's training progress. Whenever they did, Arden did his best to "accidentally" cross Olivia's path.

They developed a friendship based upon their mutual love of horses. After several months, Dolly had advanced with her training enough for Olivia to ride her and run through the new gaits. As horse and rider, they needed time to work as a team.

In June, Olivia mentioned she was being sent to finishing school. Arden's heart nearly burst at this news. *She was leaving him.*

Too stunned to comment, Arden stepped up to Dolly and tightened her girth. A girth that didn't need to be tightened. He tried to compose his face into a neutral expression before he turned around and said, "Finishing school? I don't know what that is."

"My mother is British. In England, they send girls my age to boarding school. Some schools are in England, some in Switzerland. I'm to learn things. Things I'll need to know as a wife and mother. I'm going to one in Switzerland."

He spun around. "Switzerland? In Europe?"

Her blue eyes appeared sad even as they teased him. "I don't know of any other Switzerland. However, there are several strange town names in Missouri. This is Mexico, and Paris is just north of here."

He couldn't bring himself to react to her joke. "How long will you be gone?"

She studied the ground. "At least ten months. Maybe more."

"When do you leave?"

"Next week." She handed him Dolly's reins.

"What about Dolly?"

"I'll take Dolly with me. Father has already hired a trainer to accompany Dolly on the train to New York. Then, he'll also take the ship to England to ensure Dolly travels across the ocean safely. Even though I'm going on to Switzerland, Dolly will board in England."

"I don't understand. Why take Dolly?"

"Horse shows. I'll show her in England during the school holidays. I have relatives in England, so I'll be traveling there frequently."

With his tight throat, Arden couldn't say much. "It was nice working with you. Take care of Dolly for me." Then he turned and led Dolly back to the stable.

Inside the stable, he halted at the sound of someone running up to him.

"Arden. Wait."

Olivia.

Arden turned toward her, trying to remain calm on the outside, when his insides were screaming about the unfairness of it all.

"Would you like to write to me? I'll could write to you from Switzerland and send you my address."

He smiled. "That would be a pleasure. Address letters to me to Lee Brothers' Stables. Thanks."

Her blue eyes sparkled. "Thank you." Then she turned and walked back toward the track.

Chapter Thirty-Seven

Liesl

L iesl's mission today was to wash and pack the glassware and knickknacks she and Mrs. Zimmerman had pulled from the shelves of the library. As she washed, she thought of Kurt and Hector.

What if the suspect in the video turned out to be Hector's friend? She knew the pain of living through the betrayal of someone you loved. One of her great-aunt's best friends had killed her. Pain shot through Liesl at the memory. She would do her best to help Hector deal with the situation, if his friend turned out to be the one responsible.

While she was still up to her elbows in soapsuds, her phone rang. She dried her hands on a nearby towel. It was Justin. She tried to answer without an audible surprise in her voice.

"Hey, Liesl. Are you busy right now?"

Nervousness and concern in Justin's voice was clear. "Nothing that can't wait. What's up?"

"Would you meet me at the police station in about thirty minutes? One of my co-workers mentioned Katherine Mull may have been killed. In her house fire."

Gossips in town were having a field day with the fire. Liesl searched for a proper response. "Nothing official has been announced. But why does this concern you?"

"We had an incident at Lumber City involving her. I'd like to report it to the police, and I'd prefer you were there with me."

"If you want me there, then that's what you'll get." She reached into the sink and pulled the drain plug.

"Thank you, Liesl. I'd feel better if you're there. I'm afraid I'll be talking to Kurt and his partner."

"His partner is Hector Vega."

"Yes, I've met Hector briefly, but it's the idea of dealing with Kurt that bothers me."

Liesl frowned. "Due to my relationship with him?"

Justin's tension reached her. "You think I'm comfortable talking to the guy who stole my girl?"

"Technically, he stole me back. I was his first. Regardless, I'll see you soon."

When Liesl pushed through the Public Safety Department door, Roxy was staffing the front desk.

A sergeant for the Mexico Public Safety Department, Roxy's blonde hair, as always, was pulled back into a ponytail. She was a long-standing friend to Liesl. "No more traveling contractor issues?"

"No, ma'am. Thanks for your help the other day. I appreciate it."

"You here for business or pleasure?"

"Business. A friend asked me to meet him here. He has something to report."

Roxy's eyes darted to the door behind Liesl. "Is your friend that tall, blond guy you used to date?"

"Yes." Liesl frowned. "How did you know?"

"I think that's him coming in now."

Liesl turned. Justin entered with stiffness in his stride as if hamstrung with tension. He carried a briefcase.

She'd never seen him like this before. Concern painted his features, which made her stomach twist. This was something bad.

"Thanks for being here." He managed a slight smile, but no joy showed in his eyes.

Liesl reached out, touched his upper arm, and gave it a slight squeeze. "I'm glad you called me. Together, we'll work through this."

The relief in his eyes was all the reassurance she needed. She was in the right place.

God, help me help my friend. Let me provide the support he needs to be comfortable again.

Liesl stepped aside. "Justin, I'd like you to meet my friend Roxy."

He moved forward and shook hands with her. "Nice to meet you."

"She's the backbone of this organization."

Roxy pointed a finger at Liesl. "She exaggerates."

Liesl faced Justin. "You can trust her to take care of you. Whatever you need, she'll figure out how to make it happen."

"That statement is closer to the truth," Roxy said. "How can I help you, Justin?"

He cleared his throat. "That woman who died. I had a run-in with her in Lumber City a couple of days ago."

Roxy nodded. "You mean Katherine Mull? We've had no official confirmation she's dead."

"But they found a body in her burned home?"

"I can confirm that, but it hasn't yet been identified."

Justin nodded. His eyes darted from Roxy to Liesl, then back to Roxy. "I didn't know her name when the incident began. It was a big blowup, actually. I'd never met her prior to that day."

Roxy asked, "You want to report an incident with her?"

"A co-worker told me she's dead, and someone set fire to her house. If she's dead, the police will want to talk to me."

"You think you're a suspect in her death?"

Justin visibly paled. "No. At least, I hope not. I figured I'd better report this before I *am* a suspect."

Liesl patted Justin's arm again. "It's going to be fine." Then she turned to Roxy. "Is Kurt or Hector here?"

"Both are working in the field. With that fire, they're running everywhere. Give me a moment to call them. Why don't you take a seat?"

Liesl led Justin to a line of chairs. "Would you like coffee?"

"No thanks. I'm nervous enough without adding caffeine."

"I'm glad you called me. Reporting anything to the police is stressful." She noted the tremor in his hands. "I promise you. This will be fine in the end."

"Thank you for being here."

"When my garage was set on fire, I was interrogated. It wasn't a pleasant experience. That's not happening with you. You're going to explain whatever happened. Period. It'll be okay."

Roxy waved Liesl back to the desk. "I talked to Hector. They can't stop what they're doing to take Justin's statement. They asked me to call Dennis Bates." She raised her eyebrows at Liesl. "You okay with that?"

Liesl nodded. "Yes. Dennis will make Justin comfortable." In a whisper, she added, "Justin was dreading dealing with

Kurt. You can understand, given the history between us. This is perfect."

"Good. When Dennis gets here, we'll put you all in one of the interrogation rooms. For privacy. Not for interrogation."

"Would you explain to Dennis how nervous Justin is? If Dennis approaches this in his usual calm manner, it'll help Justin."

"You bet."

Liesl returned to Justin to explain the situation. He relaxed when he understood neither Kurt nor Hector would be involved. At least for now.

"You realize the detectives might have further questions?"

He nodded.

"But if you are thorough with Officer Bates, maybe this may settle it."

Dennis Bates was a high school schoolmate, one class behind her and Nicole. He was first on the scene when Nicole's business partner unearthed old bones earlier this year. He was smart, levelheaded, and kind. Just what they needed.

When Dennis arrived, Roxy had a quick word with him at the front desk. Then he strode over to meet Justin.

Although shorter than Justin, Dennis was a lanky, athletic guy.

The men shook hands.

Dennis said hello to Liesl, then escorted them to a room and gestured for both to sit. He opened the desk drawer and removed a pen, writing tablet, and a small voice recorder.

"Do either of you care for a soft drink or coffee? I rarely recommend the coffee, but Roxy's here. She can make a fresh pot."

When they declined, Dennis turned to Justin. "With your permission, I'm going to record this conversation. That way, I'll have something to refer to when I write the report."

Justin nodded. "No problem."

Dennis stated the date, time, and people present. "You'll need to make verbal responses. 'Yes' or 'no.' A shake of your head isn't audible. Do I have your permission to record this session?"

"Yes."

Dennis took Justin through basic information. Then, he asked Justin what he wanted to report.

Justin picked up his briefcase and placed it on the table. He opened it and removed three stapled bundles of paper. He passed one copy to Dennis, one to Liesl, and kept one.

"These are copies of the official report I made of the incident at Lumber City involving Katherine Mull."

As Dennis scanned the pages, Justin spoke again.

"Our store has video surveillance, and I've made a copy for you." Justin handed a thumb drive to Dennis. "I'd like to explain what happened, and then you can watch the video. There is no audio available from our system, but I think you'll appreciate the clarity of the video."

Dennis glanced at Liesl, his eyebrows raised.

She fought back a smile at his astonishment. It must be rare for a report to be handed to them, along with video surveillance.

"Thank you, Justin. Whenever you're ready, please relay the events that brought you here today."

"I was working on Wednesday. I was in my office when my radio squawked."

Justin said, "I should explain that all employees carry radios on our belts. This allows for instant communication throughout the store. In a large operation like Lumber City, we use them all the time."

Dennis said, "Understood. Proceed."

"The call was from Arnold Griffin. He's an excellent

employee. When he asked me to come to his area, I knew something was wrong. He rarely calls."

Dennis nodded. "I know Arnie. Very competent man."

"When I got to plumbing, Arnie introduced me as the store manager to this tall, blonde lady who verbally pounced on me. She's yelling that Arnie has offended her, and she wants me to fire him."

"Go on."

"I see a crowd is gathering, and she's embarrassing the best employee we have. So, I asked her to follow me to my office."

"Is it normal to escort a customer to your office?"

"No. This was the first time. Since I was wary of this woman, I asked my assistant manager to join us. I didn't want the customer to be alone with me and make nefarious allegations."

Dennis nodded. "Go on."

"I stayed outside the office until my assistant manager arrived. I explained the problem and turned on the video surveillance for my office. Then we talked to the lady."

Liesl held up her hand. "I'm sorry to interrupt, but you have surveillance in your office?"

He turned to include her. "If we have to counsel an employee or need to correct behavior issues, we record those sessions. We use it when speaking to employees about a serious issue or terminating someone's employment."

Liesl nodded.

Dennis asked, "Is it posted in a public place that the store uses video surveillance?"

"Yes," Justin said. "Both entrance and exits have a post about video cameras and surveillance."

Dennis smiled. "Excellent. Then your recording was legal. Why did you take this woman into your office?"

"To stop the scene she was making in front of the

customers. Several people had gathered to watch her yell at Arnie. You'll see them in the video."

"What happened in your office?"

"I asked her name, and all she told me was Katherine. Then I asked her to start at the beginning and tell me the problem. She said she was there for a replacement kitchen faucet for one of her rental homes. Her plumber had sent her there to buy it. He wouldn't supply the equipment. He would just install it."

Dennis nodded. "Okay, that's reasonable. She's in the right department for buying a faucet."

"Exactly. While she was shopping, Arnie asked her questions about the mounting for the faucet. Was it one or three holes? Was it behind the sink attached to the countertop? Or was it a sink mount?"

"Nothing wrong with those questions."

"You'd think, but that set her off."

Dennis expressed no surprise about this. He and Liesl were both aware that Katherine wasn't reasonable. Justin's mistake was to assume she was.

"When Katherine explained that Arnie's questions infuriated her, I explained he was trying to save her time and money by identifying the correct faucet type she would need. My assistant manager did her best to help explain the same to her, but the lady turned her venom on both of us."

"And then?"

"I let her rant for a while, then asked for her plumber's name. I offered to call and get the details she needed to make her purchase."

Dennis smiled. "That's a nice gesture on your part."

"You'd think so," Justin said. "At that, she stood up, screamed ugly words at us and stalked out of the office. I followed her to ensure she left the store."

"Yes. Smart of you."

"Once she was gone, I had my assistant manager write a statement about what she witnessed, then did the same thing with Arnie. I also apologized to Arnie for her behavior. He didn't deserve the way she'd embarrassed and offended him.'

"Did you bring the statements from your employees?"

"Yes," Justin pointed to the packet. "You'll see Arnie's is the first report in the packet. Then the assistant manager's, and then mine."

Dennis picked up the packet.

"The video is in three parts. It starts from the time she walks into the store and goes to the plumbing area. It captures the confrontation with Arnie. The second part is the feed from my office. The last part is her exit from the store."

"Did you call the police about this?"

"Should I have?"

"I was wondering if we have a report, that's all."

"I couldn't figure out any laws she might have broken, so I didn't. She was mean and verbally vicious, so I made an incident report for internal store purposes and captured a copy of all the video."

"May we watch the video?"

"Sure."

"I'll keep my recording running while we watch, if you agree. I'd like to capture any conversation we have about your video."

"That's fine."

"I'll grab a laptop to play the video." He glanced at his watch and announced the time, then paused the recording. "Be right back."

Liesl tossed a big smile at Justin and patted his hand. "Great job."

Justin turned his light blue eyes to her. "Did you hear anything concerning?"

"No. Your encounter with her is actually not that unusual."

His eyes widened in surprise.

"She acts that way almost everywhere she goes."

"Really?"

"Yes. Been like that since she was a teenager. Maybe worse as an adult."

"I had no idea."

Dennis re-entered the room with a gray laptop. "Got one." He set up the laptop and then started the recorder again, stating the time. "We will now display the video provided by Mr. Frazier."

Justin and Liesl brought their chairs around to Dennis's side of the table to view the video. The screen filled with the image of a camera covering the entrance of Lumber City.

Dennis narrated for the recording. "We're looking at the video from Lumber City, which begins at the entrance. We see various people entering the store. Now, we see Katherine Mull entering. She enters alone. She is wearing a floral dress and has a purse of substantial size over her shoulder."

Liesl tried not to laugh at Dennis describing a Gucci bag worth thousands of dollars as a "purse of substantial size." Its cost would horrify him.

"We see Katherine turn down an aisle. Mr. Frazier, what department has she entered?"

"Plumbing."

Their narration continued through the encounter with Arnie.

Liesl recognized several people who had gathered when Katherine was yelling at Arnie. It was like a car crash—horrifying, but no one could look away.

One onlooker was Bob Mansfield, her former Sunday School teacher. Another face in the crowd was Margaret

Sterling, one of the town gossips who would relish telling the whole town about the incident.

When the video ended, Dennis asked, "Did you have any further encounters with Katherine between this experience and now?"

"No."

"Had you any contact with her prior to this occurrence?"

"No."

Dennis stated the time and stopped the recorder. "Thank you, Justin. I'll go over this with Kurt and Hector. If they have questions, they can contact you."

When they left the room, Liesl said, "Great job. You documented that incident very well."

Justin seemed able to relax. "I'm relieved that's over. Thank you for being here."

"I'm happy to help. But there's a bonus to accompanying you today. I can wholeheartedly recommend you as a manager to any company in town after seeing you in action."

He appeared pleased by her compliment.

Liesl didn't tell him he was a contender for a management position with the Community Center she hoped to develop. If she could make all the pieces fall together.

If God wanted it to happen, He would help her accomplish that goal.

Chapter Thirty-Eight

Liesl

L iesl parked in her garage, still bubbling with happiness that Justin's meeting with the police had gone well. Before she entered her house, her phone buzzed.

It was Nicole. "Hello, my friend."

Nicole's enthusiasm poured through her voice. "I'm at the office, and you'll never guess what's happened."

Liesl chuckled to herself. She knew what had happened but wouldn't spoil the surprise. "Spill!"

"We just received a contract. By email. It's representing a non-profit company in St. Louis with their purchase of our city block. Can you believe it?"

"That's fantastic!"

"Know what this sale could mean? If I can close a deal on the city block?" Nicole's excitement was electrifying.

"Tell me!"

"It means Lee and I might be able to afford a house like

yours. Not as big, but a large, historical one nearby. It makes me want to cry."

Liesl teared-up on her end of the call. "Of course, it does. It makes *me* want to cry too. It's been your dream for a long time."

"Ages and ages. But I'm getting ahead of myself. I've got to complete this sale before I look for houses in your neighborhood."

"You're going to nail the sale, and we'll be moving boxes into a beautiful old home soon."

"I am curious, though. Don't you have connections in St. Louis? I mean, why would a company in St. Louis pick me to represent them?"

"I might have dropped your name. Why wouldn't I? You're a real estate professional."

"Thank you. I'm *so* excited about this. I'm going to meet with their representative as soon as we work out a date to show them the property."

"You're going to be great." Liesl heaved an inward sigh. Finally, she could tell Nicole all the things. "In the meantime, can we meet this afternoon for coffee? I'm taking Joey to his physical therapy appointment, but maybe after that?"

"Sure. If you're buying, why don't you let me know when you're ready, and I'll pick you up?"

"I'll text you when we're back."

After Joey's appointment, Nicole came by, and they decided to celebrate with food. Liesl hadn't had lunch, and kwikis from the local food truck were irresistible.

In Nicole's car, Liesl studied her friend for a moment. Her cheerful mood over the real estate representation offer was the perfect time to reveal everything. "I've been wanting to share something with you for a long time."

"About Kurt?"

"No, but I can complain about him. He got mad at me trying to teach him the ways of having tea, and he stomped out of my house in a fit of anger."

"Has he apologized to you?"

"Yes."

"Then you're good?"

"He also thinks I'm nosey."

After a pause, Nicole said, "Is this the part where you expect me to disagree with him? If so, you'll be waiting forever."

"Hey, don't start with me. That man doesn't appreciate the fact I'm a puzzle solver, someone who can unwrap the tangles of a mystery."

"Actually, you're more inextricably linked to being nosey than a mystery *untangler*."

"Let's change the subject. If you agree with Kurt, you're putting our happy lunch in jeopardy."

"Mums the word."

When they ordered, Liesl suggested they sit in Nicole's car to eat with air conditioning running.

At Liesl's suggestion, Nicole's mouth dropped open. "You're *not eating* corn dogs drenched in barbeque sauce in my car."

Liesl froze. "What do you mean?"

Nicole crossed her arms and tapped her foot. "Nope. Not allowed."

"Are you kidding me?"

Nicole turned to take the bag with their food from the pass-through window. Then she turned to Liesl again. "Not kidding. My real estate clients sit in that seat when I'm showing them houses. I have to keep the seat and area around it pristine."

"What if I say I'm going to be one of your real estate clients?"

"When you are, then I might consider letting you dine in my beautiful van with tan leather seats. Until then, you share the same status as Claudia—no food in my car."

"Claudia is seven. You're treating me like a child."

"When you stop eating like one, I'll issue you an invitation to dine in my car."

Liesl didn't want to throw down her real estate client card just yet, so gave up the fight and chose a shaded picnic table.

The air had a slight breeze, which should keep her from melting. While they ate, Liesl shared highlights of Justin's visit to the Public Safety Department and then turned the conversation to Nicole's new contract.

With a deep breath, Liesl launched into an explanation about her inheritance and how she wanted to buy the city block to build a Community Center.

She should have paid more attention to Nicole's reaction to her news.

Once she noticed the fury in Nic's eyes and that her friend's hair was standing on end, it was too late.

Nicole stiffened and pierced her with a stare. "You mean you've kept your inheritance and this idea for developing a Community Center a secret from me for over a year?"

Liesl tap-danced around Nicole's anger. "No. Well, yes. Sort of. The money thing has been longer than a year. But I've only worked on the Community Center plan for about four months."

"Friends tell each other important things in life."

Liesl fingered her paper napkin while Nicole blinked at her in stony silence.

"You've let me down, Liesl."

Was she going to make everyone mad this week?

"I'm sorry. I had to wrap my head around receiving such a large inheritance before I could share the information. You don't even know how large it is."

"The size doesn't matter. It's you not sharing it with me that matters. I don't care about the money, and you know that. You've always had more money than anyone I know, and it makes no difference to me."

Liesl focused on the half-eaten kwiki in front of her and nodded. "You've been the best friend a girl could ever want. I had a hard time wrapping my brain around all that money. I should have shared about it long ago."

"Yes, you should have." Nicole stood. "It's time I took you home." She wadded up the remaining food and packaging and threw them in a nearby garbage container.

Liesl babbled apologies to fill in the silence during the ride back home, but Nicole had no words for her.

When Nicole pulled into her driveway, Liesl tried one more time. "I'm so sorry. How do I make it up to you?"

"I'm not talking to you right now. Goodbye."

Liesl got out of the car and watched Nicole drive away. Nicole didn't glance toward her before she left.

Later that evening, Liesl called Nicole to schedule a time to talk. She was surprised she answered her call.

"Have you forgiven me, at least a bit?" The hope in Liesl's tone was profound. "I never intended to make you mad. I'm sorry."

"Your apology is appreciated but I'm still angry. We're besties. You should have told me more than you did."

"I'm happy to explain all of my misguided actions if you'll carve out some time for us."

"You didn't trust me enough *before* to share all of your information. What's changed now?"

"This has nothing to do with trust. It has everything to do with fear. I was afraid our relationship might change."

"Change how? Due to your inheritance? I don't care about that, and you know it."

"Look, I had to figure out how to discuss a boatload of wealth without sounding like bragging."

"Fair point. But we're friends. We share everything."

"We don't share every detail of our lives."

"Agreed, but have you told Kurt about it?"

"Before you? No. I'd never tell him before you. Sisters before misters, right?"

"Right."

Liesl could tell Nicole smiled about that.

"My aunt and uncle were the best examples of caring, sharing folks. I plan to be the same. An anonymous benefactor to this community. The same way they supported the town."

"One of these days, when I'm talking to you again, you'll have to tell all the wonderful things they did. Their anonymous stuff."

"Deal."

"It's better, but I'm still not talking to you."

"What else can I do?"

"We're going to have to plan something expensive and fun for a Girl's Day Out, and you're going to pay for it with your boatload of money."

"Your wish is my command."

"But not too soon. I know you're sorry, but I'm still not talking to you."

"Okay then. Ta-Ta for now."

"Cheerio!"

Since her best friend was mad at her, Liesel decided it couldn't hurt to pull out quotes from a certain slow and bumbling but wise stuffed bear.

Chapter Thirty-Nine

Arden
Stewart Stables 1943

Arden clipped the lead on the bridle of Empress Theodora, nicknamed Emmy, and walked the magnificent animal out of the stall. He paid particular attention to the way the horse carried herself. Did her head drop when she stepped? This was one of the first indications of an injury.

Because horses were prey animals, they hid their injuries instinctively to avoid becoming dinner of something higher up the food chain. Arden helped train everyone who worked at the stables to spot wounds early. If a worker wasn't sure whether or not an animal was hurt, they were told to talk to him about it.

In addition to training horses and mules, everyone made sure all animals in their care were sound. This required help from all hands. They had to be aware of many indicators of a problem, such as feeling the heat of an injury, or reacting quickly to the first subtle signs of colic, or spotting the first signs of a change in the animal's stride.

When Arden started working as a barn boy years ago, he hadn't known much about horses, and he was totally without any experience around fancy, high-spirited show animals. Yet, his hard work throughout the years and his desire to learn had paid off. After years of experience at all levels of stable hand, grooms, and barn boy, thirty-five-year-old Arden had landed an offer from Mr. Robert Stewart to be one of his assistant trainers when Mr. Stewart purchased the stables from the Lee Brothers.

Bert, his nearly lifelong friend, was also now an assistant trainer. Arden was happy for him. He'd recently married his long-time girlfriend. Arden had the honor of standing up with Bert during the wedding in the home of Bert's bride, Kitty Flowers.

The happy couple had served a small cake to their guests thanks to several guys from the stables who donated their sugar, flour, and butter ration tickets to Mrs. Flowers as a gift for the bride and groom.

Bert and Kitty lived a few blocks away, in a tiny house they rented. Arden was a frequent guest and appreciated eating fresh vegetables from the Victory garden Kitty planted.

The war had changed so many things at the stables. Business was different, but they were making it. Mules were more in demand than Saddlebreds. With fuel rationing, farmers found it easier to pull out their old plows and work their fields with mules and draft horses.

It was the same with local vendors. Many business owners parked their trucks and hitched mules to their wagons. Even the police were back to using horses or mules while patrolling. Their use helped reduce the daily need for gas-powered police cars.

Mr. Stewart put a paintbrush in everyone's hand to paint the stables white after he purchased it. Arden considered the new color a great improvement. A new color, a new era of profitable stables.

A special lady named Virginia Jones, wife of a judge in Kansas City, was interested in Emmy. As Arden saddled Emmy in preparation for showing her off to the potential buyers, workers scurried like ants around the stable. Everyone worked hard to carry off a livestock sale.

Arden recalled that Mr. Bass had sold horses to President Theodore Roosevelt, before he became president, President Grover Cleveland while he was president, and Buffalo Bill Cody during his famous Wild West Show. Mr. Bass trained the white horse Buffalo Bill used in his performances.

Today, the stable was open to potential purchasers. People who wanted to look over each animal offered in the sale. Arden and Bert were working each trained horse so potential owners could watch their gaits.

Mr. Stewart hoped to maintain the sterling image of the Lee Brothers' Stables in his own ownership. With the stables nationally known for having excellent horses, most already trained, Mr. Stewart was in line to keep those customers.

Even in these tough times of war, some people were wealthy. They came to the sales with intentions of buying a well-trained horse so that rider and horse might place high in horse shows.

Although this was their fall sale, the warm temperatures today made it feel more like summer. As a result, the horses were dragging a bit due to the heat. Arden prayed for a cold snap by tomorrow when the sale would start. He needed all the animals to appear and perform their best.

Some visitors had arrived from Los Angeles, California. They represented a trade network on the west coast. These were men who were knowledgeable about good horseflesh, and Arden hoped they'd pay high dollar to take some animals west on a railroad boxcar. They would use these purchases as breeding stock and horse show stock.

Show horses were judged in part on how the animal moved. A well-trained horse would score high. Some buyers wanted to show their horses, while others bought them to ride on bridle paths in their cities.

Arden led Emmy past her stall buddy and hesitated as they blew their noses at each other, a pack animal greeting for others in their pack.

At the outdoor corral, people gathered along the rail of the white picket fence. Emmy threw up her head and nodded to the crowd, which caused some chuckling.

After Arden mounted, he spotted Mr. Stewart, who was always on hand to answer any questions and speak about the attributes of each horse.

Arden soon forgot about the crowds as he concentrated on the power and timing of the horse. Emmy was a five-gaited beauty, and she ran through all her gaits perfectly.

When they finished, Arden hopped down and led the horse along the fence so the onlookers, especially Mrs. Jones, could have a close glimpse of this magnificent animal.

Arden stopped when he spotted him.

A man he'd prayed to never see again. Toby.

What was he doing here? No matter the reason, it couldn't be good.

The years had not been kind to Toby. His hair was completely gray, his back hunched, and his clothes were dirty and tattered.

The only thing that hadn't changed over the years was the sneering smirk on his face. The sneer revealed yellowed teeth with one empty space. Probably some bar fight had ended with that tooth being knocked out.

By instinct, Arden didn't lead the horse anywhere near him. He didn't want her close to a man who purposely injured one of the Lee brothers' horses.

The sheriff uncovered the plot soon after Toby's arrest that night years ago. A different horse owner had bribed Toby to do it. Seems Toby was to take the Lee Brother's horse out of contention so the bribing horse owner would have a better chance of winning a high-paying horse show. Toby had been convicted and sent to prison.

Toby and the owner who planned this scheme had been banned for life from any show of Saddlebred horses.

Arden moved away from the fence and led the horse to Mr Stewart, who was talking to a man on the other side of the track. "Sir, sorry to interrupt, but I need to speak to you."

Mr. Stewart turned and frowned, but he stepped away from the potential customer. "What could be important enough to interrupt sale discussions?"

"Sorry, sir. But that old man standing by himself to the left? Name is Toby. He was fired from these stables several years ago. Got caught hurting a horse to try to take him out of a show. Bribed by one of the show competitors."

Mr. Lee straightened. "When was this?"

"Over twenty years ago. Around nineteen-twenty or twenty-one. I'd just started working for the Lees when it happened."

Both of the men turned and eyed Toby.

Toby met their gaze and held it. After a moment, he spat, then turned and sauntered toward the road.

"That man is nothing but trouble," Arden said. "I'll be spending the night in the stable tonight. He wanted me to see him, which means he's planning the revenge he promised years ago."

"Why does he want revenge on you?"

"I helped the Lee Brothers and the Sheriff catch him. I was the one who figured out he was hurting one of the horses."

Mr. Stewart frowned. "We'll need more than you in the stable. Pick a handful of guys. Have one or two stay in the maternity stable and keep the rest with you. We'll all rotate guard times."

"Thank you, sir."

"Good luck. Tell the fellows I'll pay them double for this night duty."

Chapter Forty

Liesl

Liesl pushed through the entrance of Community One Bank for her rescheduled appointment with Mr. Barnaby. She was eager to get back on track with her secret project.

Katherine would not be an interruption today. Liesl prayed her face would not leak the knowledge that law enforcement suspected she'd perished in her home fire. Kurt wouldn't forgive her if she revealed the information, no matter how inadvertently it might be.

Although Mr. Barnaby could keep secrets, she was here to discuss the Community Center, not Katherine. She needed an ally in town, and Mr. Barnaby would bring financial expertise and a Christian heart to the project. If her plans fell into place, she planned to ask him to serve on the Community Center's board of directors.

Liesl waved at the always-smiling Miranda Marquette, who sat at her desk. Behind Miranda, Liesl spotted Mr.

Barnaby in his office. The glass walls of the office allowed her to see he was with someone she didn't recognize. This gave her time to stroll over to Miranda's desk for a moment.

Miranda pushed her glasses into place on her nose. "How are you doing today? Back for your rescheduled appointment?"

"I am."

Miranda glanced over toward Mr. Barnaby's office. "He's on his feet now, so he's wrapping up with that customer. May I get you coffee or juice?"

"No, but thank you."

Miranda straightened in her seat. "Here comes Mr. Barnaby. Talk to you later."

Liesl turned to see Mr. Barnaby approaching, dressed in his usual high-class suit and tie. He had upgraded his toupee a few months ago, and the new look flattered him. Liesl adored his twinkling brown eyes, always filled with kindness

He gave Liesl a quick hug, then stepped back. "Would you care for coffee?"

"Miranda beat you to the offer, and I declined."

"Then let's get down to business."

He led the way to his office. After offering her a seat in front of his desk, he sat beside her instead of returning behind his desk.

She placed her purse and briefcase on an adjoining chair. "I'm so excited about this."

He folded his hands in his lap. "First, I must apologize for the business that necessitated rescheduling this appointment. I'm so sorry. Such things are unprofessional."

"Please, Mr. Barnaby. No apology needed. You can't discuss what happened with Katherine but please know how sorry I was at her treatment of you. You're a fine gentleman and shouldn't be treated that way."

Mr. Barnaby nodded. "Thank you, Liesl. I ran out there to

keep her from abusing my staff. She was furious, and I couldn't have her treating anyone poorly except me. That's part of my job. I sacrificed myself at the point of her sword, so to speak."

"You were noble, as I would expect. Things in life can make us angry. However, Katherine should not have abused you or your staff, regardless of the problem."

"Kurt and Hector's arrival curtailed some of her anger."

"I'm glad they helped."

He blew out air. "I'm deeply disconcerted about her home catching on fire that very evening. It makes me wonder if she is being targeted."

Liesl studied her hands, folded in her lap. He would be even more disturbed if he realized the police suspect Katherine was also a victim of that fire. She prayed her face wouldn't reveal anything.

Mr. Barnaby stood and strode to sit behind his desk. "You have my undivided attention now. How may I help you today?"

Liesl pulled up her briefcase and removed some prints she'd made of her spreadsheet related to the Community Center's development. "You know I trust you, Mr. Barnaby. You've served both my late great-aunt and uncle for decades. And recently, you've provided me with that same service."

"It has been an honor. I consider all of you family."

"I feel the same." Liesl felt her eyes water but gained control of her emotions. "I think you're aware my inheritance from Aunt Suzanne was substantial."

Color rose to his cheeks. "That is not a subject I'm comfortable speculating about."

"As a gentleman and a family friend, I will let you know that my inheritance was sizable. As my trusted banker, I'm here to discuss a special project I'm working toward."

"I'm honored to help."

She smiled. "The project is only in the planning stage.

Within the next few weeks, there may be movement forward to make this plan a reality. I hope this project will honor Aunt Suzanne and Uncle Max and will benefit the citizens of this town."

"Your great-aunt and uncle were so proud of you, and you continue to make the rest of us proud."

"Thank you, Mr. Barnaby. That means the world to me."

"Others who inherit a sizeable amount might be tempted to sell their assets and run off to France and purchase a villa or something like that. You've stayed here, honoring their memory through good deeds."

Liesl grinned. "I want to do more. I'd like to have your help to make wise investments and run a nonprofit."

He smiled. "Beyond the Butterfly House? That legacy is a tribute to your Aunt Suzanne and her friend Winnie."

She nodded. "Beyond that, yes."

"Then I guess I'd better sit beside you again to hear what you've planned."

Mr. Barnaby returned to the chair next to Liesl, and they spent the next thirty minutes discussing her plan to buy the city block and develop it into a Community Center.

"You really don't want to name it after your great aunt and uncle?"

Liesl shook her head. "God knows, and they know, this entire project is in honor of them. Of those here on earth, my financial advisers and my attorney in St. Louis know about it."

Liesl paused and studied her hands. "I've told Nicole. That didn't go well. When I spill the beans to Kurt, I hope he takes it better."

"It's good you're telling them. But why did Nicole have a hard time with it, if I may ask?"

"You may. I'd appreciate any help you can give to lessen her anger at me." Liesl huffed in frustration. "Her feelings were hurt because I didn't tell her earlier about my inheritance. It's not about the money—it's about sharing the joy and burden of it with her as my best friend."

He gave her a sympathetic look. "She'll get over it. Keep apologizing. She needs time to wrap her head about all of it. You certainly did. When you tell Kurt there's no need for anyone else to have knowledge of the provider of the funds."

Liesl straightened in her chair. "My hope is the Community Center can eventually support itself with just the building, the initial merchandise, and utilities provided by the nonprofit."

"The recent donations made by Coach Tyron Lue and Steve Ballmer to this town are exciting." Mr. Barnaby said. "Some people might associate them to your nonprofit."

"Coach Lue and Mr. Ballmer deserve tremendous praise for their donations to the town. I'd be thrilled if people believed they were the creators of this entity."

Liesl smiled. "I don't need or want any credit. Helping Mexico and the surrounding towns is reward enough for me. It's what Aunt Suzanne and Uncle Max would have wanted."

Then Liesl surprised both herself and Mr. Barnaby by bursting into tears.

Chapter Forty-One

Liesl

When she reached home after her meeting with Mr. Barnaby, Liesl walked to the front porch to retrieve her mail.

She rifled through the items quickly. When she spotted an envelope with no return address and a typed address label, she pulled it out of the group and studied it.

Advertisements weren't normally this plain. Her suspicion turned to the nomadic contractors. Was this some type of work proposal? If it was, she'd have to turn this over to the police. Could she charge them with harassment?

She flipped over the envelope and perused the back. It was a self-stick design.

Curious, Liesl used a key on her key ring to rip open the top flap of the envelope. With two fingers, she carefully pulled out the single white page.

The message was typed.

Stop sticking your nose where it doesn't belong. It might get cut off. There's a dangerous killer in town. He's delivering justice to those wrongdoers who must be stopped. You and your nosey buddy will be next if you don't back off.

Liesl's hands shook as read the threat. By the end, her nerves were so shredded it was hard to focus on the words.

Her instinct was to crumple the paper and envelope in anger or tear them to shreds. Instead, she held the letter and envelope by their left top corners and carried them into the house.

She found a paper bag in the kitchen, dropped the items inside, and realized she needed to take these items to the police station. Kurt would be upset.

But first she had to tell Nicole.

Liesl expected her call to go to voicemail, but Nicole answered.

"I've got some bad news."

Nicole picked up on her worried tone. "What's wrong?"

"It appears you and I made a potential killer mad enough to send us a threatening letter."

Nicole sucked in her breath. "What does it say?"

Liesl carefully pulled the letter out of the bag with kitchen tongs and read it to her.

"Does Kurt know?"

"He's my next call."

"I'll meet you at the Public Safety Department."

"I'll be there in five minutes."

When they both arrived, Liesl held the paper bag in her hand as she and Nicole walked into the station.

Roxy was on duty and realized something serious had occurred. "What's wrong?"

"Kurt's on his way. He's going to look at this letter I received."

Roxy bent over to open a drawer of her desk and pulled out several pairs of disposable gloves. "Use these." Then she stood and walked around her desk. "It's always something with you two. How about I put you in one of the interrogation rooms?"

"Thanks." Nicole took both pairs of gloves from Roxy.

"When Kurt gets here, I'll point him in the right direction." Then Roxy led them down the hall.

The sound of footsteps behind them caused Liesl to turn around. Kurt and Hector had arrived. She felt an immediate sense of relief.

Roxy stopped and put her hands on her hips. "Why are you guys sneaking up on us?"

Hector said, "We came in from the back, Roxy. We'll take them to our office."

"Okay." Roxy turned to the girls. "You can call me anytime if you have more problems. In the meantime, try to stay out of trouble."

Kurt frowned at Roxy. "They don't know how to do that."

Liesl spun on Kurt. "This isn't our fault."

Kurt held up both hands. "Sorry. You're right."

In silence, Nicole and Liesl followed Kurt and Hector to their detective room—a small office with two sets of desks pushed together. Plastic evidence bags filled with items covered the two desks.

Kurt waved at the mess. "What we do in our spare time."

Liesl spotted a familiar-looking item inside a bag among those scattered. She pointed to it. "What's this?"

Kurt moved to see what she showed. "It's a letter I pulled from Katherine's desk. Why?"

Liesl studied it for a moment. "May I pick it up?"

"If you keep it inside the bag, you can look at it. Why? What's wrong?"

"I recognize these. They match the note and envelope I received today." She shook the brown paper bag in her hand. "The threatening letter we brought here because it scared us."

Chapter Forty-Two

Arden
Stewart Stables 1943

That night, Arden was ready with a plan. Thanks to Mr. Stewart and his offer of extra money, Arden had plenty of men in both the maternity barn and the regular stables.

After much discussion about the situation, the men agreed that in the regular stable, they'd move the most expensive horses into the middle stalls. They'd place the mules on the ends near the exterior doors. With no place to remove the animals entirely, a shuffle was the best they could manage.

Bert, along with grooms who lived close, went home before dark, ate dinner, and brought back their dogs. Although some horses didn't appreciate the dogs, others showed no signs of nervousness.

There was only one door in the middle of the stable, which opened to the west track. Arden placed three men near that door. If he were breaking into the stables, this was the entrance he'd use.

Toby had used the north door years ago when he hurt the horse. Another door stood at either end of the stables. Arden took up his post at the north door. If Toby entered that door, Arden wanted to be waiting for him.

Bert secured the south door along with the big furry beast named Gene Autry he'd brought from home. His propensity to howl and bark earned him the name of the most famous singing cowboy of the day.

Now, all they had to do was wait.

They slept in shifts.

The darkness, even filled with all the sounds from the barn, surrounded Arden and increased his concern about the horses, the men under his authority, and his own safety. He mumbled prayers, asking God to keep everyone and everything safe from harm tonight.

When the rays of dawn lit the night sky, the men bragged about the night passing without incident.

Arden heard a sound from outside and tensed. At first, he attributed the noise to a horse misbehaving. Then he realized it was the sound of an animal in pain. "The maternity barn! Quick!"

Bert ran and opened the north stable door.

Arden turned to the men remaining inside the main stable. "Bolt this door once we're out. We have to keep him away."

Then, Arden joined Bert in their scramble to the barn.

Before they reached it, Toby stepped from behind the corner of the structure. He held a bloody knife in his fist. "Stay back."

Arden threw his hands up. "Don't hurt anyone, Toby. It's me you want."

"I want more than just you. I'm taking out everyone and everything you care about."

"Take me." Arden cut a quick glance at Bert and whispered, "Run, Bert."

Toby grinned at Bert. "I'm not particular. Both of you would serve for my revenge. A knife in the gut is a faster way to die than being locked up for years."

Bert stood resolute. "You brought it on yourself."

Toby charged toward them, his knife slashing left and right, screaming.

Arden dove toward Toby.

When Toby hit the ground, Bert pounced on him, wrapping up Toby's arms as he did.

Arden scrambled up and ran to the fighting men. He took aim and kicked the knife out of Toby's hand.

While Bert pinned down Toby, Arden pummeled Toby with his fists.

In the tussle, Toby pulled an arm free and reached for the hilt of the knife.

As Toby pointed the knife at Arden's back, Bert yelled, "No! Toby, no!"

Arden shifted his weight to hold Toby's arm in place.

Bert grabbed Toby's arm and, before Arden could help him control Toby, Toby plunged the knife into Bert's stomach.

Arden wailed in agony for his wounded friend.

Bert rolled off Toby and turned pleading eyes toward Arden.

Arden thrust his hand over the wound to staunch the stream of blood.

More fists joined the fight allowing Arden to apply pressure to Bert's wound.

Eventually, Toby lay motionless in the grass, held still by numerous men.

To one of them, Arden shouted, "Go get help!"

As a man ran away, Arden tuned to another. "We need clean towels. We've got to stop the bleeding."

Arden drove to the wealthy side of town with dread. The urgency of his mission propelled him, but concern about the reception he'd receive haunted him. Would she even bother to see him? Or would she send him away before he explained why he was there? Did she have the compassionate heart he believed her to have?

He'd dressed in his best Sunday suit. It felt uncomfortable. He only wore such clothing on Sunday, and the shirt collar chafed his neck. Although he'd scrubbed himself clean, no matter what he did, the faint odor of horseflesh followed him. Would she get one whiff of him and kick him out?

If invited inside, good manners dictated he would have to remove his hat. This would reveal the line across his forehead that divided the sunbaked skin from the skin never exposed to the sun. He'll look exactly like what he is, a laborer. Someone below her station, regardless of his promotions.

Why was he putting himself through this torture? The answer was, he owed his best effort to Bert. The best friend a man could have in this life. A friend second only to God and Jesus.

Arden strode up the front porch steps of the Victorian home, his emotions churning. It was the last place he wanted to come, hat in hand, to beg a favor. A favor that involved money. Would she turn him away?

He eyed the brass knob in the middle of the door. He'd never seen such a thing. Was that the bell?

With a twist of the knob, the sound of ringing bells inside verified it was a doorbell.

He would never, ever, ask for money for himself. Although he dreaded this encounter, he owed it to Bert to try.

He was alive thanks to Bert's bravery. He had no choice but to be brave enough to reach out to the only person who might save Bert's life.

A middle-aged woman opened the door. "How may I help you, sir?"

"I need to speak to Mrs. Olivia Thatcher. It's a matter of grave importance."

The woman eyed him for a moment. "Who shall I say is calling?"

"Mr. Arden Rahn."

The housekeeper stepped back and pulled the door wider "You may wait in the entry, Mr. Rahn. I will see if Mrs. Thatcher is receiving."

Arden stepped into the large entry way and pulled off his fedora.

The servant held out her hand for his hat, and he passed it to her. She hung it on a brass hat rack behind him, then made her way across the room.

He watched her cross polished wood floors. Rugs and expensive furniture dotted the room beyond. An enormous brass chandelier hung from the ceiling.

The woman walked to the wide wooden staircase that wound its way to the second floor. Her slow ascent of the massive staircase caused him to tense again. Was this going to take forever? They didn't have time to waste.

What if Olivia wouldn't see him? What if she didn't care enough to find out why he was here?

He shifted his weight from side to side, his hands thrust in the pockets of his pants. After a moment, he paced.

The sounds of steps on the staircase caused him to spin.

It was Olivia.

Beautiful Olivia.

She was as lovely as the first day he'd seen her wrapped in furs while riding in her father's Model T. This mature Olivia wore a lovely dress, more sophisticated yet still appealing.

He rushed to the staircase, taking her hand as she stepped down the last steps.

"Oh, Arden. It's so good to see you."

"I'm so sorry to bother you. This is a serious matter. I would not come under any other circumstance."

Olivia studied his face. "What's wrong?"

"It's Bert. He saved my life this morning but has a terrible knife wound because of it. The doctors say he needs to go to St. Louis. A specialist there might save him. But even pooling our money, we don't have enough to pay for his treatment."

Her blue eyes were as bright as he remembered. "Will they take a guarantee?"

"I don't know what that is."

"I'll explain later." She reached out and touched his arm. "Do you have a car here?"

He nodded. "Mr. Stewart loaned his to me."

"Let's go to my bank. We'll have them send a telegram to the hospital in St. Louis. Do you know which one it is?"

"The specialist is at Deaconess Hospital."

Olivia turned to the housekeeper, who was making a slow descent on the stairs. "Please tell Mr. Thatcher, if I'm not back by the time he returns home that I had urgent business. I'll explain it to him tonight."

The woman nodded. "Yes, ma'am."

Olivia guided Arden toward the front door, where she retrieved a raincoat hanging near his hat. She smiled when she held his hat toward him. "Maybe it would be better to stop at the hospital first. We can gather all the details. Then we'll go to the bank, and I'll guarantee the funds."

He felt his eyes filled with tears. He blinked them back. "I don't know how I'll ever pay you back."

She squeezed his arm.

He spotted tears in her eyes too.

"Arden, I've already received payment when Bert saved your life. Now, let's do the best we can for him."

Chapter Forty-Three

Liesl

Mrs. Zimmerman rapped on the door casing of the dining room. "Sorry to disturb you."

Liesl raised her head from her spreadsheet. "You don't have to knock, Mrs. Zimmerman. I'm just working on my computer." She didn't mention she was working on her Community Center plans. One day, she'd be happy to share the news with Mrs. Zimmerman, but not today.

"Do you have a moment? I discovered something of interest when I was packing the library."

"Really?" This intrigued Liesl.

"One of the top shelves had a box tucked in behind small books. It resembles an antique strong box or an old cash box. Did you know it was up there?"

Liesl frowned. "No. Where was it exactly?"

"Top shelf, far right corner. Come see."

Liesl pushed back her chair. "This is fascinating. How many other secrets are hidden in this house?"

Mrs. Zimmerman chuckled. "You'll be disappointed if they turn out to be your Great Uncle Myron's old baseball cards."

In the library, Liesl spotted the silver-colored box, still on the shelf. Next to it was a stepladder. She turned to Mrs. Zimmerman in horror.

"You were on that stepladder with no one holding it?"

Mrs. Zimmerman nodded.

"No more. I forbid it. No more using stepladders alone in this house. If you need a ladder for cleaning, I'll call a cleaning service with younger employees."

Mrs. Zimmerman placed fisted hands on her hips. "Are you calling me old?"

Liesl hesitated. "I'm ... I'm calling you too old to be on any ladder, even a stepladder. The truth hurts."

Although Mrs. Zimmerman glared at her, a smile pulled at the corners of her lips.

"You know I'm right."

In a sarcastic tone, Mrs. Zimmerman said, "Back to the point. Go check out that box while I hold the stepladder."

Liesl hesitated. "Why didn't we see it?"

"It was hidden behind a row of small, leather-bound children's books." She nodded to a box a few feet from them. "I put them over there. I think they're too old to be your great-aunt's books. Maybe her mother's books."

"Do they need to be somewhere besides lining a shelf? Like on display at the historical society."

"Perhaps. They're quite old, I think."

Liesl walked to the ladder and, while Mrs. Zimmerman held it, Liesl reached up and brought down the box in question.

The metal box was around five inches wide, three inches tall, and six inches long. A leather strap, which appeared dry and stiff, was laced through a metal buckle.

Liesl glanced at Mrs. Zimmerman. "Have you ever seen a box like this?"

"Never."

She undid the leather strap, revealing a bundle of yellowed envelopes held together with a pale blue ribbon. The outer edges of the envelopes were lined with blue and red marks. Below the stamps, the words "via air mail" were printed. All envelopes were addressed to Olivia Knightly in Switzerland.

"Olivia Knightly? Why, that's Aunt Suzanne's mother's name. Her maiden name."

"Wasn't this house built by the Knightley's over a hundred years ago?"

"Yes, Aunt Suzanne's grandfather built it. Her grandmother designed it." Liesl held up her find. "This is so sweet, tied in a bow. I'll bet these are love letters."

She rifled through the upper left corners of the envelopes. "They're from Mexico. But the address on the Boulevard differs isn't this address. It's from farther west on the Boulevard. Strange."

"Those were important letters to someone," Mrs. Zimmerman said. "They're hidden, but lovingly hidden."

Liesl examined the faded postmark. "I'll bet these are over fifty years old."

"The post office could tell you more about them. Someone there should be able to give you an age range. Maybe they can figure out the date."

"Another mystery! Thank you, Mrs. Zimmerman. I'm so glad you found them. I won't undo the bow, but I will pull an envelope out to let the post office inspect it."

"Aren't you going to read them?"

"I'm not sure. It feels like an intrusion into Olivia's private business."

"If not you, then who? These are pieces of history. A personal piece of history, but history none the less."

Liesl frowned. "I'll have to think about it."

"You might want to put them on display in the historical society. Or they may be too private to share with the public. What do you know about Olivia Knightly?"

"I never met her. She was Aunt Suzanne's mother. I always got the impression she wasn't a nice woman."

"What makes you say that?"

"I don't think she was very nice to Aunt Suzanne. As you know, Aunt Suzanne wasn't your typical beauty for those times. But she was so smart and inquisitive. She was friendly to everyone all of her life."

Mrs. Zimmerman smiled. "That's the woman I knew."

"I believe her mother was quite the opposite. How did Aunt Suzanne turn out so nice? Her Grandmummy, her mother's mother, was even worse."

"Perhaps these letters are exactly what you need to discover the real Olivia Knightly. It's easy to misjudge someone when you don't know all the facts."

"True." Liesl's mind tumbled for a moment. "Mrs. Sizemore certainly would have known her. I'll have to ask her."

"She would be a fine resource."

"Aunt Suzanne's grandmother and grandfather came here from Britain, and they were upper crust. Stiff upper lip people. Wealthy. Didn't mix with lessor beings."

"Pity," Mrs. Zimmerman said, using a fake British accent.

They both laughed.

* * *

Liesl called and made an appointment with Patricia Sizemore, indicating she had something intriguing for her to see. With regret in her tone, she declined the offer of tea but made a mental note to ask about her impressions of tea with Kurt.

When she arrived, the housekeeper showed Liesl into the white formal living room. Liesl eyed all the stiff, formal furniture sans color. No wonder Kurt always got nervous when he had to come here. This house was as icy as Mrs. Sizemore.

Within a moment, Mrs. Sizemore swept into the room. She took a seat at one end of her white couches and patted the cushion next to her. "Come sit with me, Liesl. I'm so glad to see you."

Liesl did as suggested. "Thank you for having me, Mrs. Sizemore ... ah, Patricia."

She found it hard to call Aunt Suzanne's best friend by her first name, but it was at her request. "Tell me how things went with Kurt?"

Patricia gave her a side-eyed stare. "You know I can't reveal anything official about that visit."

"I just wondered if you've thawed a little toward him now that we're dating again."

"I'm delighted you're dating again. He obviously adores you. He just needed to mature, and raising a son by himself has done that, in my opinion."

Liesl nodded. "I agree. The love between him and Ross is amazing."

Patricia shifted her weight and said, "So, what did you want to show me?"

Liesl reached into her large purse and pulled out the metal box found by Mrs. Zimmerman. "This. Have you ever seen this before?"

Patricia held out her hand, and Liesl gave her the box. She studied it for a moment. "No. I don't believe so."

"Mrs. Zimmerman found it on a top shelf in the library. I'm

having the floors sanded and refinished, so we have to pack and remove everything from that room."

"Quite right, you know." Patricia nodded and then turned her attention back to the box. "Have you opened it?"

"I've opened the box, but not the contents. Please look inside."

Patricia carefully pulled open the straps from the box and removed the bundle of letters. She took a moment to observe the ribbon and bow in front. Then she fingered the edges of the airmail envelopes.

"I haven't seen these before."

"My next stop is the post office. I hope they can give me an idea of their age. Do you realize these are addressed to Aunt Suzanne's mother?"

Patricia handed the bundle back to Liesl. "Mrs. Thatcher, her mother, was a hard person to warm up to. I'm not the type to get past that. Thus, we tolerated each other."

"She didn't like you?"

Patricia smiled a Cheshire cat smile. "Let's say she didn't approve that my parents were lenient in my upbringing. I was spoiled and a bit of a bother to my parents. I'm sure Mrs. Thatcher assumed I was a bad influence on Suzanne." The older woman shrugged. "She wasn't wrong. But thanks to my social status and wealth, she couldn't keep her daughter from being my friend."

"What did you do so scandalous?"

"I smoked, drank, and had a brand-new convertible. I was Mrs. Thatcher's nightmare."

Both of them smiled.

"This is a happy surprise. Aunt Suzanne never breathed a word of such things to me."

"Of course not. She was my best friend, and she'd never say a harsh word against me, even if true."

Liesl's face fell. "I've made Nicole mad at me. I've apologized, but she's still angry. I don't know when she'll forgive me."

Patricia frowned. "Don't worry. If you've apologized, she'll forgive you. Give her time. She loves you as much as I do."

Liesl stared wide-eyed at Patricia.

Patricia waved a hand at Liesl's shock. "I've always cared for you, Liesl. From the moment you belonged to Max and Suzanne."

"You could have fooled me." Liesl immediately regretted her words. "I'm sorry, Mrs. Sizemore. What an ugly thing to say."

"It's Patricia, and I don't mind you speaking the truth. I have a hard time being warm and friendly. I've struggled with it all my life."

"I admit to being uncomfortable around you as a child."

Patricia nodded and focused on the interlaced fingers resting in her lap. "Your aunt was one of the few people who understood me."

She raised sad eyes to Liesl. "I wasn't raised with cuddles and outward signs of affection. Neither of my parents were like that. Suzanne's father was the loving person in their house."

Liesl felt pity for Patricia. Even though Liesl's parents died young, she'd been raised with great love from Aunt Suzanne and Uncle Max.

"My father bought me expensive things to show his affection. My mother showered me with clothes and jewelry. Neither gave me much attention."

"I was unaware of that."

"Your aunt would have considered it rude to talk about such things with you. Suzanne's mother was like me, stiff and cool with people. Her mother and I recognized the hard outside shell of our similar personalities. The kindness and consideration for others was there. It's hidden inside."

"Then Aunt Suzanne understood you because you were like her mother."

"Exactly."

"Everyone needs a friend."

"She was a great friend. Your aunt forced me to go to church with her, and I began to thaw." Patricia's eyes filled with tears.

Liesl patted Patricia's hand and fought back her own tears. "You have me, now. I'm not afraid of you anymore. My aunt cherished your friendship. She always said you were honest and forthright."

"Perhaps too much of both."

"But I like straightforward people. You must always be honest with me. No matter how hard the truth is."

Patricia smiled. "I miss your aunt so much, but I feel she's left you as a gift to me."

Liesl chuckled. "I have a charitable idea brewing. It's not ready to be revealed yet. But I hope to get you involved in the work. Are you game?"

Patricia pulled out a dainty handkerchief and wiped tears from her eyes. "It would give me the greatest pleasure to work with you—in any capacity."

Chapter Forty-Four

Nicole

Everything was going wrong today.

From the moment Nicole had rolled out of bed, she'd been one step behind. The suit she'd ironed last night had slipped from its hanger and lay wadded and wrinkled on her bathroom floor. Lee was out of town, so she got Claudia ready for daycare all by herself, and Claudia had been out of sorts this morning.

In an act of desperation, she'd bribed Claudia with a drive-through doughnut from Ralph's. That wouldn't win her any parenting awards, but it saved time.

When she got to the office, the printer wasn't working. Marc, her business partner, was off in the far corner of the county showing a farm property, so he wasn't available to fix it.

Thank the Lord for sweet Penny at the Chamber of Commerce. When Nicole reached out to her, she'd been happy to help print what Nicole needed on the Chamber's printer.

When her documents were ready, Nicole ran over to Penny's office as fast as her four-inch-high heels would allow. As she made her way back to the real estate office, she decided Penny earned a gift card for her emergency printing services.

The only bright spot in her day was her ten o'clock appointment to show a house to a family for a second time. Fingers-crossed that a second look would convince them to make an offer.

Once she had everything printed and ready to go for the showing, Nicole allowed herself a moment to make a much-needed a second cup of coffee. As the wonderful aroma filled her nostrils, Nicole's thoughts turned to her foul mood this morning.

Was Claudia's bad mood related to her own? She'd admit she'd been in an obvious depression since her argument with Liesl. Was her daughter picking up on her sorrowful vibes and reacting to them? The last thing she wanted was to have her adult problems upset her sweet little girl.

Liesl's failure to share an important part of her life with her hurt her heart. She'd talked it over with Lee, and he said, "Time would heal her wounds." But would it?

Why hadn't Liesl trusted her when she was grieving over her great-aunt's death and trying to comprehend a large inheritance? Was she not as good of a friend as she thought she was? Or was Liesl being truthful about needing time to work through it on her own?

When her phone rang, she jumped. With her luck today, it was probably her house-hunting couple canceling their appointment. She braced for bad news. "This is Nicole."

"Mrs. Smith? Mrs. Lott, here. I'm calling because Claudia is running a fever. I'm afraid she feels bad."

Nicole felt a pang in the pit of her stomach.

"She wasn't acting like her usual, happy self this morning,

and then I noticed her cheeks were red. Her temperature is one hundred and three. Figured you'd want to come get her."

Nicole's mind raced as she glanced at her watch. The people for the showing were probably on their way. Lee's in Jefferson City for sports trainer training, and Marc was too far away to substitute for the house showing.

With a stammer, Nicole said, "I have some logistics to resolve. May I call you right back?"

"No problem. Do I have your permission to give her some fever reducer?"

"Yes, please. And use cold cloths on her forehead and neck to bring down her fever."

"We're doing that. Just call us when you have something worked out."

"Thank you." Nicole hung up the phone.

Liesl. As mad as she was at her, Liesl loved her daughter and wouldn't hold their argument against her. Perhaps Liesl could pick up Claudia and take her to the doctor? She'd meet them there when her showing was over.

She felt guilty about failing to realize Claudia was sick this morning. Her focus had been all about herself and not on her daughter. Now she needed Liesl's help.

Perhaps this was God's way of providing a much-needed lesson in forgiveness.

She swallowed her pride and called her bestie.

Liesl sounded anxious when she answered, "Are you still mad at me?"

Nicole kept her tone to pure *concerned mother*. "Yes. I'm still not speaking to you. But I have an emergency with Claudia."

Liesl sucked in her breath, then said, "Oh, no."

"The daycare called to say your goddaughter is running a high fever and feels terrible."

"What can I do?"

Nicole explained why she couldn't immediately pick up Claudia. "Could you take her to Dr. Johnson's office?"

"Of course. Let Doc know I'll be right there. I'm at the post office, so I'm already halfway to the daycare."

Nicole breathed a sigh of relief. "Thank you. I feel better already."

"Don't worry. I've got this. We're in luck because Ross's booster seat just happens to be in my car."

"Text me everything you find out. I'll come as soon as I can."

"I'll keep in touch. It'll be fine."

Nicole's voice wavered with emotion. "I'm still not talking to you, but you know I love you, right?"

"Of course I do. I love you too."

Nicole heard the smile in Liesl's voice before they ended the call.

* * *

Liesl

Liesl pulled into the parking lot of Claudia's daycare three minutes later. This fever? What did it mean? Claudia was rarely sick.

Mrs. Lott held open the door for her. The daycare owner was in her sixties and had taken care of children most of her life. She was a smart woman, always one step ahead of toddler shenanigans. She'd babysat Liesl when she was young.

"Nicole called and said you'd be getting Claudia. I'm so glad you made it here quickly. She's miserable."

"Thank you for taking care of her." Liesl searched the room for Claudia. "Where is she?"

"I've got her on a daybed in our break room. Its sole

purpose is for sick children who don't want the other kids bothering them. Follow me."

Mrs. Lott led her to an ill Claudia. With her light brown skin tone and big brown eyes, Claudia was the image of her mother. But today, her eyes were ringed by dark circles, and her cheeks were flushed red.

Liesl rushed over to squat on the floor near Claudia. Her stomach clenched as she took in the watery, dull eyes that lacked their normal sparkle. Liesl reached for Claudia's hand and felt the warmth of her fever.

She had little experience with children but now wished she did. How serious was this? "I'm sorry you feel bad, sweetie. I'm taking you to the doctor. Okay?"

Claudia nodded.

"I'm sure you'd rather have your beautiful mother here, but she'll join us as soon as she can."

Claudia pushed herself into a sitting position but appeared wobbly.

Liesl picked her up, wrapping her arms around the child. Claudia melted onto her shoulder.

On their way out, Mrs. Lott trotted beside Liesl. "Do you have a car seat?"

"Sort of. I have a booster seat. She's a little young for a booster seat, but that's all I have."

"I have an extra. I'll run and get it."

"Do you know how to hook it up? I don't."

Mrs. Lott laughed. "I sure do. I'll have it fixed in seconds. Be right back."

Good to her word, Mrs. Lott strapped in the car seat, and they poured Claudia into it.

"Thank you, Mrs. Lott. I'll get this back to you as soon as I can."

"No worries. You just take care of our girl."

They arrived at Dr. Johnson's office without incident. Liesl sat in the car with the feverish child and called the receptionist.

"Nicole told us you were coming. Come on in with her. Sherry Hill will take you straight to a room. Since we don't know if this is something contagious, we're cautious."

"Great. Thank you."

Liesl got Claudia out of the car and explained her friend Sherry, an experienced nurse, would take care of them.

Sherry was a tall, blonde-haired woman. She was also one of the few people who could carry off wearing scrubs.

When they entered the reception area, Sherry immediately called out from the back, "Go to room three, Liesl. I'll be right there."

Liesl had been a patient of Dr. Johnson's since she was a child, so she knew the way to exam room three. Claudia kept her head against Liesl's shoulder as they walked.

Liesl had never seen Claudia this lethargic. Her worry increased. Children ran fevers all the time. But that didn't make her any less anxious.

Please God, let these wonderful, caring medical providers help our girl.

Liesl had sad memories of Dr. Johnson calling her in to explain he suspected her aunt had been poisoned. That memory made her hug Claudia closer. She found the right room and snuggled Claudia in her lap.

Once settled, Liesl sent a quick text to Nicole assuring her they were in an exam room. She also reported Claudia was doing as well as expected.

When Sherry came in, she said to Liesl, "Try not to worry. Claudia's going to be fine."

Sherry then turned to Claudia. "I'm going to put this thermometer in your ear and take your temperature, okay?"

Claudia nodded with her head lying on Liesl's shoulder.

After the beep, Sherry announced, "One hundred and three."

Sherry walked across the room and returned with a tongue depressor. "May I see if you have any frogs in your throat?"

Claudia lifted her head and turned to face Sherry.

"Thank you, sweetheart. Say ah."

Claudia said, "Ah."

"By the look of that throat, I may have spotted the problem." She threw the tongue depressor into the contaminated container. "No frogs there. But your throat is red. I'll see if Doc is ready."

Sherry stepped out of the room and then returned with a swab in her hand. "Doc will be right in. He'll probably want to check her for strep. That would be one explanation for that fever and her red throat. But we'll wait for him to make that call."

Claudia relaxed back against Liesl.

Liesl rubbed Claudia's back and made small talk with Sherry while they waited. "Has it been a busy day?"

"We had several firefighters with some smoke inhalation complaints on Monday, thanks to that big fire on Friday night. Today has been calmer."

Liesl nodded. "The fire at Katherine Mull's house has been the talk of the town."

Sherry's eyes twinkled. "I have a hard time being sympathetic about her losing her home. Couldn't happen to a nicer person, if you know what I mean."

"I understand." Liesl hoped her face wouldn't broadcast anything related to the Katherine saga.

"I know lots of horror stories about her. I've had a few harrowing experiences of my own. The worst involved a patient of this clinic."

"Really?"

"Our patient suffered from asthma and couldn't tolerate mold or mildew. Her husband did everything he could to get Katherine to fix the house they rented from her. He even tried to sue her, but Katherine's attorney from Columbia got it dismissed."

"I'm sorry, but I'm not surprised. Seems like all her tenants have complaints."

"This wasn't a small lawsuit. He filed for wrongful death after he lost his wife. He believed she died from an asthma attack caused by the wet, moldy, unrepaired property."

"Katherine was accused of wrongful death? Why haven't the town gossips been spreading that juicy detail?"

Sherry shrugged. "They probably weren't aware of it. I've said too much. Patient privacy laws, you know."

Liesl asked, "Any idea if the widower used a local attorney?"

Sherry didn't have a chance to respond as Doctor Johnson entered the room.

Normally, Liesl would have given him a hug, but she remained seated with Claudia in her lap.

Dr. Johnson understood her inability to move, and they shared a smile.

He reached out and patted Claudia's back as he asked, "Where did you find this beautiful girl?"

"She arose from the ocean last time I was there. She must be a mermaid."

"I don't see many mermaids in my practice. This one sure is pretty."

Claudia smiled, her eyes following him as he walked across the small room to grab an instrument.

After a quick look at Claudia's throat, and a swab of her throat to test, he pronounced the mermaid "Very brave."

"Just like her mother," Liesl said.

As the nurse slipped away to get the results, Dr. Johnson continued his exam of Claudia, making her smile when he asked her if all mermaids have unicorns in their ears or was it just her?

Sherry returned, announcing the test was positive for strep.

"I have the perfect medication for getting mermaids to feel good again," Dr. Johnson said. "I'll send it to the pharmacy listed on your chart. You and Miss Liesl can pick it up. I promise you'll feel better in no time."

Claudia gestured for Dr. Johnson to come close.

When he leaned toward her, she wrapped her arms around his neck.

Dr. Johnson smiled as he straightened. "You've made my day, Claudia. It's not every day I get hugged by a mermaid."

To Liesl, he said, "If she doesn't feel better by tomorrow, call me."

In the car, Liesl tapped out a report to Nicole and Lee via text. While she drove to the pharmacy, she tried to tempt Claudia with fast food or a frozen drink, but she declined all offers.

Liesl pondered the information mentioned by Sherry. Somewhere in town was a man who blamed Katherine for his wife's death. Could something like that push a man toward murder? Perhaps.

"I'm going to give you your medicine as soon as we get to the pharmacist. The doctor said it will help you feel better soon."

Liesl glanced at Claudia in her rear-view mirror. Her eyes were closed. Had she fallen asleep? Poor thing. Liesl was sure she wanted her mother, but she'd put up with her as a second choice.

Soon, Nicole should swoop in and make her daughter happy. Would she make Liesl happy by forgiving her?

When they arrived at the pharmacy drive-through, the attendant told her the prescription wasn't ready. Could they come back in twenty minutes?

Another glance at Claudia provided proof she'd fallen asleep on the drive.

Instead of driving somewhere else, Liesl parked in the parking lot and left her car running so they wouldn't fry in the heat of the day. Claudia could sleep until the medicine was ready.

Liesl called Kurt to tell him about the man who blamed Katherine for his wife's death.

He answered after two rings.

"Are you busy?" She had hoped for a chance to talk since he hadn't answered with his cop voice.

"Not too busy for you. Hector and I are reviewing surveillance tapes. What's up?"

"I have a potential suspect for you to investigate. This guy has a motive to kill Katherine. I just don't know exactly who he is."

"So, you have a potential suspect, but you don't know his name?" Kurt chuckled.

She frowned. Kurt smirking about this wasn't appreciated. "That's not an accurate way to describe my information. Could you at least hear me out?"

Contrite, Kurt said, "Sorry. Go ahead."

"At the doctor's office today, I was told there's a man who blames his wife's death on Katherine."

"Wait. Are you sick? Why were you at the doctor?"

"Claudia is sick, Nicole had a showing, and Lee is out of town. I was the only one available. Claudia and I are at the pharmacy, waiting to pick up her medicine. I had a moment to call you."

"Is she doing okay?"

"She is pitiful, but she'll be fine. She has strep throat."

"I hope you don't catch it."

"I'm not worried about that. Poor thing. She only wants to lie on my shoulder. The little dancing queen doesn't feel like dancing."

"I hope she's better soon. So, what did you hear?"

"This man's wife had asthma. They lived in the mold and mildew of one of Katherine's rental houses. He tried to get Katherine to make repairs, but she didn't. Then his wife had an asthma attack and died. He blamed her death on Katherine. I was told he even sued her for wrongful death."

"Wrongful death? That's a civil matter. I'd suspect there wasn't enough evidence of a crime to charge her, so the man chose a civil suit."

"Do you think you could see if your department had any complaints about her? Maybe the man filed one."

"We've already pulled all the reports with her name. This would require searching the courts for a lawsuit. That takes time."

"Aren't court records online?"

"Almost all of them are now."

"Could Roxy research it? You know she's smart. Use your influence on her or her supervisor to have her do it."

"You think I have influence?"

She smiled at his question. "Beg Roxy to search in her spare time. She seems to know her way around a computer. Ask her boss to let her help with this enormous case you've been saddled with."

"I could talk to Roxy."

"In the long run, won't you have to pull any lawsuits she was named in?"

"This is my investigation, not yours. You're telling me what I need to do and who to assign to help?"

"I'm only trying to pass on information given to me. Like those IE's or CC's or whatever you call them."

"You mean CI? As in confidential informant? If that's what you mean, they only pass on information. They restrain themselves from trying to tell me what to do with the tips they give, unlike what you're doing."

Sounds of shuffling came from the back seat. Liesl saw Claudia was awake.

"I've got to go, but give the Roxy idea some thought, please."

Kurt grumbled. "I do have some news, but you can't share it with anyone except Nicole. The body discovered in Katherine's home has been identified. It was her."

Liesl sighed. "Not unexpected but still not good news."

"Keep this under your hat for now. Talk to you later."

She hung up and whispered a quick prayer. When she looked at Claudia, she said, "Hey, sleepyhead. We'll be heading to my house soon. You can see Barney as soon as we have your medication."

Claudia nodded but still didn't smile.

The second time through the drive through, they retrieved the medication. She also received a text from Nicole that she was finally free.

Liesl told her to meet them at her house.

"Now, Miss Mermaid, we're off to my house. You have your choice of several couches to lie upon, and Barney will be delighted to join you. Your mom is meeting us there."

Chapter Forty-Five

Kurt

This was the second time Hector and Kurt had spent hours huddled in front of the station's largest computer monitor, watching the surveillance video copied from the Poindexter home in slow motion.

Kurt pointed at the image on the screen. "There. Stop it right there."

Hector did as he requested.

"Doesn't that look like David Whittier?"

"Are you back on the *David* theory again?" Hector stared lightning bolts at Kurt, then rubbed his hand across his mouth and chin. "I don't believe Dr. and Mrs. Johnson have a killer who dog-sits for them when they go out of town."

"I haven't convicted him. But as a computer science teacher, he'd have the skills to handle the clever banking transfer and access to Katherine's security system." Kurt waved an arm at the monitor. "And this guy looks like David. Same age and general appearance."

Hector turned toward Kurt with eyebrows raised to his hairline. "Does this guy look black to you?"

Kurt shrugged. "I admit skin color is hard to determine from this video."

"Get real, Kurt. These images aren't clear enough for this to be proof. A lot of joggers look like David."

"Look, man. He's your friend and you want to protect him. I get that. But you have to keep an open mind."

Hector pounded his hand on the table. "I *am* keeping an open mind. You're the one who's pointing fingers."

"Because I think it's David?"

"Because David has an alibi. He was helping coach at the high school track that night. Let the facts guide you, not the other way around."

Kurt sighed. "Okay, if that's not David, could it be James Kellar?"

Hector spun toward him. "He has an alibi too. Also, Kellar is too tall to be your guy here. Kellar was a professional athlete. Compare this guy's height to the mailboxes nearby. The guy in the video is only six feet tall. Both Kellar and David are taller than this man."

"Then who is this?"

They both turned back to the image and stared in silence.

An idea came to Kurt. He grabbed his laptop and pulled up the spreadsheet he'd made. "Do you remember Mrs. Overton talking about a guy who mowed lawns part-time in the neighborhood and still had the energy to jog through the neighborhood?"

"I do. Do we have a name for him yet?"

"No. But here is what she said, and I quote, 'You'd think his lawn work would get him enough exercise to satisfy himself, but apparently not. I've seen him almost every evening for months now … His wife died about six months ago. I understand he was really torn up about her death.'"

"Liesl just told me something about a patient of Dr. Johnson who lost his wife and sued Katherine for wrongful death because of it. She said the case was dismissed."

"She get a name?"

"Nope. Patient confidentiality. But how many middle-aged guys in this town have lost their wife within the last year?"

A knock on the door of their office preceded the entrance of Roxy, holding two large Styrofoam drink cups. "Although I hesitate to offer you guys more caffeine, I think both of you need something to cool you off. Literally and figuratively."

Hector smiled at her and took one of the drinks offered. "You're a lifesaver. Thank you."

When Kurt reached for his, he motioned to the monitor. "Who does that look like, Roxy? Anyone you know?"

She stared at the frozen image for a moment and shook her head. "I don't recognize him." Then she took a step closer. "But I think I recognize the jogging suit."

Hector screeched in surprise, "You do?"

"They look like some on clearance at the second-hand shop. See that stripe down the side of the leg?" She pointed at the video. "You don't see that as much in newer fashions."

Kurt asked, "Was this recently?"

"No." Roxy thought for a moment. "Probably several months ago. Must have been in the spring when I saw them on their clearance rack."

Hector stood and said to Roxy, "Let's go to the second-hand store and talk to them."

"Now? I'm on duty."

"Who's covering your desk right now?"

"Dennis. But he's at the end of his shift."

Hector motioned her toward the door. "I'll bet he'd be

happy for a free dinner at DeAngelo's in exchange for a few minutes at your desk."

Kurt called to his partner as Hector and Roxy exited the room, "Don't mind me. I'll just stay here, watching video and searching for guys who are middle-aged and lost their wife in the past year or two."

Chapter Forty-Six

Arden
Summer, 1953

The sound of the boys playing reached Arden before he could spot them. A smile spread across his face at the crack of a ball against a bat. Squeals of excitement followed, as if there was a close play on a base.

Music to his ears. These sounds resonated with him differently than when he was a boy. Today he heard the enjoyment of his sons, some of his nephews, and their friends playing baseball.

These boys didn't have to work to support their families. Instead, they played and practiced for hours with real baseball bats, regulation gloves, and baseballs on a field designed specifically for baseball.

That feisty young man he'd met in 1929, had made good on his promise to hire Arden as a trainer. Art Simmons purchased the original Clark and Potts stables in 1948, and the newly renamed Simmons Stables was flourishing.

Art agreed to sponsor the boys' uniforms and equipment, so they voted to call their team the Simmons Sluggers. Arden was one of their coaches. He didn't know much about baseball, but he understood the need for his children to chase their dreams.

Bert's son, named Oliver in honor of Olivia and the money she spent to save Bert's life, was the team's best pitcher. Tall and broad like his father, Oliver was the best player on the team. His hitting was nearly as good as his pitching.

Bert helped coach the team, too, when he had time. He'd moved from horses to cars and was now a salesman at Pearl Motor Company.

Every day, Arden thanked God for the people He'd placed in his life.

He prayed Olivia was happy with her husband, Thomas Thatcher. At least she still lived in Mexico, in the Victorian her grandparents built at the corner of the Boulevard and South Jefferson.

His thoughts turned to that day he'd gone to Olivia to help Bert. Although he imagined he would need to beg her to help, she'd jumped to act. Her fast actions saved Bert, thanks to her willingness to fund the special medical treatment he needed to recover.

Once Bert was out of danger, the first accidental meeting between them was awkward. But time helped them overcome those feelings of uncomfortableness. Because her son Myron played with the Simmons Sluggers, she and Arden frequently interacted.

Few in town remembered or cared about their long-ago doomed romance. With deep gratitude, Arden thanked God for sending Sheila to him. His beautiful wife loved him despite his broken heart over Olivia. God sent her to him so she could heal his heart and build a family.

He had much to be grateful for, even though he and Olivia couldn't be together. He prayed Olivia felt the same.

At the ball field, his eldest son was catching, so he walked up behind him when the batter struck out.

"Hey, son. Good job of stopping that foul tip."

The teenage boy with shaggy blond hair pulled off his facemask and wiped the sweat from his brow with his forearm. "Thanks, Dad. We haven't been keeping a score this afternoon. We've just been playing for fun."

"Just what I want to hear. Playing for fun is a wonderful thing."

Chapter Forty-Seven

Liesl

A few days later, Claudia was back to dancing, and Ross had returned from his time at the Lake of the Ozarks with his grandparents.

Kurt was still putting in long hours, so Liesel had stolen Ross for a fun morning with her before he spent the afternoon at a birthday party. Kurt consented to stop by for a quick lunch but couldn't stay longer. They were hot on a suspect's trail, and he was only taking a break to eat with her and Ross.

Ross finished his food in record time for Nicole to collect him for the birthday pool party at The Oaks. Nicole insisted on driving and attending, mainly to monitor the health of Claudia.

Liesl left Kurt devouring a second ham sandwich while she walked Ross to Nicole's car. After she waved at his smiling face as Nicole dove away, Liesl turned and spotted Joey.

It was rare to catch him spending time outside of his apartment, but there he was, elbow deep in mulch, working with the flowers in his flower box. She took a moment to walk over to Joey's apartment.

"Hey, there, Joey. Did you enjoy your sandwich?"

Joey nodded, intent upon his work.

"Could I bring you some dessert?"

Liesl smiled when her suggestion caused Joey's head to pop up like a gopher out of a gopher hole.

He turned toward her, hands clad in gardening gloves. "What are my choices?"

"Ice cream, chocolate chip cookies homemade by Mrs. Zimmerman earlier today, or a combination of both."

Joey considered. "Flavor of ice cream?"

Liesl grimaced. "Only vanilla. I promise to pick up some strawberry tomorrow."

He sighed in obvious disappointment. "Just the cookies, then." Once again, his full attention was on his flowers.

Guilt accompanied Liesl as she made her across the backyard. Disappointing Joey was something she didn't like to do. Joey didn't ask for much. She vowed to make a better effort to keep everything he loved in stock.

At her back door, a man's voice she didn't recognize came from inside the house.

She hesitated on the steps. Strange. Did Lee stop by with Nicole, and she missed him? She mentally shrugged. Odd.

She opened the door, then realized Barney wasn't there to greet her. He was her Velcro dog. Where could he be? His leash hung in its usual place. She glanced up and down the hallway for him but didn't see him.

Liesl felt a pull at the pit of her stomach. Something was wrong. Barney certainly hadn't been in the backyard, and now he wasn't inside waiting for her. Where he? What happened?

She strode toward the kitchen, fear wadded in the pit of her stomach. She stopped when she spotted Kurt standing in front of the banquette with his arms up, facing the hall to the pantry.

A man's voice yelled, "Is that you, Liesl? Get in here!"

She swallowed her fear and made her way there, her mind racing. What happened during the three minutes since she'd walked out the front door?

Mr. Mansfield stood in her kitchen, and in his hand was a pistol pointed at Kurt.

Everything fell into place. Her stomach lurched. This was Katherine's killer.

This man's wife had died of an asthma attack and they'd lived in one of Katherine's rentals.

Sherry, the nurse, had given her all the details but a name. Her brain had refused to connect the dots to a sweet man like Mr. Mansfield. He was a Christian. He'd been her Sunday School teacher years ago. How could he have chosen this path?

The hand holding the pistol was unsteady.

Please God, give me the ability to reason with him. Or to calm him down. Guide me to do whatever is needed for this to end without violence or injury.

"Mr. Mansfield, how did you get in here?"

"I watched you take that kid out and walk over to Joey's place. I waltzed inside, but your stupid dog heard me, and then Kurt found me."

Kurt said, "I locked Barney in the bathroom at Mansfield's request."

She nodded and took another step closer. "Why are you here?"

"You have to be stopped."

Liesl was afraid of the red, angry Mr. Mansfield. She'd never seen him like this. "I'm sorry, Mr. Mansfield. I shouldn't have stuck my nose in your business."

Her brain bounced around for anything she could say to improve the situation. "You taught me in Sunday School that only God is perfect. The rest of us are working hard to be worthy of His love."

"There is no God. Or if there is, He has no mercy. Why would he let my sweet wife suffer under Katherine's negligence?"

Liesl held her hands up, as in surrender. "I don't know, but Kurt and I never wished you or your wife harm. Mrs. Mansfield was a wonderful woman. She was kind to everyone."

Tears rolled down Mr. Mansfield's face. "That's right."

"Why are you pointing a gun at Kurt?"

"He found my stuff in the woods. It won't take long before they know I killed Katherine. I can't go to prison. I can't."

"Please don't hurt Kurt, Mr. Mansfield. Mrs. Mansfield wouldn't want that."

He turned toward her. "She wouldn't want any of this."

"It's not too late, Mr. Mansfield. God forgives us of our sins."

"Thou shalt not kill. It's a commandment. I've broken His commandment." With a sob, he added, "It was easy to kill Katherine. She was an evil person. But both of you help people, in your own way."

The ping of a text received on her phone broke the silence in the room. Liesl grimaced. *Why now?*

Anger resurfaced in Mr. Mansfield. "Throw that phone on the floor! In front of you." Mr. Mansfield pointed his gun toward her to emphasize the command.

Liesl pulled her phone from her back pocket and crouched to place it on the floor.

Mr. Mansfield looked at Kurt, who stood a few feet away with his hands up. "Same for you."

Kurt nodded, reached behind him to remove his phone,

and dropped it on the floor with a bang. Kurt had two phones, but Mr. Mansfield assumed he had one.

She kept her eyes on Mr. Mansfield and prayed her face remained neutral. Could she distract Mr. Mansfield enough for Kurt to call 911 on his other phone?

Mr. Mansfield took a step closer to Kurt and kicked the phones away from them.

She stole a glance at Kurt. He rolled his eyes toward his right hand. With his right thumb and pointer finger, he made a quick "gun" gesture, then returned to holding his hand upright.

His gun! Kurt's gun was locked in the library.

When Mr. Mansfield bent over to pick up the phones, Kurt launched himself at Mansfield's legs.

She turned and ran down the hall toward the library. A loud explosion behind her made her scream, followed by the sound of glass shattering and hitting the ground.

Barney howled from the bathroom.

The only window in the kitchen was large, facing the backyard. The bullet must have shattered it. *Had the bullet hit anyone before it hit the glass?*

With a hammering heart and dread for Kurt's well-being, Liesl continued her race to the library.

Another explosion erupted from the gun. A splinter of wood flew from the wall in front of her.

This killer was shooting at her!

She rounded the corner of the library at full speed, sliding into the empty built-in bookshelves where the locking shelf was located.

Her eyes darted across the vacant shelves. Where would Kurt have hidden the key? She'd been playing with Ross when he arrived and hadn't followed him in here.

Where was it?

The enormous mantel clock sat on the fireplace mantel. They had not yet packed it, thanks to its size and weight. She rushed toward the timepiece and ran her hands behind it. She felt the key.

She grabbed the key and ran to the locking shelf. With shaking hands, she inserted the key and turned the lock, then pulled out Kurt's service weapon with care. There was a round in the chamber. This model type didn't have a safety. It wouldn't help to blow off her foot when she needed to stop a killer.

With a solid grip on the short handle of the pistol, she turned. She quelled her desire to run to the kitchen the way she'd come. Instead, she turned and ran into the adjoining music room.

With rapid steps and the gun pointed in front of her, she crossed the music room and exited the door leading to the front entrance. At the alarm panel, she pressed the panic button. Immediately, a cacophony of alarms rang throughout the home. Barney howled again.

Liesl ran through the living room, then slowed. She needed to step silently past the dining room and the butler's pantry to catch Mr. Mansfield off guard.

Over the screaming alarms and Barney's howls, the sound of a struggle came from the kitchen.

Inching beyond the threshold of the kitchen, she spotted the bloody floor where Kurt and Mr. Mansfield wrestled in the broken glass, fighting for the pistol.

Kurt! Dear Lord, please keep him safe.

"Stop!" She shouted over the alarms. "I've got a gun."

When her screams failed to halt either of them, she pointed Kurt's gun toward the already broken window and pulled the trigger. The sound of the gun firing was louder than she expected, and her nostrils filled with the sulfurous smell of gunpowder.

Kurt used the intruder's surprise to his advantage and rolled on top of his back, pulling Mr. Mansfield's arms with him, securing them behind his back.

Areas of blood dotted the clothes and skin of both men.

"Grab the cuffs out of my jacket pocket."

She scrambled to get them from the jacket hanging on a kitchen chair.

Once the handcuffs were in place, Kurt faced her. Small bleeding cuts speckled his face. "You okay?"

"Better than you. Are you hurt?"

Kurt grinned. "My shoulder is killing me. Who would have believed I'd be wrestling like an alligator so soon after an injury?"

Liesl raised her eyes to the ceiling. "Thank you, God!"

In seconds, patrol officer Dennis Bates arrived at the scene.

"How did you get here so fast?" Kurt asked.

"Joey called nine-one-one. Reported the sound of a gunshot and a window shattering."

Chapter Forty-Eight

Liesl

Three weeks later, Kurt, Liesl, Joey, and Ross arrived at Plunkett Park, eager for a summer evening picnic. Simultaneously, Lee, Nicole, and Claudia parked beside them.

Liesl turned to Kurt. "Great minds."

"It's spooky how you and Nicole wind up at the same place at the same time. It's like you planned it that way or something."

Liesl laughed. "Okay, smart aleck. Let's unload the food. Not you, Joey. Would you go pick which tables we need to use in the Lawrence Shelter?"

Joey nodded and jumped out of the car.

"I'm coming, too, Uncle Joey," Ross said as he unhooked his seat belt.

Ross diverted his path when he spotted Claudia. Together they ran, laughing and squealing to play at the adjacent playground.

Kurt walked around to help unload food from Liesl's car, but she waved him away. "Don't even think about it. That sling on your arm means you only carry potato chips today."

Kurt rolled his shoulder around. "It's getting better."

"And that shoulder will only continue to improve if you give it two more weeks of rest, like the specialist ordered."

It was an evening for grilling hot dogs and hamburgers. A get-together to celebrate friendships and to acknowledge the conclusion of a case.

Justin had been invited but had declined. He said it was still too soon for him to be friends with Kurt.

They set up a snack table for watermelon, deviled eggs, chips, and dips, and soft drinks. All the essentials for hot dogs and hamburgers, including coleslaw, potato salad, and desserts, were laid out on the adjacent table.

Hector surprised Liesl when, after he'd accepted the invitation for an evening picnic, announced he was bringing a date. He refused to give her name, only saying she'd arrive late because of a prior conflict.

Liesl and Nicole were more than curious about his date. Who was she? Was it someone they knew?

Hector wasn't talking. Instead, he'd challenged Lee to some hoops, leaving one-armed Kurt in charge of the grill.

Kurt announced it would be twenty minutes before the charcoal was ready for burgers and dogs.

Nicole glanced over at where the children were swinging. "No sense doing anything more. Let's give the kids a chance to play."

Those not swinging or playing basketball sat at the snack table, munching and talking.

Liesl leaned toward Nicole and, in a hushed voice, said, "Let me know when you're speaking to me again, because I really do want to share with you about my project. Oh, and you'll never believe what Mrs. Zimmerman found in my library."

"What?"

"So, are you speaking to me now?"

Nicole swatted playfully at Liesl. "It depends. How interesting was her discovery?"

"She found a box of family love letters that had been hidden."

"Really? Do tell! Who wrote them? Are they old?"

"Yes. Very old." Before Liesl could elaborate on the metal box or its contents, Kurt sauntered closer and interrupted.

"Speaking of old things, did I tell you we received the Civil War soldier's DNA results?"

"You certainly did not, and that's a big fail on your part," Liesl said. Sharing with Nicole about the box Mrs. Zimmerman found and whatever secrets it held would have to wait. The mystery of the Civil War remains trumped a bunch of worn love letters any day.

Nicole moaned. "I'm so tired of talking about those bones. Will they ever go away?"

Liesl shot a look at Nicole. "Pay no attention to her." Turning back to Kurt, she asked, "Did the results conclusively determine the soldier was Colonel Michaels?"

"No," Kurt said. "The opposite, actually. The DNA doesn't match the family the soldier was supposed to have come from."

Liesl straightened. "Does that mean he really was a spy? He was wearing the Colonel's uniform, but he wasn't really the Colonel?"

Kurt nodded. "That's what it means."

"Fascinating." Liesl rubbed her chin. "Was he posing as Colonel Michaels the whole time?"

Kurt grinned at her. "I'd say you need to do more research

about him." He winked at Nicole. "Sounds like good book material to me."

Nicole moaned again. "I'll never be rid of those bones. They're going to haunt me forever." She elbowed Kurt. "Why don't you change the subject and share the details about notifying Katherine's next of kin?"

With a grin, Kurt said, "I can't tell you everything, but I will say Nelson Palmer is a good guy. We figured he wouldn't be upset about Katherine's death. What surprised him was Katherine's lawyer explaining that he and his brother and sister would inherit all of Katherine's assets."

Lee and Hector rejoined the group, panting and sweating. Men of a certain age could only go one round on a sultry afternoon like this.

"Are you talking about Nelson Palmer?" Hector asked.

"I am," Kurt replied.

Hector grinned. One would assume he'd be ecstatic to inherit, yet he regarded it as corrupt money."

Nicole asked, "So they inherit everything since Katherine didn't have a will?"

"Basically," Hector said. "She could have given the money to anyone. Or left it to a charity in a will. But, because she never made a will, the state's law of inheritance kicks in. That's what determines where one's assets are distributed."

Liesl asked, "So, her nearest kin were these cousins?"

Kurt nodded.

"And they objected to the money?"

"Nelson balked. He didn't want money that had been taken from the pockets of the poor."

Nicole said, "He sounds like a great guy."

Liesl turned to Nicole. "I agree. We need to get to know him."

Hector said, "He was afraid this inheritance would bring

him bad luck. I suggested he speak to an attorney. Maybe donate it to a charity or charities."

Nicole grinned at Liesl. "Great suggestion, Hector. There are charities who would put that money to good use."

Liesl frowned. "How did I miss Mr. Mansfield as a viable suspect? Most of us were aware his wife had died. I didn't know the reason for her death, but I should have put that together."

Kurt patted her hand. "It's hard for anyone to think a friend would be capable of murder, right Hector?"

Hector laughed. "You were mistaken about my friend."

"I'm delighted about that."

Hector explained, "Mansfield had just landed on our suspect list, thanks to Liesl's tip about the wrongful death suit. We just didn't have enough time to work the tip before he outed himself at Liesl's place. I mean, the man didn't have a criminal record and was well-regarded in the community. Hard to imagine what he did."

Hector reached for a chip. "Enhancing the video let us identify Bob carrying gas cans into Katherine's house, but it took time to get the enhanced version. We don't know how he accessed her security code, but he used it regularly. He'd been watching her house for weeks before the fire. We imagine he's the one who moved her bank accounts."

Liesl felt pity for Mr. Mansfield. Life's circumstances had caused him to break. "Poor man. What's going to happen to him?"

"I don't know," Kurt said. "He may end up in a mental health unit. He lost his mind when his wife died. A good defense lawyer will argue that."

Liesl asked, "Does he have a good defense lawyer?"

Kurt shrugged. "I don't know." He turned toward Hector.

"Didn't he file for a court-appointed defense attorney since he's broke?"

Liesl shot a look of interest at Nicole. "Perhaps a good citizen will provide him a good defense attorney."

Nicole nodded. "He needs something to give him back his faith in the Lord and in humanity."

Liesl and Nicole shared a look that meant, "We'll talk more about this later."

Hector rose to his feet as a car pulled into the parking area.

Nicole nudged Liesl. "Hector's date has arrived."

They were stunned to recognize Roxy as she stepped out of her car.

Liesl turned to Kurt. "Did you know about this?"

He grinned. "You're not the only one who can keep a secret."

Author's Note & Acknowlegements

This book contains historical figures as well as fictional characters.

Cyrus Clark of Mexico, Missouri, a banker in the 1890s and 1900s, built what was to become the Simmons Stables in 1887. Originally, the barn was painted red. The beautiful fan-shaped stained glass window over the main entrance is original to the stable's building.

Clark and his brother-in-law, Joseph Potts, started the Clark and Potts Combination Sales Company in the stables that auctioned all breeds of horses. The stables were also the location of the B.O. Tucker Stable, Dincara Stable, along with many others. The Lee Brothers (George and William) leased and then purchased the barn. Eventually, R. G. Stewart purchased and remodeled the stables, painting the stables white. When Mr. Stewart passed, his friend, fellow owner and trainer Bill Cunningham, placed an ad to sell the stable in June 1948.

The advertisement for the sale of the stables in Saddle and Bridle read, "Modern up-to-date saddle horse barn and five acres of ground in the city of Mexico, Mo., 254 feet long, 20-foot wide center aisle, 36 box stalls, beautiful large office, wash rack, tack room, grain storage room, hayloft will hold 5,000 bales of hay."

Mr. Art Simmons bought the stables in 1948, and Simmons Stables operated at that location for 53 years. In 2001, James Simmons, Art's son, moved the horses and equipment to a new modern training facility just outside of Mexico, which continues today.

Thanks to the hard work of Bobette Balser Wilson, Mary White Littrell, and so many others, the Simmons Stable Preservation Fund was formed. Numerous donations and grants have allowed Simmons Stables to be preserved as the International Saddlebred Hall of Fame and Event Center.

Simmons Stables is the oldest known building continuously devoted to boarding and training champion American Saddlebred horses. In 2004, it was placed on the United States National Register of Historic Places.

Murry Tate, a trainer, is a fictional character representing hundreds of skilled trainers who crisscrossed the United States. These men learned their craft beside famous trainers. They worked hard, learned the trade, and were free to move from stable to stable as their skills improved.

All names of horses are fictitious except for the famous Rex McDonald 833. You can learn more about Mr. Bass, the Bass bit, Rex McDonald, and Belle Beach at the Audrain County Historical Society and Simmons Stables/International Saddlebred Hall of Fame. There is a monument for Rex McDonald in East Lawn Cemetery, near the monument for Mr. Bass. The information about Rex McDonald being stuffed and put on display at the Ringo Hotel is true, as well as being moved to the Bass barns after a fire burned down the hotel.

Audrain County Sheriff James G. Ford was the acting sheriff

in 1920. The events related to his participation in the arrests of Toby and Frank are fictitious.

Mr. Cyrus Clark, Mr. Joseph Potts, the Lee Brothers, Art Simmons, Robert G. Stewart, and Tom Bass are as historically accurate as I could make them. Any misrepresentation or mistake in this work is my own.

Thanks to Jane E.B. Simmons for the book about her father, *Arthur Simmons: American Icon of the Horse World—A Daughter's Memories*. I also appreciated all the information included in Bill Downey's book *Whisper on the Wind: The Story of Tom Bass, Celebrated Black Horseman*. These books were invaluable to the writing of this book.

About the Author

Ellen E. Withers is a retired insurance fraud investigator, which helps provide realism and intrigue found in her new dual-time mystery series, *Show Me Mysteries*. Set in Ellen's picturesque hometown of Mexico, Missouri, each book features a historical structure, a dual-time plotline, and intriguing mysteries.

Ellen has earned nearly 100 awards for her short stories, including a prestigious Pushcart Prize nomination for published short fiction. Her debut novel, *Show Me Betrayal*, was the Scrivenings Press 2023 Readers' Choice Award Winner and the 2023 Book of the Year, 2023 Best Mystery/Suspense, and 2023 Best Debut Novel. It was also a finalist in two categories for the 2024 ACFW Carol Awards, in Mystery/Suspense/Thriller and Debut Novel.

She is a columnist for *Writers Monthly PDF*, a guide for professional writers about writing for contests. As a freelance writer, Ellen has written over 75 nonfiction articles published in local, regional, and international magazines.

Ellen is a member of White County Creative Writers, American Christian Fiction Writers, Sisters in Crime (SIC), and Tornado Alley, a local chapter of SIC.

Also by Ellen E. Withers

Show Me Betrayal

Show Me Mysteries—Book One

Two deaths occur decades apart. Is it possible these deaths are related? What motivates a killer, who got away with murder sixty years ago, to kill again? Was it uncontrollable rage or the hope of silencing someone who fit all the puzzle pieces together and deduced who committed the crime?

Set in the picturesque town of Mexico, Missouri, *Show Me Betrayal* takes flight in words and emotions of rich characters woven together into a story you won't want to put down.

Voted 2023 Book of the Year, 2023 Best Mystery/Suspense, and 2023 Best Debut Novel for Scrivenings Press Readers' Choice Book Awards.

Get your copy here:

https://scrivenings.link/showmebetrayal

* * *

Show Me Deceit

Show Me Mysteries—Book Two

Present Day: Liesl Schrader is once again involved in death investigations. A body is discovered inside a charitable museum where Liesl serves on the board of directors. She and her best friend Nicole are drawn into a police theft investigation stemming from the death at the museum.

When Liesl and Nicole uncover a set of historic bones, questions arise. Are they related to the Civil War-era encampment in their town? The unit, commanded by General Pope, guarded one of the biggest supply chains of the Union Army—the railroad lines located in Mexico, Missouri, throughout the war. Was this a battlefield death, or was it murder? Surrounded on all sides by Southern sympathizers, did the Rebels kill this Union soldier?

1862: United States Army Lieutenant Cormac O'Malley has a problem. He knows there is a Rebel spy in his camp, and he needs proof of the spy to save the lives of Union soldiers. He has no choice but to work with his sweetheart from town, Enid Connelly, and her local friends to uncover the proof. Are they trustworthy and loyal to the Union in a state divided between North and South? Can he reveal the identity of the spy before the spy can silence him—possibly forever?

Take a walk through time with Show Me Deceit, book two of the Show Me Mystery Series. The mysteries are set in Mexico, Missouri, where death encompasses two eras—Civil War and contemporary times. Liesl, Nicole, and Detective Kurt Hunter, have previously put a killer behind bars. Now they must combine their skills again to stop the plunder of local charities and solve the mystery of a Union soldier's death. Can Liesl and Kurt work together again as friends, putting aside their former romance, to solve these mysteries?

Get your copy here:

https://scrivenings.link/showmedeceit

* * *

A Collection of Three Christmas Novellas

by Tonya B. Ashley, Jenny Carlisle, and

Ellen E. Withers

A beautiful hand-carved nativity set travels from its original home in Germany to a riverboat in Van Buren, Arkansas, in the mid-1840s, then to Mexico, Missouri, at the beginning of the American Civil War. More than a century later, it resurfaces in a tiny town in the Arkansas River Valley.

Three stories tell of the impact this treasure has on the families who own it. God's love survives tragedy, turmoil, and even abandonment. His love is the gift for all, for all time.

Get your copy here:

https://scrivenings.link/agiftforalltime

* * *

Stay up-to-date on your favorite books and authors with our free e-newsletters.

ScriveningsPress.com